D1527170

Sins of Commission

A Martha Beale Novel

Cordelia Frances Biddle

ISBN: 1978039794
ISBN 13: 9781978039797

Also by Cordelia Frances Biddle

The Martha Beale series:
The Conjurer
Deception's Daughter
Without Fear
The Actress

Beneath the Wind

Saint Katharine: The Life of Katharine Drexel

Twelve Crossword Mystery titles written under the pseudonym Nero Blanc

Renascence

Edna St. Vincent Millay

Thou canst not move across the grass
But my quick eyes will see Thee pass,
Nor speak, however silently,
But my hushed voice will answer Thee.
I know the path that tells Thy way
Through the cool eve of every day;
God, I can push the grass apart
And lay my finger on Thy heart!

CHAPTER 1

Thomas Kelman

*I love Martha Beale. This I freely admit, though I recognize that my senti-
ments will come to naught. She and I are too different in parentage and
in our current positions in the world. None in any level of society would
approve a match between us. Martha would be regarded as marrying beneath her; I would be reviled as attaching myself to her for financial gain.
I must put away all expectations.*

THOMAS KELMAN'S PEN stabs at the last word; the ink has run dry, making the
letters no more than a ferocious scratch that rips the paper. He dips the nib into
the well, intending to continue writing in his pocket journal, but he instead looks
away from the page and stares into space while a black splotch drops upon the
page.

There's nothing he can add to the argument; he has considered every facet
of this inner dialogue before. Many, many times before. For four long years, in
fact. And what has he done during this period? Has he acted nobly and excused
himself from her acquaintance so that she might feel free to encourage acceptable suitors? No. And no again. And again. Instead, he finds excuses to be in her
presence. Weekly excuses, if not daily ones. Yes, he journeyed to South America
with the intention of removing himself from Philadelphia forever. But what was
the result of that sojourn? Mere months later, he crept home, the business endeavor he had intended to embark upon forsaken, the fortune he'd hoped to
accrue no more than a pipe dream.

So he remains the man he was, a person born into poverty whose self-
will propelled him toward an education and livelihood the like of which his

parents could never have envisioned. But how can a position that requires him to spend countless hours investigating crimes and consorting with cut-throats, cutpurses, counterfeiters, and hucksters be of adequate stature for a woman of Martha Beale's cultivation and wealth? She was born into the highest ranks of Philadelphia society, he into its dregs. The answer is that, as a couple, they are irrevocably mismatched. And no amount of wishful think-ing will alter that fact.

Kelman frowns, his eyes coal-dark and hard, ancient scar slicing his left cheek turning silver against his skin. Were he not such a handsome man, he would appear fearsome—to which any criminal would attest. Thomas Kelman isn't someone whom any of that brotherhood wishes to confront. None of them will ever see the gentle smiles he lavishes on Martha; none would even believe him capable of such frailty.

He returns the journal to his coat pocket, the fabric as somber as mourning garb; Kelman never dresses in the fashionable, bright colors of other men of his generation. In part, the choice is dictated by his work, but mostly it's because he disapproves of men donning showy raiment when laborers are starving. It galls him to witness mill owners clothed in brocades when their earnings come from making cottonade to sell to southern slaveholders: earnings that depend upon chaining children to the looms and hiring women who earn half the men's wages. No wonder the weavers and other laborers have been rioting since the great conflagrations of 1844. Kelman should disapprove of those lawless acts, which he does officially. His heart, however, decrees otherwise.

His thoughts return to Martha. Martha, whom he must protect from her own iconoclastic nature. Why can't she see that a union between them is im-possible? And why doesn't he try harder to renounce her, or even depart from Philadelphia entirely so that there'd be no chance of their marrying?

A shout disturbs him; it's so loud it travels through the two doors separating the inner room of his office from the corridor on the upper floor of Congress Hall. Running feet follow, then an insistent rap on the outer door. He rises, preparing himself for bad news. No constable ever races upstairs to bring good tidings.

"Mr. Kelman, sir. Come quick, if you will. A fire has broken out."

"Another riot?" Locking the door, he strides down the hall, his regimental bearing authoritarian and his footfall decisive. The constable, who's not only short but also round as a field squash, has difficulty keeping up.

"I can't say, sir. I was told there were no protesters. Or none to be seen. But the blaze is very bad."

"Which location?"

"Sixth Street, sir. Between Pine and Lombard."

"Ah" is the sole reply. Kelman knows the area well; Lombard Street is full of brothels—"fancy houses," as they're called—but Pine is also home to many of the city's once-fine residences. The streets south of Washington Square were elegant spaces forty-odd years ago, but then that lauded statesman, George Washington, was still alive and the nation a hopeful place.

Realizing that he's outpacing the wheezing constable, Kelman tells the man he'll proceed on his own, which appears much to the fellow's relief. Kelman is difficult to match both physically and intellectually.

Hastening first south along Fifth Street, then west on Walnut, he hears the blare of fire brigades racing to the site; their clanging bells increase in volume and urgency. Around him, other men are hurrying toward the scene, while women, either strolling together or in company with theirs or their mistress's children, draw back, pulling close to walls in order to avoid the crush of those flying past. The crowd swells: curiosity seekers, genuine good Samaritans, and the usual peddlers and pickpockets who attach themselves to every throng. No one notices that the afternoon has turned lovely: a perfect May day, with high clouds glowing against a lilac-blue sky, with azaleas in bloom, with trees unfurling new life within each leaf, the green as resilient as faith.

→⊶═◉ ◉═⊷←

Arriving at the blaze, Kelman finds that all is chaos. Day watchmen and constables struggle to hold back the crowd, but to no avail. People dart forward shouting, or they rush into the burning edifice, only to reappear moments later, holding aloft a lamp or a vase or some other costly object. The firemen toss their leather water buckets, man to man to man, but often the chain is broken, and the liquid splashes on the ground instead of on the conflagration. Women in various states of undress huddle together, cowed by the jeers the churlish rain upon their heads. They take no solace from one another; in fact, the opposite is true, and they deliberately avert their gazes. The men among them, also hastily clad, behave in the same fashion. Kelman understands the reason for their mortification. The house is a well-known place of assignation for married ladies and their lovers. He imagines most of its current patrons wish themselves anywhere but here, then wonders if people too fearful of discovery to flee the burning building are still inside.

In a trice, he's across the road and thrusting himself through the scorching, cindery air, his lungs heaving as he gasps for breath. With his handkerchief held over his nose, he pushes inside, yelling to the victims he envisions trapped on the upper floors. "Help is on the way!" he shouts.

But no sooner does he start to mount the stairs than a wall of flame roars down to meet him, the heat carrying with it a deafening crack of splintering timbers, tumbling bricks, and collapsing plaster ceilings. He leaps backward, the fire in pursuit as if bent on consuming the entire block of residences. Screams erupt as the flames gush from the house; horses rear in their traces or snap their harnesses and bolt, stampeding first into the crowd before careening off. One fire wagon overturns, knocking its still-coupled beast to its side; lying in the street, it bellows in pain. Three women and one gentleman client from the establishment faint, but no one pauses to revive them. Instead, everywhere is noise and panic and horror, while the fire brigades, rather than banding together and sharing supplies of water and buckets, begin to battle one another. Fists fly; a cobble is wrenched from the roadway; soon there are other projectiles in other hands. Kelman bellows at the men to stop.

"Desist, I tell you. Desist, at once! You men. Return to your wagons." Which, miraculously, they do, eyeing the speaker with an aggrieved surliness. Some attempt obscene gestures, but Kelman's steely gaze inhibits their efforts.

The blaze is far from finished, however; more water is hurled upon it; a third and fourth bucket brigade is formed, but the original structure collapses in a heap as if it had been made of no stronger stuff than a cardboard doll's house. Free from one building, the firemen and volunteers next concentrate on its neighbors, three-story homes whose exterior walls soon turn black with liquid ash.

With the adventure finally waning, the thrill seekers start to depart, but the erstwhile patrons remain, staring at the ruins as if trying to ascertain whether they've conjured up a nightmare and will wake to find themselves reclining on perfumed sheets while engaging in an afternoon's dalliance. Many shut their eyes, hoping the false reverie to be true. In vain, Kelman urges them to provide him with their names before they leave and seek their homes; he promises utmost discretion. Receiving no response, however, he orders two constables to procure blankets and distribute them so the stunned group can escape exposure. While issuing this and other directives, his eyes alight on a new arrival: Martha Beale, come from her afternoon's work among the children at the Asylum for Colored Orphans. Seeing him, she hastens to his side, then stops, noting the scorch marks covering his clothing and soot smears on his face and hands.

"You put yourself at risk, Thomas. As is your habit" is all she says at first, then she turns her gaze to the smoldering building rather than reveal how distressed she is to find him thus. Her bonnet successfully hides her expression, but her shoulders, wrapped though they are in a cashmere cloak, betray her emotions.

Remorse at causing her pain softens the furrows on his forehead and the stern pinch of his mouth, an expression his underlings wouldn't imagine him possessing.

"I thought people might be trapped on an upper floor."

"Were there?"

"We won't know until the rubble cools. The fire was already too far advanced for me to mount the stairs."

"But you attempted to do so?"

His silence is response enough. She turns to regard him. "I wouldn't have you become a less courageous person, even if you cause me to worry. I hope you understand that fact."

Again, he makes no reply. Not because he doesn't wish to assuage her fears, and not because he believes his position precludes personal revelations, but because his heart is too full. At war with himself, he says nothing.

She reads his thoughts but keeps her reactions to herself until she smiles, a half-mournful note of forgiveness and admiration.

Watching her expression alter, he also ventures a quiet smile. For a moment, the two stand amid the grumbling firemen and acrid smoke. They might as well exist in a world apart.

"Mr. Kelman. A word, if you please." The man speaking is well known to Thomas—known far better than he'd like. Freers is his name, a writer for the penny press who's free with hyperbole, invention, and every type of fraudulent fact that sells newspapers to those who prefer scandal to truth. "Any names to supply regarding customers at the bawdy house? Oh, excuse me! 'Place of assignation,' I should say."

Martha, who hadn't yet divined the building's function, takes an involuntary step backward, which causes Freers to eye her, his expression as sly as a cat inspecting an unguarded dining table. Because he's short, and Martha's tall for a woman, the disparity in their heights makes him look more diminutive and greedier, too.

"Was the lady among the clientele?" he asks Kelman while continuing to watch Martha.

"What do you want, Freers?" is the brusque answer.

"The basics as always, Mr. K.: names of injured or deceased parties, how the blaze started, and whether or not—in your estimable opinion—it was a case of arson."

"I have no response at this time."

"And the lady?"

"She has no reply, either."

"Surely, she can speak for herself? Madam, may I appeal to you as a good citizen to supply a statement to the press? For instance, did you hear any cries of anguish issuing from the building before it—"

The request is cut short as Kelman grabs the man by his showy cravat. "Get out of here, you ghoul."

"I don't take my orders from you, sir. Not from the likes of you. Now, unhand me." Which Kelman does, albeit grudgingly. "If you won't permit open conversation with your charming companion, then I'll seek statements elsewhere." Straightening his mangled cravat, he fluffs the linen into a cone that nearly engulfs his chin. "But mark me, sir, I'll mention in my report that you appeared more interested in your female confidante than in your work. That's a dereliction of duties, to my mind."

Martha opens her mouth to correct the error; Thomas lays a restraining hand upon her arm, which Freers describes in his notes as: *Said lady was forbidden to utter a sound. Has this scrivener uncovered a plot to conceal a lawless act from the populace?* With that, he moves away, padding toward the now blanket-bearing survivors, who start to scatter at his approach.

"Freers, leave my witnesses alone," Kelman calls after him.

"Witnesses, are they, Mr. K? I'd say 'participants' would be a better choice of word."

"Leave them alone. If not, I can and will have you hauled in for obstruction of justice."

But Freers isn't to be cowed. He pursues Kelman's dispersing witnesses with an ingratiating and high-pitched, "Sir…madam…a moment of your time is all I desire," while Kelman snarls at his back and orders the constables to escort him from the scene; he then focuses on Martha again.

"Forgive me. That was language you should never hear."

"I pass along these streets every day, Thomas. I've heard indiscreet terminology before. As a spinster three decades old, I'm no longer considered young. I hope I'm as seasoned intellectually as my years permit."

"You're no spinster, Martha, however proud you are of your age. And I never wish to lose my temper in your presence."

She laughs. "And I'd rather have you talk and act according to your nature, which is one I esteem, if you'll recall."

The conversation is drawing perilously close to intimacy, a situation he has sworn to avoid. "May I have one of my men escort you home? I'm afraid I must remain here for some time."

"No. I can make my way alone quite well. As I do every day. The 'brazen Miss Beale walking abroad, as if she were a man'!" She smiles at this description, then the bright expression disappears. "I'm sorry you must always encounter the direst of human suffering, and I pray you won't find additional victims in the rubble."

"Yes" is all he says, but his face shows he's far from confident that this will be the outcome.

She studies him and then looks away, gazing at the remnants of the building. "And was this a house of…what that unpleasant little man suggested?"

"It's better you don't know, Martha."

"Oh, Thomas, I'm not a child who needs to be protected from the world's vices. Haven't I had experience with the city's netherworld? Ella, whom I rescued from the streets after being consigned to a bawdy house—"

"True. Though I'd rather you—"

"Perhaps you'd prefer me to be like the prim ladies who swoon upon hearing a coarse word, or who refuse to believe that poverty forces parents to sell their children into—"

"No. I don't want you to be anything like those women."

"I'm glad to hear you say it."

"Could you doubt me?"

She gives him a brief smile. "Let me go on my way and leave you to your duties; I'm afraid I'm a distraction during these trying circumstances. I dine alone tonight. If you're not too weary to join me, I'd welcome the company." As she starts to move away, her gown stirs up a cloud of charred papers that have begun to blow along the walkway. She picks one up. Her face turns pink as she regards the image. "From that house, I assume," she says as she hands the picture to Kelman, "and part of a book, if the ripped binding is any indication. I didn't realize such pictures existed."

"These and worse, I fear. They're part of the 'fancy book trade' from which many publishers derive a fortune."

Similar images blow past her feet. "*The Education of Celeste…Two Cousins….A Lustful Turk*…Oh, Thomas, these are despicable!"

He bends to pick them up but then is undecided how to discard them, or whether they should be saved as visual evidence of the house's former purpose. "Human nature is a complex mechanism; our baser instincts often win out against our better selves."

She frowns, gazing from the folded pages in his hand back to the onetime house of assignation. "So I understand. I don't stand in judgment against the men and women who frequented this place; that's between them and their consciences. But I do judge the men who produce such 'reading material.' They're worse than the customers to whom they pander." Her frown deepens. "Calico printed here in Philadelphia traded for human cargo in Africa; match girls punished if they fail to sell a night's product. We're a nation whose economy is based on exploitation. How can we change that situation? Or can we not? No, I've said enough. Let me leave you to your work. Send me word if I can expect you this evening. No, better yet, simply come to the door. You may wash the grime from your face in peace in my home, which is always, always open to you."

Touching his arm in farewell, she departs without waiting for a reply, while Kelman, fighting and losing his private battle, crosses the street to begin examining the fire's aftermath.

CHAPTER 2

In the Ashes

WORKING INTO THE night, Kelman neither pauses for food nor quits the scene. A courier conveys word to Martha Beale that she should not expect him; sending the message is the only moment his pace slows. Torches and gas jets assist the search, lighting the sky with a yellow, hissing flare and casting those toiling among the wreckage in misshapen shadows that look like ghostly spirits rather than men hoping to rescue other human beings.

Word circulates that a voice or voices have been heard in the house's cellar. Ruined beams are hauled aside, brick and other rubble cleared until the exterior cellar door is found. Miraculously, the wood, though charred, remains intact, but when the heavy doors are prized open, a rumble of sooty smoke blows upward through the space. And heat, too, because the coal piled in boxes on the cellar floor has been enkindled.

More water is called for, the embers attacked, but the flickering, orange sparks refuse to be quenched; instead, they slither out of reach, creating new spurts of color. For the firemen, the waste of such a valuable commodity is inexcusable. Coal burned for nothing useful. Might as well dump whole barges of the stuff into the Schuylkill River! They curse the smoldering heap; they curse the night; they curse one another, as well as their hot and sodden boots, while Kelman moves among the wreckage looking for anything that might prove useful in detecting the cause of the conflagration. By now, he's convinced it wasn't accidental; the fire was too extensive to have been produced by an uncontrolled blaze emanating from the kitchen or cellar, or an unattended lamp. If that had been the case, then the fire brigades could have rescued a sizable portion of the building.

All this time, unbeknownst to him or to the men under his charge, Freers stands watching. The constables have driven away other journalists and so-called journalists, as well as the ever-present beggars hoping to retrieve something, anything, of value—even a lump of still-hot coal. But Freers has bundled himself within a narrow passage between two buildings facing Sixth Street, the space only wide enough to permit a person entry to the shabby courtyard in the rear and the "trinity" house sequestered there. Dressed in black, surrounded by black, Freers is invisible.

And so, the moment Kelman makes his discovery, Freers hears of it: a body of a woman, her face scorched beyond recognition.

→∔═◉ ◉═∔←

A certain house of assignation, owned by one Mrs. Celestine Lampley, was the scene yesterday of a hellish blaze that consumed it: rafters, pianofortes, draperies, cordial cabinets, and all, leaving nothing but a smoking husk. In vain did our noble firemen strive to tame the inferno; in vain did its patrons—most unsuitably clad, as they'd been driven out of doors against their wills—cry out against the tragedy. In vain, also, did this scrivener attempt to query a certain Thomas Kelman, who, as a public servant, should have been ready and willing to supply information and direction. Alas, he was not, because his attention appeared divided between the conflagration and a certain lady companion. Was this writer mistaken in intuiting that the quintessentially taciturn gentleman has an amorous interest, and might the lady's initials be M. B.? No matter, faithful readers. That shall be meat for another literary repast. Our readers need only know that a female corpse was discovered among the rubble. May her soul rest in peace eternal, despite the supposed nature of a crime against conjugal amity and propriety…

Martha puts down the newspaper and looks at Kelman. Haggard though he appears, he has had time to bathe and change his attire before presenting himself at her house, newspaper in hand. Fresh linens, combed hair, and a scrubbed face, however, can't conceal the burn marks she knows are seared into his soul.

"I thought you should receive this from me instead of hearing your name bandied about elsewhere. By noon, I imagine Freers will be haunting your service door—if not banging on your front entrance or attempting to accost you in the street."

"You haven't slept, have you?"

"No."

"Nor eaten?"

"No…I think not. No, I'm certain." Finding the correct response seems critical to him, as if remembering that mundane detail is more important than identifying either the arsonist or the victim. Martha has never seen him so spent.

"Sit, and let me order you some breakfast. A beefsteak, *oeufs au plats*, toast, preserved cherries—"

"I require nothing. I should return to—"

"Thomas, if you don't take sustenance, you'll collapse at my feet."

The image produces a wry, weak smile. Instinctively, he touches his breast pocket, wondering whether she's capable of discerning the words he has confided in his portable journal. Hasn't he already thrown himself at her feet? And isn't he hoping—attempting—to do the opposite? "No, I must leave. I apologize for disturbing you at your work." For Martha had been seated at the desk in her second-floor parlor when her visitor had been shown into the room. Ledgers from the Beale Brokerage House now lie forgotten while she stands at his side.

"I'm delighted to forsake those endless columns of numbers. My chief clerk, Mr. Newgeon, is forever advising me to approach the accounts as if I were perusing an historical narrative, but I can't do it. Decimal points and numerical calculations aren't people and events. At least, they aren't to me." She folds the newspaper, hiding Freers's report, then draws Kelman away from the table upon which he'd spread it. "This investigation of yours can wait until you've eaten."

So saying, she walks to the bellpull, summons the footman, and requests breakfast for her guest. "Now, will you sit? I don't require conversation. You may keep silent, or muse aloud, or anything you wish." Seating herself near him, she folds her hands in her lap. Despite her occasional displays of impatience, Martha has a facility for waiting.

The clock on the mantle chimes the half hour. Elsewhere in the house, other gongs sound, some deep and sonorous, some delicate. By habit, Kelman pulls out his pocket watch and glances at it. Regarding him, she smiles. "I trust our minute and second hands are in agreement?"

"Pardon me?"

Her smile increases, the chestnut-colored curls framing her face bouncing with mirth. "I believe you're so tired, Mr. Kelman, that you don't know where you are." Seeing a look of sorrow return to his face, she tempers her good humor. "I shouldn't jest. You've reason to be exhausted. Discovering that dead woman must have been horrific; not knowing her identity heightens your difficulties, because a family should be contacted. Given the circumstances, though..." The words trail off. "Oh, what a tragic mystery."

Passing a hand across his eyes, he releases a leaden "Yes." Then he apologizes for being such poor company.

Martha interrupts before he can finish. "Cast aside your regrets. Aren't we friends? More than friends. You are company—dear company—even if all you do is stare at the carpet and ruminate, and I am honored to have you talk or not as you see fit. I realize your mind is troubled at yesterday's events. Know that you have a sympathetic ear in me, if you wish to unburden yourself." She says no more, because a tray is produced, laden with so many gold-rimmed plates that it seems impossible to believe that actual food can be found there. But it is, and piping hot and in plenty.

Kelman takes his fill, while beyond them the city sounds fill the air. Near and far are the clatter of hooves on the cobbled streets, the roll of iron-bound wheels, the squawk of a pie-seller, a murmured conversation passing below the parlor windows, each noise comforting in its familiarity, as are the echoes of everyday labor within the home. There's the clink of a bannister brush in the stairway, the muffled tread of a servant passing along the corridor, and the sudden lilt of song warbled by one young voice, then two: Martha's adoptive children in the third-floor chambers—bedrooms and a communal study area for use when they're not in school.

The song rouses Kelman from his breakfast. His eyes glisten. "How pleasant to hear those two so happy."

"Yes." Having said that, she sighs. "Cai is joy itself, although he continues to be—and doubtless always will be—troubled by his former complaint, the 'falling sickness,' as he insists upon calling it. In all other aspects, he looks and acts like a normal boy. Not knowing his birthday, I provided one. So, he's now eight, which is appropriate to his size and sensibilities. What I haven't yet told you is that a few gossipmongers have begun to insist that he looks like me, which is hardly possible, given that he's a mulatto. I always cast aside the remarks. Not Cai, though. If he hears the sneers, he reacts with pleasure. It makes him proud to think we might be physically linked. I never dampen his enthusiasm. I tell him he's my dear child, whether we're related by lineage or not." Martha pauses. "Ella, though, Ella...Oh, girls of fourteen can be a trial."

"Not when I've seen her."

"She's on her best behavior then. She wants to please you, as does Cai. Alone with me, she can be a hellion. Perhaps the root of the problem is that I'm not her mother, for whom she continues to pine, although the woman's identity will never be known, and Ella's memory of her is minimal. Or perhaps, it's the place from which I rescued her that has left lasting scars; after all, her parents sold her into that bawdy house when she was ten. During her most loving moments, she embraces me and calls me her savior, but at other times she's full of wrath. I know she's justified in feeling anger, but the emotion is so sweeping it encompasses everything: me, Cai, the cook, the maids, Mademoiselle Hédé in her role of governess—all of us dwelling here." Martha pauses again. "When her anger wanes, it can transmute itself into sullen silence. At those moments, I understand she's berating herself for her actions but isn't able to curtail them."

Watching her, Kelman frowns. When he speaks, his words are measured. "Some time ago, I said I'd find her mother. With one thing and another, my search was curtailed, and there the matter rested, which I assumed was for the best. I can take up the investigation again, if you believe—"

"A woman who abandoned her child while consigning her to a life of depravity? No, Thomas—though I thank you. It's better that Ella forget her past altogether."

"Which she seems unable to do."

"With time, though, don't you believe—"

"Not necessarily. Hardened criminals who appear devoid of compassion can have psychic wounds that render them as weak as children. In my opinion, the phrenologists and craniologists who insist they can divine a person's capability for goodness or evil are misguided. Positing which 'humor' is prevalent in an individual disregards our uniqueness as people. So, no, I don't believe Ella can ignore her history. Just as you and I can't."

Martha doesn't reply. She knows Kelman's reasoning is sound. Her father was a cold, demanding parent; although dead these four years and the mystery surrounding his demise never resolved, nor his body recovered, his influence remains.

"What do you suggest, then?"

"That I resume my search. I can't promise to find Ella's mother. Women of that ilk generally don't live to old age, but knowing her fate will be better than not knowing." Seeing her face cloud, he changes his approach. "You fear that if I find this parent, she'll reclaim her child—or worse, will demand remuneration for her. Is that it?"

"Yes." She leans forward in her chair. "Both situations are possible. But worse is that Ella might choose, *gladly* choose, to leave me."

"Why? When she possesses all this?" His glance encompasses a room that displays every accouterment of a woman of wealth: paintings, statuary, tables covered with objets d'art. In his estimation, no child born into poverty would ever willingly forsake a home that afforded spaces as comfortable as these.

"What were you like as a youth, Thomas?" is the quiet answer. "I was often rebellious—not that anyone recognized that quality in me, but I can recall the emotion perfectly."

"And you're a rebel, still, I'm afraid."

"My father would never have permitted me to act on those volatile feelings, but I remember how painful it was to keep them pent up in my breast. There were times when I loathed my life, when I felt I was being suffocated. Even the notion of a future marriage met his disapproval. And, of course, I had no female ally."

"Something altered those perceptions, though. When I first encountered you, it wasn't desperation I saw, but strength of purpose. Ella is certain to outgrow her resentment—"

"I never 'outgrew' my discontent. Rather, my circumstances altered, and I found myself becoming a different person. When you met me while investigating my father's disappearance, I was fighting that ancient battle. You entered my existence when I most needed to prove my worth."

"Which you did."

"Not without your aid."

Neither speaks. Both are returned to the past: Martha, as she was when her father disappeared, and Kelman, who offered her practical assistance at the time, only to have the great Lemuel Beale's confidential secretary interfere.

"There's something else," she begins, before hesitating again. "You remember that strange boy from the almshouse—"

"Findal Stokes," Kelman says. "Yes, of course. He's no longer a boy, I imagine."

"No. That's just the problem." Frowning, she pauses anew. "He and Ella have struck up a friendship."

"How is that possible? Young Stokes should have little to no ability to spend time with her."

"One of the downstairs maids tells me that he's often seen lingering by the service door." Before Kelman can suggest that it's possible to prevent unwanted people from loitering nearby, she adds, "Ella's aware of his presence. She brings him food. And meets with him secretly."

Kelman's expression turns grave. "Did she tell you this? About these clandestine meetings?"

"Yes."

"That's good. She's not attempting to deceive you, then."

"I won't call it deceit, but I was forced to confront her before she revealed the truth. She didn't give it freely. You know her background. You know human nature. She appears to believe him courageous and clever. She insists that he once saved my life." Again, she pauses.

"Did he?"

"Rescue me? Yes. *If* it was he. Unwittingly, I stepped into the path of a runaway horse. A boy yelled out a warning. I leapt out of the roadway, but when I looked in the direction from whence the shout had come, no one was to be seen."

"Have you told Ella?"

Martha doesn't immediately answer. When she does, her tone reveals her misery. "No. I've feigned disinterest. Or I've told her the city is full of boys and men—and women, too—ready to warn strangers of impending peril."

Kelman's fingers clasp together, a habitual and meditative gesture. "Between us, do you or do you not believe this boy was Findal Stokes?"

Her voice a mere whisper, she murmurs, "Yes." Then she adds an anguished, "But what am I to do? I don't like hearing her laud him. It makes me uneasy. More than uneasy. It fills me with dread. I fear that in one of her fits of pique, she'll run away from my home, and that young Stokes will be her refuge—"

"If she left your house without permission, I could find her."

"And then what? Drag her home forcibly? No. I can't and won't imprison her. I want her to feel free to do whatever she wishes, and to be whomever she chooses. I don't want to raise another young Martha Beale, frightened of her own emotions, and always, always living in some netherworld where love and joy are denied. No, I won't permit Ella to be stunted in that fashion. Human beings need light and air. Not the silence of the tomb." Martha's face contorts. She turns aside to hide her distress, but Kelman has already leaped up and is kneeling at her side.

"My dearest one. Put your mind at ease. Remember that without you, Ella and Cai would have nothing. Neither home, nor kindness, nor perhaps their lives. Consider what good you've done, rather than regretting what you can't accomplish."

She's too full of emotion to answer. Instead she turns her face into Kelman's shoulder while he holds her tight. If, for one moment, he were to consider how this pose contradicts his former resolve, he might waver, but he doesn't.

CHAPTER 3

Becky Grey Receives a Visitor

LESS THAN HALF a mile from that tender scene, a less amiable one is in progress. The setting is the Southwark Theatre, famed as a favorite of George Washington when Philadelphia served as the nation's capital. The property currently belongs to Becky Grey, once wife to a man whose family was counted among the city's elite. Now she's happily a widow, though unhappily, not a wealthy one. Becky was a noted thespian in Great Britain and on the Continent; marrying William Taitt was her life's great error. In his estimation, it was, too. Having decided he'd wed below his station, he made his opinion known daily. He never believed in curtailing his speech or his blows.

The ill-fated union did produce a child, however: little Will, for whom Becky now labors long hours. For him, she struggles to have society accept her as "respectable" despite being a performer and the manager of a company of performers. She's determined that her past fame, combined with the wise administration of her artistic and financial resources, will bring her success, and she understands that it's imperative for her to maintain a certain sangfroid, as if earning her bread and board were done by choice rather than by necessity.

Her visitor appears undaunted by Becky's imperious pose and handsome demeanor, for the actress is the ideal beauty of the age: golden-haired, amply curved, a woman meant for décolletage and glittering ornaments. The private receiving room where she greets her visitor is decorated like a fashionable parlor, the furniture à la mode, the drapes Nile green, the carpet figured in gold and crimson. Impressive as this backdrop is, it fails to intimidate Becky's guest.

"You don't know me, Mistress Grey? I must admit, your disregard pains me." Shrouded in expensive widow's weeds, a long black veil concealing her face, the woman has a voice full of the drawling irony of someone accustomed to wielding power.

Becky reexamines the carte de visite that was delivered into her hands before the guest was ushered into the room. "Mrs. D. Willoughby Anspach. No, I have not had the pleasure."

"I assure you that you have, madam. Think back."

Trained in the dramatic arts, capable of changing timbre of voice as well as her appearance, Becky tries but fails to imagine who this person could be. Certainly, none of the actresses with whom she journeyed to America five years past. All decamped to England as soon as they could, promising to send letters that never arrived, promising undying devotion, too. By then, Becky was wed and her marriage sufficiently brutal to make any former acquaintance seem of little consequence.

"And I'm equally certain, Mrs. Anspach, that we've never been introduced. If you saw me perform in London—"

"I've never been to London."

"Or here, or in New York, when I first arrived from abroad—"

"I never had that pleasure, either." With these words, Becky's visitor sits, settling herself as though she intends to remain for some time.

"Mrs. Anspach, at the risk of appearing rude, I must ask you your business. I have work to attend, and my leisure time, I'm afraid, is limited. Perhaps, if you lifted your veil, I might recognize your face, but your voice I do not—"

"Becky, Becky, for shame."

"Madam, I repeat—"

"Not to recognize your own Leonora."

"Honora!" Becky's mellifluous tone has become a gasp.

"Or Honora. Either one, my dear. I have a plethora of names from which to choose. You knew only two, but I've always had other aliases."

Hurrying to the door, Becky closes and locks it while her visitor calmly raises her veil.

"What are you doing here?"

"That's all the thanks I get after—"

"You must realize that you're in peril in this city. Grave peril."

"Not as Mrs. D. Willoughby Anspach" is the smooth reply. With that, Honora—or Leonora—tosses aside her headdress, her smile complaisant, her manner assured. The costly lace, gauze, and crepe fall to the floor. "Fret not, dear friend. No one but you can identify me. Which you will not do—" Becky attempts to interrupt, but her guest hasn't finished her speech. "Which you will not do, because to do so would cast you in an unfavorable light. Worse than unfavorable. Isn't that true?"

Becky stares at her. The eyes are just as calculating as they once were, the hair as fiery red, her complexion as pallid. The color, though, is less reminiscent of human weakness than of alabaster. Honora, or whomever she has chosen to become, is a stony woman.

"I also recall telling you that we might have been friends under other circumstances; do you remember that, my dear? True friends, not acquaintances."

Becky, for whom speech is as natural as breathing, merely nods.

"Of course. How could you have forgotten the little snuggery we shared?"

Finding her voice at last, Becky interrupts her visitor. "Why are you here?"

"Why, to resume our sadly curtailed attachment."

Walking to her desk, Becky pulls open the top drawer. "I assume you want money."

A laugh greets the suggestion. "When have I ever wanted money? Don't I know men who manufacture the stuff—and in any denomination they choose? Or raise one bill's face to mimic a more valuable one? When you and I first crossed paths, wasn't counterfeiting my lover's trade? And wasn't he a prince among his peers?" She smiles again, but her eyes remain inscrutable. "I think you must call me Adelaide. Adelaide Anspach has a respectable ring to it, don't you agree? And you may tell people that you and I have been bosom companions since...no, that scenario won't work. Not bosom companions. Instead you're—"

"What is it that you want of me?"

"Impatience was ever your fault, madam. We'll come to that in time. First, let me think."

Becky can't help but obey, although finding herself again commanded by this woman is excruciating. A year and a half of hard-won autonomy, of placating those whom she felt required it, of currying favor and doing favors in return, then of creating her own company. Must it all have been for naught? Thinking of her little Will, at home with his nursery maid, she weighs obedience with rebellion but cannot decide, while her guest, sensing her hostess's ambivalence, strikes while she can.

"I require your assistance. I wish to purchase a certain property. Your good standing will aid me in securing a line of credit."

"My 'good standing'? I'm an actress, Honora—"

"Adelaide."

"Adelaide. Do you understand what you're expecting of me?"

"Of course. Why would I have approached you if I had another choice?"

Becky's heart sinks. How often has she feared this day, and if not this conversation, then one remarkably like it? "The property's here? In Philadelphia?"

"Just so. Don't you desire that we should be sister citizens of this glorious metropolis?"

"Why should I?"

"That's unkind, my dear. Remember, it was I who rescued you."

"Yes. And it was the lies you forced me to make that allowed you to escape."

"Precisely. Which tidy arrangement I doubt you've shared with anyone. If you had, you would have been accused of abetting a crime by permitting two wanted criminals to flee. But I see before me not only a free woman but also a prosperous one, someone who has every intention of triumphing in the artistic and social spheres. Am I right, or am I not?"

Becky's heart flutters; her palms turn damp. This is worse than any opening-night qualms, she thinks. Instead of giving into her fear, however, she straightens her spine and then pats the ringlets framing her face as if attention to her coiffeur were uppermost in her mind. "You're mistaken, Honora; I did supply the information to the constabulary—"

"Adelaide" is the repeated correction, but Becky doesn't heed it this time.

"You and I made a pact. I kept my part of the bargain and created a diversionary tactic, which provided you the opportunity to flee. If I hadn't, you and your lover would have poisoned me. All of this the legal authorities know."

"You're lying."

"Am I? You may be capable of returning undetected to a city where you and your lover are wanted for murder, but I doubt you're able to detect what's said—or isn't said—in the privacy of a constabulary office. So, I repeat, why have you come here? For it's not to reminisce about old times and your devotion to Gideon Sark, master counterfeiter—"

Honora glares. "Never speak his name again—"

"And well-known libertine."

"Don't mention him again. I warn you."

Becky shrugs. "Don't threaten me. I protected you once. As you also protected me. But the compact we made is finished. Now, I must ask you to leave and to let me return to my affairs." Saying this, she wills her heart to cease pounding. Nerves have parched her throat. Her charade is in danger of becoming exposed. Steadying her hands, she reaches into her desk, pulls out a small stack of bills, and holds them out to Honora. "Take this. Genuine currency. Don't come to me for more. And don't expect my further involvement."

"How's your son?" is the sole reply, but the words are a hiss; and Becky's fingers, in the midst of proffering aid, jerk back.

"Leave me alone, Honora, or Adelaide, or whoever you are."

"No. I told you I need assistance. I won't quit this room until you provide it."

Becky sits, or rather drops into her chair, while Honora, separated by the width of desktop, regards her. Neither of their twin expressions is victorious; neither is resolute; neither serene.

"I've dispensed with the black-leg trade. Without my Gideon to guard me... well, no matter. The truth is that I have no protector now. After what occurred here. No, I can't let myself think about that dismal night. Please. Do you wish me to throw myself on your mercy?"

"Why should I help you?"

"Because you're frightened of what might transpire to your precious career—and even more precious babe—if you didn't—"

"Didn't you hear me? I revealed all to the police eighteen months ago. I have nothing to hide; therefore your threats are useless."

"I think not, Becky."

The two watch each other: Becky attempting but failing to vanquish her opponent, and Honora succeeding in the same effort. When Honora speaks again, her voice is a honeyed coo: "None of my former colleagues knows where I am. To them, I've vanished. 'Good riddance to a bad penny' is how they must feel, and I took care to cover my trail. So, Mrs. Anspach, as you read on my card: Adelaide Anspach. A woman with certain well-developed feminine charms who finds herself in pecuniary embarrassment and as a result decides to open a house of pleasure where gentlemen of breeding can partake of attractive ladies' company. What I have in mind is a first-class establishment, none of your old and ailing whores: first-class, with pretty girls, aged wines, and well-furnished chambers. Such places can turn a considerable profit. It's not as though this city has a dearth of bawdy houses, so you needn't wrinkle your nose and sneer."

Which Becky is indeed doing, although the reaction is an affectation to mask her anxiety.

"And you do want cash to finance your venture, I take it?"

"Yes. I lied to you. I need money. Not these paltry bills you offered. Help me, Becky. I never wanted to hurt you. Or your child. It was Gideon's plan. Not mine."

Becky stares, but she makes no answer. *Or your child*, her thoughts repeat: *or your child.*

"What he revealed to you was untrue. I wouldn't harm a baby. I wouldn't. Gideon, however—"

"Yes. I saw what he could do. But you were his match."

"Didn't I spare you? And your little one? Didn't I?"

Becky doesn't speak, but her mind's eye fixes itself on her little Will. *Little Will in the hands of this witch-woman.*

"So, let's let bygones be bygones. No good comes from dredging up the past."

Sinking back in her chair, Becky asks a hollow, "Why here? Why not another city?"

Honora laughs. "Why, Mistress Grey, judging from your tone, I question whether my decision meets your approval." The attempt at joviality ends. "I can promise you a share of the profits. I'm prepared to offer a very satisfactory percentage."

"Not from peddling flesh. I want no part of your earnings."

"Aren't you the high and mighty one? All women are whores. You should know that as well as anyone. I saw your husband, and I saw what he was, too. I won't accuse you of marrying for profit, because that might upset your delicate sensibilities, but that's what it was: an actress joined in unholy wedlock to a blue-blooded pig. Oh, dear me, no, I intended to say *prig*."

Becky remains silent. She thinks about the life she's built and how precarious their existence now appears. *Honora and Will*, her mind repeats. *Honora and my darling boy. She'd kill him for spite, or pleasure if the spirit moved her.*

"Tell me how much you require. I'll provide what I can. And then, I wish never to behold your face again."

CHAPTER 4

A Chance Encounter

THE SURGEON EXAMINING the body discovered in the fire's wreckage can find no physical clues that would help reveal the woman's identity, which leaves Kelman in the unenviable position of waiting for some forsaken family member to come forward and report that a loved one is missing. Or rather, he hopes that her absence will be reported. If, like most of the clientele, she has come from wealth, then inquiries will be made, albeit discreetly. On the other hand, if she was a woman hired by the evening or hour, then the task of providing a name and history will be well-nigh impossible.

Rather than wait for a knock on his door, or a circumspect letter, he embarks upon a study of those involved: the owner of the establishment, Mrs. Celestine Lampley; the staff employed on the premises that day; and a fragmentary list of clients. It's doubtful the last group could supply information and equally dubious that one of them would have started the blaze, but all eventualities must be considered. Arson is arson, and those who commit it are driven by a multitude of motives: some for profit, some for notoriety, and others for revenge.

He decides to begin by interviewing Mrs. Lampley and her staff, but there he meets another obstacle, for the owner, fearing legal action, has quit the city for an indeterminate period. The maid who informs him of her mistress's flight reveals that "Mrs. L." understood Kelman's orders to remain in Philadelphia but that she didn't want "no bother from the constabulary, and took herself off on the boat bound for Baltimore." Where she intends to travel next, the maid has no idea. A large woman with a bovine cast to her body and wide, belligerent eyes, she's only too glad to belittle her employer. Once she begins talking, Kelman need pose no further questions.

"Could be anywhere by now, Mister. Heading south. West. I don't know and don't care," he's told. "Left me in the lurch, she did. Said I could stay in these precious, small chambers of hers till the rent comes due, but what happens then, I ask you? If she's not back, I'll be pitched into the street. Pitched straight into the street. Which is all the thanks I get after serving her nigh on fifteen years. Fifteen years with that woman! Oh, she can be smooth as molasses when she wants to and sweet enough to make your teeth ache, but isn't she a devil when alone with me? That's not a question, Mister; that's a statement of pure fact. 'Heavenly' is what she says Celestine means, but I'd say it's just the opposite."

The animosity in these remarks makes Kelman wonder whether the maid might be lying about Mrs. Lampley's disappearance, which leads him to consider if the female corpse could be the house's owner, but, as if the maid has second sense, she sneers a response to the query he hasn't yet asked.

"Oh, she wasn't burned up in that blaze, if that's what you're wondering. Not her. Likely as not, it was her viciousness that got the flames a-going. She's got a tongue on her that's hot and mean. No, she ran off as fast as she could once the blaze took hold and then flew up here and hid. Didn't even wait to see if I was all right. Let alone all those others who pay for her upkeep. You can ask the scullery boy, if you doubt me. Or the serving girl. Mrs. L. left them to their own devices, too. They were worse off than me, 'cause they didn't have a roof over their heads that night and may not still. They lived over in the house, you see, in case the clients wanted anything special after hours. Not that I'd call the miserable quarters where they dossed *living* as much as being stabled. As for me, the mistress doesn't mix business with her private affairs, which is why we're here. Or why I am—as long as it lasts." Pausing only to reflect upon the injustice of her treatment, she adds a final note. "But them two are younger and don't mind sleeping under the stars, or wherever they've got themselves to. Bridgid's the girl. The boy's Borcher. Last name. Don't know his first." Then the door is shut before Kelman can ask anything further.

⇥▰◉ ◉▰⇤

As Kelman begins his hunt for Mrs. Lampley's additional servants, Martha's adoptive daughter Ella starts a third slow promenade around Washington

Square. She's alone, which she shouldn't be, but she's become so adept at eluding the governess, Mademoiselle Hédé, that she does so for no other reason than boredom. Supposedly retired to her bedroom for an afternoon repose—*un repos*, according to Mademoiselle—she crept down the rear stairway and thence to the road, where she walked from Martha Beale's residence on Chestnut Street to Walnut Street. Sometimes she considers taking Cai on these excursions, because wandering here and there can be a lonely pastime, but she knows he'd never be able to keep their clandestine rambles a secret. Besides which, he's excitable and given to fits, which makes him less than ideal company.

Thinking of him, she sighs. Trying as he can be, she envies his cheerful disposition. He delights in everything he's given, everything—including the lessons in arithmetic and history and geography and composition Mademoiselle assigns. *How can we two be so different*, she wonders, then decides, as she always does, that it's because Cai was young when he was adopted. He has fewer bad memories to forget. Or maybe he doesn't remember anything other than being Caspar Beale. Whereas she—

She sighs anew. Pouting, her face takes on a coquettish prettiness that makes her look older than her years. Young men, as well as their elders, pause to take note of the finely dressed young lady who appears so self-assured, and, truth to tell, so likely to become a flirt. If she were with a female companion, some might tip their hats and hope for an opportunity to exchange pleasantries. Alone, though, she's forbidden game.

Not so for another woman also strolling the park, also in a solitary state, and also expensively arrayed in a costume that makes her look newly arrived from Paris. The lustrous blues of her mantilla and gown would complement her red hair, but Adelaide has hidden it beneath a brown wig. Despite her nondescript coiffure, she epitomizes regal aloofness. Approaching Ella, she condescends to nod before passing on, while Ella, her boredom instantly gone, begins to invent a glamorous history for the stranger. The minutest details of her garments and carriage help create the story. *A countess, maybe, or a princess. French, of course, because her clothes are elegant and foreign. And maybe a friend of the count who owned the chateau on the banks of the Delaware…Bonaparte, the emperor's brother.* Ella knows all about the compte de Survilliers, because Mademoiselle Hédé told her. Mademoiselle's parents were employed by the *compte*, so her facts are correct.

Ella's flight of fancy continues. She adds more fantastical embellishments to the tale. Then, unconsciously, she turns and follows Adelaide, rapidly gaining on her, because she's still half child despite her years. When she's close to her quarry, she experiences momentary shyness, but nothing ventured, nothing gained. She coughs to indicate her presence, and the lady turns in surprise.

"Ah, chérie, que voudriez-vous. *Pardon*—let me converse in English. What may I do for you, pretty one? You desire to speak with me, *non*?"

Ella's heart comes near to bursting with excitement. A real princess speaking to her! And to think that she could have been trapped at home for *un repos*! She drops a curtsy, because she knows that's polite, but before she can decide what to do next, she blurts out her name. "I'm Ella Beale." And then she compounds that impropriety by shaking the lady's hand.

The faux *princesse* laughs in false delight, though Ella mistakes the reaction for genuine enjoyment. "Ah, you Americans, so bold, so full of *joie de vivre*. In my native land, such temerity would be regarded with suspicion, if not scorn. I'm pleased to make your acquaintance, Mistress Ella. But I think your *maman* might be dismayed by your impudence, *n'est-ce pas*?"

Ella's shoulders sag. *Maman! How can anyone call Martha Beale my mother? Don't I have a mother, a real mother, who may now be missing me terribly? Maybe she's ill or suffering; maybe she's very, very poor; maybe she's even near death from starvation.* These thoughts flood her brain, turning her face a mottled pink. She had a younger brother, too, she recalls. He fell into the cooking fire one day, which left his face half purple-red, half white, as if he were part demon and part angel. Where is he now? Where are they both?

Adelaide watches the emotions transform the attractive girl with the creamy curls into a stormy beauty. Passion in a female, whatever its form, can be a powerful aphrodisiac, as Adelaide well knows. After all, how many men seek out tempestuous companions rather than stay home with their placid wives? She smiles. "I should not have mentioned your maman, chérie. I had no right to intrude upon your privacy. Forgive my faux pas." She stretches out her hand and takes Ella's. "Promise me we'll part as friends, for I must be hastening on my way. Now adieu. Or, rather, au revoir, for I hope that someday we'll meet again."

With that, Adelaide strolls out of the park, passing without noticing a gangly youth with oversize ears who has covertly witnessed the exchange. Before Ella can spot him, however, he hides. Findal understands when to keep his distance from this girl he adores and when to make his presence known.

→≡◉ ◉≡←

Having made the acquaintance of Martha Beale's adoptive daughter, Adelaide returns to her chambers. Locking the door, she walks to the small looking glass set atop the chest of drawers provided by the landlord. There, she gazes at her reflection, a smile of conquest playing across her lips. "Now we begin," she whispers while regarding her silent double. "A-de-laide An-spach," she adds, drawing out the syllables. "What do you say, ma chérie? Will we meet with success? Non? Oui?" At this, she laughs. Mirth is absent from the exercise.

Then the manufactured smile vanishes. Her lips relax into a bitter line. She touches the glass, the expression in her eyes transformed to grief. "Gideon," she murmurs, "my love. You watch me. Wherever you are. You watch what I do to them." Her fingers stroke her reflected brow, then her cheeks and earlobes, the caress lingering and bereft. "What I do, I do for you." With that, the image and the genuine woman forsake sorrow for fury. "Thomas Kelman and his doe-eyed Martha. Unsuspecting and so very sweet. You needn't wait long."

She turns her back on the chest of drawers and dresses again in her widow's weeds, carefully returning her French finery to the muslin wrappings in which they were stored. The wardrobe contains other changes of costume that suit the onetime Honora's aliases. She can garb herself in muted Quaker gray, or in the coarse black dress of a serving girl, or in country fare that makes her look especially naïve and easy to deceive.

The glittering jewels (paste, alas) are exchanged for jet beads, a mourning brooch, and mourning bracelet—all purchased from a pawnbroker in New York City. The mementos give her a moment's pause; it seems ill luck to wear another woman's memorials to loss. She shrugs off the weakness, pulls on kidskin gloves, then glides down the building's rear stairs and begins to stroll the town, a figure clothed head to toe in black.

Thus concealed, she meanders this way and that. The day is fine and pleasant. Her spirits begin to match the weather's mood, and she reflects with pride on her current status. Having begun her career as a petty thief when still a child, she soon graduated into the confidence game, becoming so adept at passing false bills that she was revered among her peers. Now a new career lies within her grasp—if she wishes it. *If.* Or perhaps not.

Strolling, she envisions herself ensconced in a private parlor in her new abode, accepting the best clientele for the choicest of girls. She'll advertise—discreetly, of course, because discerning gentlemen require discretion—and will list her business in a local publication, *The Guide for the Stranger in the City of Brotherly Love and Sisterly Affection*, as "a house where charm and gentility can be found in abundance." In her mind, her future bawdy house becomes a kind of seminary for young ladies where they learn deportment and etiquette—with the mistress of the household acting as a gentle, if exacting, matron.

Thus fantasizing, she finds herself in the city's northern, industrial heart. Gone are the fine mansions and tree-lined boulevards, gone the pavements along which the rich and highborn saunter, gone the governesses with their young charges. Instead, she sees and smells commercial wharves and a continual whirl of people clothed in shabby browns and grays. Every garment has been patched; most have had multiple owners. Here, where the textile mills produce bolt upon bolt of pristine fabric to be purchased by those who can afford such luxuries as damascened silk or brocade, the ragmen ply their trade, shouting out "old clothes for sale!" and buying them, too. A housebreaker entering the home of a wealthy family is wise to search the wardrobes as well as the plate-silver chests, for a pricey piece of clothing is a valuable commodity indeed.

Adelaide steps past the hawkers and peddlers, the vendors purveying soups or cooked potatoes, the fishwives displaying basketsful of eels pulled from the Delaware—none of which look fresh. Escaping the maelstrom, she turns down a small court leading from Noble Street, which is anything but noble, and there encounters an abbreviated funeral procession: an undertaker's carriage followed by mourners on foot. It's clear from the paltry trappings that the family of the deceased is poor. The customary black is made up of newly dyed old garments, and the color has run, turning any exposed skin a dirty slate-gray. Supported by a man, a woman sobs; if he weren't clasping her, she'd fall. Accompanying the pair is another woman who coos and pats the mourners' shoulders, although these ministrations appear tentative and not entirely welcome.

Adelaide pulls back within the shadow of a building lest the group spot her and mistake her presence as being intentional. The undertaker's assistant does spot her, however. Passing close, he moves to her side and touches his hat in a sign of respect for the elevated status her garments show her to possess.

"You the manager's wife?" he asks in a muted tone.

"No," she says, shrinking closer to the wall. "No, I was only passing by."

"Ah…I thought those folks might be doing right by the poor kid. I was wrong. No surprise, there. Them folks think kids are no better than mill ponies. Worse, probably."

"The deceased is…was a child?"

"You can see the coffin, Missus. That wasn't made for no circus midget." He wipes his eyes on a black-edged handkerchief. "You wouldn't imagine a fellow in my position weeping, would you? After all the burials I've attended in my time. But I'm softhearted when it comes to the little ones. I've got eight of my own. This lad here, well, to look at him when he arrived at our shop would have made you sick. Caught up in the cogs of one of the looms he was, and his hands nearly wrenched off. He lingered a few days, which was no blessing for the parents, or for him. Though the mother kept expecting a miracle. It would have broke your heart to hear her. Should be wearing mourning white, shouldn't they? Seeing that he was such a wee thing. But it's cheaper to cover the old with a black tint, so there you have it—the niceties can't always be observed." He pauses, and then adds a sorrowing, "I wish you was the manager's wife. It would have eased their pain to know an employer took note of their grief." With that, he rejoins the somber group while Adelaide, vengeful, merciless Adelaide, presses her unforgiving back against the wall and gives way to silent tears.

CHAPTER 5

What Remains Unsaid

AT SIX O'CLOCK that evening, Martha is astonished to have her footman announce that Mrs. Becky Grey is waiting downstairs and wishes to pay a call. The hour is unusual, for it's approaching the time when dinner is taken, but Martha understands that rehearsal schedules can be erratic, and she immediately sends for her friend, walking into the corridor to meet her when she ascends the stairs.

"You'll stay for supper, I hope?" are the cheerful words Becky hears as she mounts the steps. Other than her footfall, sound is negligible, the absence of noise being another manifestation of wealth. Becky's lips tighten in an expression of envy tinged with regret; she doesn't begrudge Martha her inheritance and elevated situation within the city's elite, but she would like to be afforded a similar ease; she also knows the impossibility of that dream.

"No, I must return to the theater. I came to see you because I desired company not given to histrionics. Staging a comedy like *The School for Scandal* shouldn't induce fits of furor, but it has. The actor portraying Sir Benjamin Backbite is the worst of the troupe when it comes to melodrama. His temperament is better suited to portraying a villain like Iago."

"Perhaps he's taking the character's name to heart."

Becky smiles. "They say Mr. Sheridan's play was George Washington's favorite—thus my decision to revive it in his favorite house of entertainment. I ally myself to your nation's history while providing an evening of wit and verbal parrying."

"Your nation, too" is Martha's small rebuke.

Her guest makes no answer. Instead she toys with the ribbons of her bonnet, untying them as if to remove her hat, but then she stands irresolutely, studying the room as if summoning the courage to speak. The pose isn't one her public ever sees. Martha recognizes it, however.

"Something's troubling you. What is it?"

"Can't I pay a call for no reason other than pleasure?"

Martha comes close to mentioning the hour but stops, lest she insult her visitor. It's difficult enough for Becky—and Martha, too—to combat the inescapable truth that society's elite regard performers as inferiors. Certain acquaintances of Martha's snub anyone who treads the boards. *Backbite, indeed*, she thinks. *That character would never win a competition among the supposed ladies of Philadelphia.* "Of course you may. Tell me about *The School for Scandal*. We'll sit and be sociable, and you can describe all the greenroom gossip." Which Becky doesn't do, thus forcing Martha to also remain standing.

"No. I don't want to consider Mrs. Candour or Lady Sneerwell or my own portrayal of Lady Teazle. I want reality, not paint and posturing." Saying this, Becky frowns and then takes a step away. "If you heard something about me… something untoward…or…or even evil, would you believe it?"

Martha gauges her guest's behavior. Becky's face is hidden, so it's impossible to ascertain the veracity of the emotion. Her friend, she knows, can be given to hyperbole. She replies as though the question were authentic. "Are you asking if I'd forgive you if I thought you'd committed an unkind or cruel act?"

"Yes…I suppose that's what I'm asking. What would you decide?"

Martha ponders both the question and the anxiety of the speaker's voice. "Forgiveness isn't something we humans can measure out. True forgiveness comes from God."

"I know that. But I'm talking about you, not a deity."

Martha doesn't immediately reply, which causes Becky to become more restive. "I assume this isn't idle discourse but a valid concern, and if so—"

"Don't preach to me about God. He'd never forgive me as readily as you. It's your opinion I want, not some invisible being who may or may not exist."

"Oh, Becky! How can you talk so rashly?"

"With perfect equanimity. You believe one thing, I another. Your faith provides you with hope and consolation, but no beneficent deity would condone suffering—"

"Becky!"

"Therefore, there can be none—"

"You don't mean what you say!"

"I do." Her posture softens. She affixes a bright smile, though Martha recognizes its lack of sincerity. "Pay no mind to my query. It was merely idle chat. We actors become apprehensive and volatile toward the conclusion of a rehearsal process. But enough of my prattle about deities and otherwise. How is your Mr. Kelman? Thriving, I hope."

"Is that what you came to discuss?"

"Why not? Don't I want to see you happily wed?"

Martha regards her friend, who now stands firm and tall. Nothing in her pose recalls the woman who entered the room, nor the person she was one minute past. "I've learned that certain events and emotions can't be rushed. And so it is with Thomas Kelman."

"Oh, pooh. Don't sit on your hands and wait, or pray for a proposal of marriage. You must show passion." She pauses. "I'm not the best person to provide marital advice, though. As you well know." With that she sits—or, rather, flings—herself into the nearest chair.

Martha says nothing for several moments. Nor does her companion, although her disquiet intensifies. "Becky, I doubt there's any act or sin you could have committed that wouldn't be justified in your eyes. If so—"

"Let's not speak about that. My question was pure badinage and nothing more. Oh, but look at the time! I must leave you to your supper." Rising, she hurries to Martha, kissing her cheek in a distracted manner. "You've been so kind to me. Too kind. Befriending me when everyone abhorred me. Becoming my champion when my husband reviled me, and during that terrifying episode last year when...but oh, we needn't mention that. It was frightening enough to live through."

"Dear friend, if there's—"

"I'm ever thus when a play is in the final stages of rehearsal. All actors become as fluttery as caged birds. I apologize if I've caused you concern. In truth, there's nothing to worry over."

"Please. I'm your friend. Confide in me."

Becky forces a laugh. "Oh, I will. I will. I shall tell you all about Sir Benjamin Backbite's intrigues. But not tonight."

"Don't go. Dine with me—"

"No, no, I leave you to your happy domesticity. I must hurry back to the theater. A manager's work is never finished."

As she speaks, the door open, and Ella appears. Her surprise at not finding Martha alone makes her hesitate. She's about to retreat, but Becky beckons her in, walking toward her and giving her a warm embrace. "And here is the family beauty come to remind her mama that dinner is awaiting. Ella, my dear, you grow lovelier daily. It seems that every visit I make to this house, there's a new and wondrous change in your demeanor." Looking at Martha, Becky smiles, the expression in earnest this time. "You must take heed of unwanted beaux circling round our Ella. I have a strong feeling that she'll become a veritable siren. If she isn't one already. Now, let me leave you to your pleasant evening hours."

The meal Martha shares with her adopted children and their governess isn't the scene of placid domesticity Becky envisioned, for Ella is uncommunicative, which inspires Cai to grow more voluble, which in turn induces his sister to berate him. Martha and the governess intervene, but the remainder of their dinner is far from tranquil.

⇢⊨◉ ◉⊨⇠

While the four sit at their troubled table, Kelman undertakes his search for Celestine Lampley's missing servants. The dinner hour suits him because, attempting to elude the police or not, people must eat. And he's found that generally they congregate in places they've frequented before. The girl Bridgid is the first he locates, though it's difficult to interview her, as she has negotiated paying for her meal by washing the other diners' dishes. The result is that Kelman must attempt to converse with her over the sluicing noise of the pump in the rear alleyway of a small, insalubrious eatery on the inaptly named Queen Street. Householders and others wait their chance at the water pump, thus forcing Bridgid to expend additional energy on growling at them to "keep clear." She's a solid, ungainly person with a lowering gaze and broad back, as if accustomed to bearing heavy burdens since childhood. Kelman's astonished to learn that she's sixteen, for her barrel-like stance and dull glare make her look twice that age.

"The missus wouldn't have kept me around if I'd been pretty" is the brief assessment she makes of herself. Then, like Lampley's lady's maid, she launches into a recitation of complaints about her ill-usage: working in the house from the time she turned twelve in order to support a drunken mother; the clients who scarcely noticed her, or if they did, turned away with a sneer; the few who crossed her palm; the many more who didn't; and finally her disgust with the "low moral state of the clientele"—accompanying which judgment, she curls her lips. In vain does Kelman query her about the names of those in the house on the night of the fire, or about anyone's identity during her period of labor. Bridgid cannot supply them. "It was only Mistress and Master, and like that," she states as if he should know better than to raise nonsensical questions. When he concludes the interview by asking whether Mrs. Lampley might have had an enemy willing to burn down the place, she forsakes the pump and folds her arms across her chest. "'How many of them' is what you should be asking, not 'whether.' Beelzebub doesn't have more detractors than Celestine Lampley. And now she's left me to starve. Well, I say she can go straight to Hell. It's where she belongs."

Borcher is more difficult to locate. Kelman searches from oyster house to rum cellar, from itinerant soup purveyor to pie seller. All have seen him, but none tonight. To a person they express approval of the young man's habits, for he spends freely when he has money in his pocket. About to relinquish the hunt and begin again the following day, Kelman's informed that Borcher sometimes takes his ease among a group of ragtag youths on a corner of Christian Street above the docks. And this is where he's found.

Unlike Bridgid, Borcher is delighted to be the focus of an inquiry. He gives his age as twenty-two, though Kelman doubts he's older than eighteen. There's nothing gangly about his limbs and torso, though; instead, he's boxy as a trained bear. "And what may I do for you, my dear sir?" he asks, giving a knowing wink to his fellows, who arrange themselves close, the better to watch the show. Although Kelman represents the constabulary, his quarry is a free man and supposedly a victim of the blaze, like anyone else on the premises. He knows he must tread lightly.

"Borcher at your service. And always happy to help out our noble enforcers of the law."

Kelman doubts that this is the case but decides to humor his subject. He begins by asking if "Mr. Borcher" can recall names of clientele or others present on the evening in question.

Like Bridgid, the young man can't provide the identities of those who frequented Lampley's establishment, either on the night of the fire or on previous occasions. This doesn't stop him from naming anyone who has appeared in a city newspaper, however. "Cadwaladers, of course," he announces, grinning at his mates rather than at Kelman. "Male and female both. And a Rittenhouse or two—no, three—during the space of my employ. And a Wharton, too. Mrs. Lampley catered to the finest folk in the city. It was a privilege to work there. Anyone bound in service to a single home can't hope to rub elbows with the swells I've encountered. A privilege, as I said." He finishes off the claim with another nod to his neighbors.

Kelman decides to prod a bit. "So in your estimation, Mrs. Lampley was a good mistress, is that correct? Or is it only due to the 'swells' you met? Bridgid's opinion was the opposite."

"Silly cow. What would she know about class? Nothing, is what I say. Mrs. L. was forever trying to get that ugly hunk of cheese to improve her appearance. Would she do it? Not her. Which is why she spent most of the time cooking and cleaning, while I was sent to serve the ladies and gents. I was like Celestine's— Mrs. Lampley's—footman, instead of a lowly scullery boy."

Kelman notes the inadvertent use of the lady's Christian name as well as the fact that Borcher's already-ruddy face turned scarlet when he made the mistake. "And yet this exemplary employer left you with no labor and no letter of reference."

"Who says so? Maybe she treated those two drabs in that fashion, but not I." Another wink is bestowed upon his friends. "If I don't choose to seek current employment, that's my affair. As long as I'm in good standing with my boon companions here, that's all that matters."

Kelman regards the company. He's well acquainted with these types of young men. They'll work for honest wages if they're offered; if not, they pilfer anything left unguarded, or else do so at another's behest. The only constant is the esteem they bear one another. Criticize one, all receive the wound, and all react in outrage. It can take a trifle to turn them into an angry mob, constables being a preferred target of their rage.

He asks whether Mrs. Lampley might have had an enemy who could have set fire to the house, and he receives his first surprising response.

"I'm guessing she did the deed herself. She's a remarkably resourceful woman, and if she had creditors, well, what better way to escape those bogeymen?"

"You're suggesting arson, are you, Mr. Borcher? That's a nasty allegation, especially considering how well your mistress treated you."

"What's nasty about it? The lady has style as well as class. And she's clever, too. It wouldn't have taken any effort for her to pull off a trick like that—"

"The 'trick,' as you put it, claimed the life of a woman."

"An accident, I'm sure." Borcher waves his hand as though dispersing a cloud of gnats. "At any rate, everyone was present and accounted for after the fire took hold, so maybe that female came from elsewhere. Maybe somebody was trying to damage Celestine's—Mrs. L.'s—reputation."

"Your mistress ascertained her guests were safe, did she? Or did you?"

"Not I, but Mrs. L. would have. She's very particular about how she runs her business."

"But you can't swear she did, can you?"

Borcher remains silent one second too long. "Course I can. And do."

"You seem to be certain of yourself in all respects, Mr. Borcher."

The young man nods at his peers. "That I am. And should be. For I'm bound for finer things than idling my days away here in this dreary old town. Mrs. L. liked to tell me about the fortune a man could make out in the wilds to the west. Pittsburgh is the place to start, she said, where the three rivers run together in such a torrent of water and foamy spray that it looks as if the earth were rising up out of the ocean that formed it—"

"Is that where she's gone?"

Wary in an instant, he ducks his head, a nervous gesture not previously displayed.

"Is that where your mistress is, Mr. Borcher?"

"How would I know? A footman or a scullery boy's naught but a flunky, isn't he? Why would a lady as estimable as her tell me her plans? Lady's maids and majordomos and like them, they're flunkies, too. Neither master nor mistress blabs to those lowly folk. Leastways, none I've met."

CHAPTER 6

An Act of Consolation

THE NEXT MORNING, Adelaide clothes herself in yet another set of garments—this time as a matron married to a moderately prosperous gentleman of trade. Her hair is now a black wig and all but concealed within a bonnet that's remarkable only in that it's unornamented by silk flowers or velvet trimmings. The bonnet type, known by the common name of "coal scuttle," for that's what it resembles, hides the wearer's face like blinders concealing the eyes of a horse.

Thus transformed, she makes her way toward the Northern Liberties, where she encountered the funeral procession the day before. Ella would never recognize the Parisian princess of her dreams. Traversing the city, Adelaide could be venturing out early to visit a sick relative, or to make purchases necessary for her household, or to call upon her husband before he begins his day of labor. Not even the street urchins follow her; from their point of view, it's obvious she carries no extra coins to disperse, and even if she did, she wouldn't share them. In their well-seasoned opinions, ladies wed to merchants, whether grocers or purveyors of dry goods, aren't of a philanthropic nature.

Reaching Noble Street, she stops and studies her surroundings, trying to ascertain in which direction the lodgings of the dead boy's parents might lie. Not spotting any sign of mourning, she asks a passerby if he knows of a child killed as a result of a mill accident.

The question elicits a glare of contempt. "The Jervis boy, you mean? You're from the company, then?"

Although she denies the accusation—for it sounds very much like an accusation—it's clear that he doesn't believe her. With ill will, and without even the tip of his battered hat, he points out "the Jervis *manse*," sneering the last word in a manner intended to cut Adelaide to the quick. How mistaken he is about this woman. If she had a mind to, she could do more than upbraid or "cut" him in return, for she was early trained in the art of wielding a knife.

Meekly, however, she climbs the stairs to the one-room, second-floor apartment that comprises the Jervis home and knocks on the door. Smells of cheap cookery fill the stairwell and corridor: cabbage stews, fish-head soups, and boiling trotters; the walls are greasy to the touch, the original color beneath the grime impossible to ascertain. There's a distant wail of an infant and the crash of something thudding to the floor, and then brutal silence. Adelaide knocks again.

A woman who might once have been considered pretty opens the door. Fair hair turned the color of dust, skin of an equally ashy hue, eyes limned with red, and a mouth held in a perpetual grimace to conceal its missing teeth.

"Mrs. Jervis?"

"Who wants her?" The question is posed in a tone as downtrodden as the woman's appearance. There's so little inflection to it that Adelaide wonders for a moment what has been said.

"I'm Mrs. Adolphus Green, from the Bureau for Betterment among the Bereaving." There's no such organization, but she states the name as if it were as genuine as the Association to Rescue Drowning Persons. "I understand your son—"

"Not mine. My sister-in-law's. Her only surviving child." The grimace crumples in a silent sob. She turns away from the door and addresses a man half slumped over a table. "Jervis. Some fine lady wants to see you."

Then she quits her post and trudges with heavy steps to the curtain that partitions the room and disappears from view. Adelaide can hear her crooning words of comfort to someone who remains invisible.

Jervis raises his head. He's a gaunt man whose eyes are sunken in their sockets. The act of focusing on the unexpected visitor requires effort, but not, Adelaide surmises, because he's been drowning his sorrow in gin, but because he hasn't moved for many hours.

"You from the mill?"

"No, Mr. Jervis, I represent the—"

"Because we don't want you here. The missus and I, we never want to set sight on any of your wicked faces again."

"Sir, if you'll hear me out—"

"Sir, is it? When was I ever 'sir' to the likes of you? When I was toiling over them looms myself? Or when my missus was? Or our little boy—" The words break off; his lips part wide as if to cry out, but no sound comes.

Adelaide waits for him to compose himself, but his mouth remains fixed in a rictus, as if he were gasping for air.

"Mr. Jervis. I represent a group of citizens who help parents in distress."

"You're trying to buy us off, that's what you are. Well, my missus and I won't have it. You know why I can't work, and why the little fellow went to help his mother the best he could."

"I'm not—"

But Jervis, frozen as he's been, now becomes galvanized by anger. He shakes his fists at her; both hands are missing their thumbs and forefingers. "If you've come to gloat about how powerful them steam looms of yours are, Missus, I'm living proof of their efficiency. And you wouldn't keep me in any other employ, would you? Never mind how faithful I'd been all those long years."

Adelaide permits him to rage on. If her former acquaintances were to happen upon the scene, none would be able to reconcile her changed demeanor. Has fierce Honora ceased to exist, or is this merely another disguise? Probably she doesn't understand herself.

"Mr. Jervis, no one I know belongs to the mill that killed your child and maimed you. I haven't come here to bribe you, or to mock your grief, or to cause you and your wife and sister-in-law further distress—"

"Then begone. You and your fine clothes and pushing ways. Forcing your way inside my home when it's clear we want to be left alone. It's unseemly. That's what it is. Begone, I tell you."

"No, I will not leave," says Adelaide, again transformed, for the tone she has assumed has a resolute edge at odds with her deferential posture. "I will not quit this room until you allow me to help you." So saying, she thrusts her hand into her reticule, pulling forth every bit of authentic currency she owns: banknotes crumpled together with coins of minute value, some shiny, some mossy with age. She dumps this heap onto the table. The display is hardly that of an official representing a charitable bureau, but Jervis doesn't seem to notice.

He gawks at the pile, then at her, and then touches the tip of one of the bills as if he's never seen its like before. Finally, he stares into her face, or at least what can be seen within the wings of her bonnet. "How much is this, Missus? Months and months of work, I'm thinking."

"Not enough to assuage your grief" is what she says, though the statement is prompted by her inability to name the amount. Remorseless and conniving, she should know the value of her gift, but the fact is that she doesn't. Nor does she question her seeming lapse in judgment. Those who have known poverty open their hearts more spontaneously than those who have been taught to save and hoard, lest they end their days in want. At this moment, she represents the best in human nature. "I give you all I have—all I've been commissioned by the association to supply," she adds as an embellishment, "in hopes that it brings you and your family some relief."

With that, she turns before she can be queried further or reveal emotions whose source she doesn't wish to examine.

Hurrying down the stairs, and then walking south and westward, she's a full six blocks away before the three residents of the Jervis household realize they don't recall the lady's name, or the beneficial agency she represented.

"She was like an angel," the dead boy's aunt mutters. "Like the queen of the angels."

CHAPTER 7

Devotion

FINDAL STOKES WATCHES Ella's maneuverings as she departs Martha's home. First, she opens the subterranean service door fronting Eleventh Street, and then she utters a loud "shoo" to a nonexistent cat while keeping her face turned toward an unseen person within the vestibule. After that she coos an exaggerated, "Oh, you poor, poor thing. Here, I'll bring you some milk." Finally, she emerges, walking up the six steps to the pavement, but without a saucer of cream in hand or looking for the phantom feline. Ella has developed numerous ruses for leaving her home. If queried, one of the maids will state she heard her young mistress walk outside to feed a stray animal. Because Martha is loath to curtail the girl's freedom, none of the servants have been instructed to watch her movements.

Findal extricates himself from the preferred hiding place, where he observes the house—it's a two-foot-wide alley leading to a rear courtyard of another home on Chestnut Street—and follows. If Ella's aware of his presence, she doesn't reveal it, but then she's too engrossed in her own emotional maelstrom to notice anything but herself. Traveling north on Eleventh Street, she turns west when she reaches High Street, then pauses before setting her course for Penn Square, long ago a bucolic gathering place replete with statuary and a fountain but now merely a grassy sward. Some vestiges of the square's elegance remain, but Ella chooses to ramble there because of its relative desertion.

Reaching Filbert Street, she walks northward. The late-springtime sun is nearly overhead, and the grasses and other greenery glow with a countrified air as if the coal docks on the Schuylkill River weren't within a half hour's stroll. She takes no heed of the weather or landscape, however. With anger and sorrow in her heart—toward what and whom she doesn't fully comprehend—she marches along. Findal trails behind, waiting to spot a momentary softening of her scowl or spine. When this doesn't happen, he approaches her.

"Miss Ella."

Without turning or slowing her pace, she orders him to go away and leave her in peace.

"No, Miss Ella, that I can't do. You shouldn't be walking out here on your own. Not in your handsome clothes. There are too many pickpockets about, and—"

"What do I care?" She spins around and levels her wrath on the boy, then allows her high emotion to slither into something underhanded and cruel. "You look like a cutpurse, yourself, if you want my opinion. You've gotten so tall you've outgrown your clothes."

The accusation wounds him, as she intended. It also causes a sickening wrench in her stomach, as if she'd ignored a fledgling bird kicked out of its nest and left dying on the pavement. She bites her lip. Tears spring into her eyes; she blinks them back. She yearns to apologize for her mean words but cannot bring herself to do so. "Go away, Findal. I don't wish to talk to you, or anyone else."

"I can't do that. I'll move off a bit so you don't have to speak with me if you find me ugly and ill formed, but I'll not permit you to stroll about here without a man to watch over you."

"A man, are you, Master Stokes? When did that transformation occur? Yesterday? Today? You're sixteen; that doesn't make you a man of the world."

"Sticks and stones, Ms. Ella. Sticks and stones."

In her unhappy fury, she flings herself away from him, but he plucks at her sleeve, forcing her to remain. "Let me go, Findal. Let me go, or I'll shout aloud that there's a street urchin pestering me."

The threat is genuine enough to cause him to relinquish his grip. Released, however, she remains where she is.

"You shouldn't creep away from your home the way you do. It's not safe."

"Do you think I'm unaware of the danger? Wasn't I born into the same miserable world you were? Don't you try to tell me what to do."

When he doesn't reply, her eggshell-thin veneer begins to crack. "I don't want you here," she mutters, but the words carry little weight, and so Findal makes no move to desert her.

"Come along home to your mother—"

"She's not my mother!"

"No, she's not. That's true. But a better one you couldn't hope for—"

"How would you know? How would you know anything, except trailing after me in order to pester me?"

He regards her, his expression serious. Notwithstanding his youth and his ill-fitting clothes, which leave his wrists and ankles exposed and his neck perpetually stretching away from his shirt collar, he can assume an air of sagacity.

"Don't be unkind for unkindness's sake. That's a sin, that is. Old Stokes got vicious for no reason other than to beat me. Oftentimes, I thought it was the sole reason I was born."

Ella nods her silent assent. She and Findal have shared all aspects of their early lives. "I swore I'd never become like him. Not so long as I drew breath."

"I know that."

"So, don't you carry on in this foolish fashion. You're not one of those prissy-faced young ladies always looking down their noses when they spot beggar children. You need to remember where you came from."

"How can I ever forget it?" The question is a yelp of hurt, but he isn't finished with his lecture.

"I'm thinking it must be easy to forget when you're surrounded day and night by all the comforts in Miss Beale's house." This is the wrong approach, and he realizes it before he has finished speaking.

"I don't want to live there any longer, Findal. I don't. What do I care for fine dresses, and lessons on deportment and geography, and…and singing? Why should I wish to become an old maid like Martha Beale, who does nothing but—"

"Ella, what you're saying isn't right."

"I'll say what I choose."

"But you'll not bite the hand that feeds you—"

"I'm not a dog. I'm a person." With that, she bursts into tears, while he, private counselor and secret swain, pats her shoulders and eventually holds her in an awkward clasp.

It's fortunate that no member of the day watch is patrolling Penn Square, for the boy would be chased away before he or Ella could attempt to explain. Findal surveys the scene with the lofty gaze of protector and champion.

"Tell me what you wish me to do for you, Ella. Anything at all. I'd move mountains for you if I could."

Comforted at last, she gazes into his face. "Can you find my mother? My real one?"

He relinquishes his hold and looks at her for a moment before speaking. "Do you know what you're asking?"

Frowning and nodding at the same time, she answers with a quiet, "Can you do it?"

"I'm not saying whether I can or can't. I'm asking if you understand what might happen if I succeed."

"I do."

"Oh, Ella! Miss Beale's so very fond of you, and she's given you more than any other girl your age could dream about—"

"I don't want those trappings. I've told you—"

"You'd rather be sold into one of those bad houses again, is that it? Or live by your wits, as I do. Or marry some brute just because you need a roof over your head."

No. Of, course not. I'd like to see her, that's all—"

"But what about Miss Beale?"

"I don't know. I don't know! Please. Can you help me?"

He shakes his head, his expression grieved and impotent. "I don't see how anyone could manage that impossible mission. Not after all this time. And you with so little memory of your onetime home. Who am I supposed to hunt for? A lady who looks like you? We imagine we're different from other folks, but hundreds of people in this city could be our kin. " Then he adds a nearly inaudible, "Besides, she might be…she might have died."

"But you can do anything, Findal. Anything you set your mind to. I know you can. And you're brave, too. Braver than anyone."

→┤═◉ ◉═├←

A similar group of questions is surging through Thomas Kelman's brain. In anticipation of commencing an official search for Ella's birth mother, his thoughts have become a battleground of warring possibilities. Found, the woman could have any number of repellent characteristics. She could be a drunkard, a thief, or both, and live in an unsavory household with all conditions of odious partners. She could be dying. She could be dead—which Kelman deems would be the best outcome. Given that she sold her daughter, she could deny their relationship, though that reaction is unlikely. Or, she could utilize the relationship between her "lost" child and Martha Beale for financial gain.

Examining the various loathsome scenarios, he ponders presenting Martha with a lie: *the search was made; the mother, alas, succumbed several years past.* Tempting though it is to report that fabrication, he realizes he can't deceive her. A falsehood might spare her future grief, but he wouldn't be able to live with himself if he betrayed her trust. So how to proceed? The query next leads him to speculate whether to move with haste or methodical care. A leisurely investigation could forestall pain, but it might augment the girl's anxiety, and with it, the friction between her and her adoptive mother.

Kelman walks the city as he thinks, passing the Merchants' Exchange on Third Street, then continues south before abruptly turning east to the Delaware and its commercial docks. In the space of a few city blocks, a new populace appears. The noise becomes a din of foreign voices—Plattdeutsch, Hochdeutsch, Ligurian—the women shouting as loudly as the men, and employing as many oaths.

He moves on, his ears attuned to what clues he cannot yet identify. Habit makes him listen; habit makes him watchful. Continuing his haphazard journey, he turns north again, passing ropewalks and chandleries until he comes to the public landing at the foot of Walnut Street. There he pauses, gazing out at Windmill Island: three small landmasses clustered in the middle of the river.

Compared to the overcrowded stench of the wharfs, the island appears lost in its virginal vegetation, like something dreamed and not real. Even the waters lapping its shoreline look clean and blue, while the sails of the vessels closest to it are blinding white rather than the salt-stained, gray canvas of cargo ships. The scudding craft seem as illusory as the place.

Kelman closes his eyes, thinking the vision will vanish and the spot turn into dirty scrub, its beaches flecked with scum and the detritus left by thousands of tides. The picture remains, however, unblemished and beckoning. He can almost feel the saline tang of the marshland bathing his face, and hear the cries of rails and curlews as they chase the minute waves. He imagines rowing there with Martha sitting in the boat's bow. Facing him, she smiles. They both smile.

His mind's eye watches him beach the craft, then step ashore. He holds out his hand to help her debark; her fingers press his, the skin warm, her grip sure. Alone in this solitary realm, they begin to ramble here and there, their hands clasped, their arms touching. He can smell the perfume of her hair and the heat rising from her body as the sun climbs the sky.

The reverie continues as he removes his coat and spreads it on the sandy soil. Bay laurel bushes scent the air and provide a shelter, but there's no one here to watch them recline side by side. They gaze first at the sky and then turn toward each other. "Oh, my dearest," he says, the words spoken in both his fantasy and the reality of the workaday world.

CHAPTER 8

The Carte de Visite

HER HEAD CRADLED in a linen-covered pillow, the woman turns toward her lover. Her eyes are soft with sleep, and the smile she gives him is muzzy and replete. His back to her, he doesn't notice the expression, how its slides across his bare shoulders and then follows the line his spine cuts down his back. Her smile grows. She yawns, the sound a purr.

"Nicholas, we must arise."

The answer is a rhythmic rise and fall of his breath. Fully awake now, she shifts to gaze upward into the bed's canopy, but he remains asleep. Her hazel-colored eyes darken with impatience. Susannah Rause has always been an exacting woman.

"It will be luncheon soon, and one of the maids will come to remind me. We must be up and dressed before anyone knocks." Saying this, she kicks aside the coverlet; her foot is still clad in its white stocking, and her leg must untangle itself from several layers of petticoat before she can arise.

"Up, up, sleepyhead. There's no opportunity for dallying today." So saying, she stands, dragging the lengths of underskirts out from within the welter of sheets, and begins the task of readjusting her clothing. "Up, Nicholas. You must help me tighten my stays, for I can't ask a servant for help. Not under these circumstances." She laughs.

When he doesn't respond, she leans across the bed and gives his buttocks a sharp pinch that startles him awake. "Arise, Sir Knight. It's time you were gone from my home."

Nicholas Hendricks attempts to grab the hand that pinched him, but his mistress is too quick. She yanks off the coverlets, leaving him naked and exposed. "You've given me a bruise," he complains, to which she laughs again.

"Your other ladies will wonder at the rough company you keep; is that your fear?" The mock-playful tone turns serious. "Get up, Nicholas. We've had our sport. You must leave."

With a noisy groan, he springs out of bed, then stands, leering at her. He's not a tall man, but he's perfectly proportioned and so blond and fair-skinned that he'd resemble a marble statue if he posed in one position long enough. He's also a decade or more younger than Susannah, but, as she keeps her age a secret, the exact discrepancy in their years is unknown. "What would your husband say if he happened to return home early?"

"He'd challenge you to a duel, of course. My husband dotes upon me. Now, hurry, Nicholas."

But he hasn't yet finished preening. "Are you as agile a lover with him as you are with me? Or are there tricks you share with Master Rause alone? Or ones you bestow upon me that you deny him?"

"I am…a wife" is the smug reply.

"That's scant answer, my dear. I want to know whether your liege lord enjoys himself in this bed as much as I."

But Susannah has grown weary of the game. She turns her back on him. "My stays. Then your clothes."

Padding silently over the carpet, he pulls the ribbons and strings as he's been commanded. She gasps at each adjustment. "Not so firm. I need to breathe."

"Let someone else clothe you, then. I'm not your servant. What happened to your lady's maid?"

She grimaces, though he can't see the troubled expression. "She's no longer in my employ."

"You should keep your servants longer. Loyalty comes with longevity of service." So saying, he tosses back his white-blond hair and then pulls on trousers, shirt, stockings, and fitted coat. "Satisfied? I'm dressed, and you still look a scandal." Having delivered that statement, he opens the door leading from the bedchamber into her private sitting room and takes a seat, while Susannah struggles to smooth her rumpled garments and fix the hennaed ringlets that have come unpinned. Failing to replicate the coiffeur created that morning, she dons a lace cap and then slips her arms into a formless morning gown. Sumptuous though it is, and fashioned of gold satin and *pointe d'esprit* lace, it's a graceless garment.

"Very grandmotherly, Susannah," Nicholas tells her when she joins him. "The great Darius would never guess his matronly wife was practiced in the wanton arts."

The remark stings. She gives him a thin smile. "And how should I dress to receive an unexpected visitor who arrives before noon on a day when I'm not 'at home' and expecting callers? In clothing I'd wear for a carriage ride? Jeweled and in full décolletage?" When he doesn't reply, she asks a querulous, "Did you leave your carte de visite in the foyer salver, as is customary?"

"Doesn't proper etiquette require it? And don't I always follow society's rules? To wit: when visiting a married lover, a gentleman always places his carte de visite on the entryway table, or in a designated receiving bowl, while being privately entertained upstairs."

She shrugs but doesn't speak. Now finished with their lovemaking, there's little ardor or compassion between these two.

"So, what does the Merchant Prince make of my visiting cards when he returns home?"

"Don't call him a merchant, Nicholas."

"Ah, the title's too déclassé for my lady, is it? You'd prefer 'mill owner'?"

"Enough. You're not here to discuss my husband nor his business affairs. Now, let me examine your attire to make certain you didn't neglect anything. I can't risk having the servants suspect anything untoward—"

"Especially that lady's maid of yours."

"No need to discuss her. Besides, I paid her enough *not* to question anything—"

"Thanks to the Merchant Prince."

"Have done. Your jest is in exceedingly poor taste."

"Poor Susannah, ashamed because her husband must earn his daily bread."

"That's enough. My husband's riches help support you, too." She steps toward the door to indicate that their conversation is over, but Hendricks doesn't move.

"An investigation is underway into the fire at Mrs. Lampley's, you know," he says.

Her back to him, she freezes, then turns to face him, another forced smile on her lips. "I expected there would be."

"Did you?"

"An accident of that magnitude? Yes, of course."

"I've heard word that this Kelman fellow is in the process of interviewing everyone who was there that night."

If the information troubles Susannah, she doesn't reveal her discomfort. Instead, her expression remains masklike. "What's your purpose in explaining this to me?"

"Well played, my lady. Brava! Very cool. Very cool, indeed."

She glares at him. Despite her flawless complexion (for the maintenance of which she consumes minute quantities of white arsenic) and tinted curls, she suddenly appears old and haggard. "Are you asking for more money? Is that the purpose of your revelation?"

"Don't I always require additional funds, my dear?"

Attempting to stare him down, she doesn't immediately speak. When she does her tone has a swagger that lacks conviction. "You've as much to lose as I do if our presence there becomes known."

"I disagree, my love. I'm not wed to a rich merchant—forgive me, industrialist. What difference would it make if Nicholas Hendricks—rake, roué, bon vivant, and gentleman of leisure—were discovered to have been disporting himself in Celestine Lampley's pleasure dome—"

"We weren't 'disporting' ourselves."

"A small inconsistency. We were there. The fact that the blaze began before we'd undressed is irrelevant."

Again, she grows silent. In the absence of a reply, Hendricks leans back in his chair. "Which permitted us an anonymous escape. Unless Lampley identifies us, which apparently she can't, because she's left Philadelphia for parts unknown. How convenient for you, don't you agree?"

"How much do you want this time?"

"You make me sound like an opportunist."

"Well, you are." This time she smiles in earnest; he does as well. Then he rises and walks to her side, touching her mouth with his perfectly manicured fingers.

"I want nothing, my dear Susannah. Nothing but your ardent kisses and the sweet, sweet memory of your many kindnesses."

"And I can do without your mockery."

"My lady has fallen into a pique. Alas and alack. But her Nicholas must depart, and take his magical curative powers with him." He raises her hand and kisses it, though she receives the gesture with undisguised hostility. "'La belle dame sans merci'…and I thy 'wretched wight, alone and palely loitering' while 'the sedge is withered from the lake and no bird sings.' Make certain you continue to pay for your servants' silence. I doubt Darius would be pleased to find himself supplanted."

⇥⊨◎ ◎⊨⇤

As Hendricks reenters the flow of affluent pedestrians attending to their daily appointments—ladies making morning calls, or gentlemen preparing to lunch with others of their elevated breed—Ella arrives home to find Martha waiting for her in the formal parlor. Anxiety has given way to frustration, frustration to anger. In vain has she warned herself to remain calm, to recall that she's the adult and Ella a child who has recently turned wayward, because that's the heart of the problem: a girl who either doesn't appreciate the dangers she's risking or who's actively courting them in order to flaunt authority.

"Where have you been?" is what Martha demands the moment Ella enters the room. This isn't the speech she rehearsed, nor is her tone the even-tempered one she intended.

"I went for a stroll. I should have asked permission." Ostensibly, the response seems respectful, but Martha surmises that it is not.

"Permission isn't what's at issue here; it's your safety."

"I don't want to walk about tied to Mademoiselle Hédé as if I were a baby, like Cai. Besides, here I am. Safe and sound and back home." Ella glares defiance, although there's a measure of longing within her eyes that unfortunately Martha can't detect.

"That's an unacceptable reply."

Helplessness makes Martha angrier than she should be; Ella's reaction is to raise her jaw in opposition. Then she makes a brief curtsy, as if accepting the reprimand, and prepares to leave the room.

"Remain here, Ella. You and I need to discuss your actions." So saying, Martha crosses the room and pulls the double-door panels closed. After they've slid into place, she turns back to her adoptive daughter. "Don't I provide you with everything you wish and desire?"

"Yes." The tone is sullen, but Martha accepts the answer.

"Then what prompts you to repay me in this fashion?" No sooner are those last words spoken than she regrets them. She can hear her father demanding the same thing, as if love were a business agreement in which one commodity is traded for another. "What I mean to say is: Why are you unhappy when you have everything you want?"

But Ella has already reacted to the first question and doesn't hear the amendment. "I'll endeavor to repay you better in future."

"That's not what I intended. Nor what I ask or expect. I've never requested payment of any kind. I don't attempt to buy affection. And no one should be in a position of being beholden for a sentiment that should be freely given. I brought you into this house because I couldn't turn my back on you, nor could I permit the authorities to send you to Blockley."

"Yes. You rescued me, and I've thanked you for it."

"It's not your thanks I wish." An irate sigh accompanies this statement. "I simply want you to understand that you're no longer living as you once did—"

"Don't I know that?"

"Don't interrupt me, young lady. You're no longer living as you did before. The circumstances bring benefits as well as responsibilities. The benefits are obvious; the responsibilities—"

"But I don't want to be like you," Ella says, wailing. "Always doing what's proper. Never being free—"

"I am free. In fact, I have a great deal more freedom than my peers."

"Then why don't you marry Mr. Kelman?"

"Ella, enough! This is not a discussion we should have. You're far too young to know what you're saying, or to venture an opinion on a matter that's private. I won't permit you to query me in this fashion."

Hurt and anger bring tears to the girl's eyes, but she ducks her head so that Martha can't see them. The result makes Ella appear more obdurate than she is.

Martha also undergoes a transformation, because the reference to Thomas has increased her sense of dislocation. Like Ella, though, she hides the reaction, so both appear to the other to be inflexible and harsh. When Martha next speaks, her tone reinforces the image.

"I don't want to fight with you. But you must understand that your former circumstances no longer apply. Perhaps the people you saw daily were accustomed to other modes of communicating—"

"That doesn't make them lesser than you."

"Ella. Listen to me. For pity's sake. This isn't a battle. My house, and everything else I have, are yours. Can't we have a conversation without it becoming a war?" Irritated in the extreme, Martha is tempted to end the discussion, but she forces herself to persevere. "I never said anyone was lesser or greater, only that habits vary from one group of human beings or one individual to another. I was raised in affluence, but my father didn't believe pleasure was healthy for a child. I was forced to remain silent until he spoke, and then to converse on subjects he chose, rather than any of my own. I've endeavored not to replicate that model with you and Cai. I do understand, though, that wealth brings certain strictures that you may not find agreeable but are necessary nonetheless. One of those regulations is that young ladies don't go off gallivanting on their own."

Then, seeing that her adoptive daughter is about to speak up again, Martha raises her voice. "The reason for that may be viewed as nothing more than the niceties of etiquette, and you may think that etiquette is foolish—let me finish, please—but it's practicality that dictates where you go, and with whom and under what circumstances. A girl as well dressed as you becomes easy prey for pickpockets and worse. You could be robbed; you could be abducted, and a ransom demanded for your return. In each case, the criminal would achieve monetary gain, while you could be seriously harmed. We live in lawless times; desperate people will stop at nothing when they need to feed themselves and their own families."

Ella doesn't answer. Nor does her pose soften.

Recognizing how little an impact her message has had, Martha asks a beleaguered: "Do you understand what I'm telling you?"

"Yes, I understand."

"And will you promise me not to leave the house without someone accompanying you?"

"May I go now?" is the intractable response.

"Not until you give me your word."

"My real mother wouldn't treat me so cruelly."

The words to refute this statement are in Martha's mouth in a trice. She swallows them, instead stating a measured, "It will please you to know that Mr. Kelman has begun an official search for your mother." Without waiting for a reply, she dismisses Ella and then walks to a window while the girl exits the room.

Martha hears a door slide open and close and listens to footsteps climbing the stairs while she tries to control her emotions. The impulsive act of bringing Ella into her home now seems a mistake from every perspective. How could she have hoped to undo years of the girl's ill-treatment? Or make a polite little lady out of someone who wants no part of that role?

Criticizing herself, Martha imagines her father sitting in a nearby chair and scoffing at her foolhardiness. He would have told her that the poor are irredeemable because they adhere to bestial instincts. Then he would have insisted that her predicament was of her own making, because she had a woman's soft and useless heart. He would have shown no compassion or empathy. Nor would Martha have expected it.

She sighs anew as she pulls back the undercurtain to gaze into the street. The day appears incongruously cheerful in comparison to the bleakness of her soul. Closing her eyes momentarily, she feels the sunlight cover her face, but its warmth can't revive her spirit. *A failure in love*, she thinks, *a failure in my efforts to act as a parent, a failure as a daughter, a failure from my youngest days.*

She lets the drapery fall and turns back to the room. The furniture has been changed since this was her father's abode. Gone are the neo-Gothic tables and sideboards, the unforgiving high-backed chairs, the draperies of such a dense purple they looked black, but the ghost of Lemuel Beale remains, mocking her with its incorporeal presence. "Even as a child, you were a disappointment."

CHAPTER 9

Open for Business

ADELAIDE HAS LOST no time in procuring a rented house in which to conduct her business, nor in finding a young woman to become her "star resident." The former family dwelling is on Wood Street near Vine, or "Mulberry Street," as some still call it, a newly fashionable section of town where many of the rich German burghers dwell. Anspach is a name that carries a certain national recognition here; "the widow" Adelaide makes full use of the invented connection.

The property is appropriately demure: three stories of quarried stone, the windows tall, the marble front steps turned, the recessed door surmounted by a fanlight. In all respects, it looks like a place where gentility resides. When the business begins to achieve success, the number of gentlemen daily ascending those handsome entry stairs will give the neighboring housewives cause to query what sort of woman Mrs. Anspach is, and she may be forced to change locations. For now, however, not a single client has appeared, which gives the house's madam time to concentrate on the décor.

Like the building, the furnishings are also rented. Draperies, carpets, looking glasses, beds, settees, wardrobes: all have been hired, some using the cash Becky Grey provided, but the majority of items have been procured by credit. Although Adelaide still possesses enough counterfeit currency to cover her costs, she refuses to use it out of fear that her former compatriots will find her. The amount serves as a secret treasure trove in case she must escape Philadelphia for another community.

At the moment, that dire situation is far from her thoughts. She's' too busy rearranging furniture: putting an inlaid escritoire in the front parlor, then moving it to the landing, then returning it to the reception room. Her majordomo does the lifting; Adelaide oversees. She treats the man with unfailing courtesy, taking no notice of his awkwardness when carrying the little desk, or the way he hides his hands when finished with a task.

Jervis is the man, and like the establishment itself, he's bedecked in borrowed finery: his swallowtail coat hired on a monthly basis, his linen and neckcloth, trousers, stockings, and shoes purchased thirdhand, or bartered for "future favors provided by one of the house's young ladies"—which Adelaide intends to make certain never occurs.

"You may no longer be fit for mill work because of your unfortunate accident," she tells him, "but you perform your duties here admirably. I'm delighted to be able to aid you and your family in your hour of distress."

He says nothing, although he nods his head in a deferential manner, wishing all the while that the employment he accepted two days past was the job he imagined it to be. And the one his wife believes he has: a servant in a respectable lady's home. His only consolation is that he never supplied the exact address. The secret will remain his own.

A knock at the door disturbs his thoughts; he goes to answer it while Adelaide retires into a rear parlor. The routine she intends to establish will provide an illusion of decorum; like a genuine lady, she'll wait in seclusion until her visitors are announced.

Jervis returns with a carte de visite in his hand. A neighboring woman has left it with an invitation to call at her home on Tuesdays, which are her receiving days.

It's all Adelaide can do not to tear the thing to shreds; instead she thanks Jervis, places the calling card in the desk where she keeps her accounts, then walks upstairs to visit her "perfect pupil," a woman of twenty-three who has the ability—for now, at least—to appear as fresh as a girl of seventeen. Adelaide found her in New York, where she stole her from a large establishment by offering dazzling sums and the chance to become a "queen among courtesans." She even hinted (though this was a lie) at a share in the profits. But Solange, as she has styled herself, is easily bored, and, having never known solitude, is frightened by quiet and peace. Adelaide realizes she must find another girl quickly, even if she's no more appealing than the donkey that's put in a thoroughbred's stall to soothe it.

And so the day wears on, with timid, neighborly knocks at the front of the house and more importunate ones at the rear: tradesmen delivering yet more goods, as well as a steady stream of comestibles, until Adelaide begins to worry that she'll never be able to pay off her debts. A tedious afternoon gives way to early evening, evening to suppertime, suppertime to the hour when gentlemen begin to seek entertainment, yet still no one comes. Adelaide is about to dismiss Jervis for the night when another person presents himself at her front door.

Accoutered à la mode and carrying a cane with an ivory knob surmounted by an emerald, he appears too good to be true: handsome, youthful, and debonair, like an actor portraying a gentleman of quality. Warily, Adelaide greets him with her most winning smile. "You bring me luck, monsieur," she tells him. "My humble abode is only now opened for service, and you shall have the company of my choicest mademoiselle."

With that she trips upstairs, calling a sweet, "Solange, *ma chérie*. Please to descend and meet *un vraiment gentilhomme*. No, no, my other pets. Be still, *s'il vous plaît*. It's Solange I wish."

As requested, Solange descends the staircase, her progress slow and preening, while Adelaide oversees the meeting between practitioner and customer, noting with approval, and more than a touch of ardor, that when the man doffs his hat, his hair is the color of purest gold. It's an aristocrat's coloring, combined with an aristocrat's natural grace. His physique is equally flawless, leading her mind's eye to strip away jacket, linen shirt, and trousers. Perhaps he'll become a randy young plaything for the future use of the lady of the house. "May I ask your name, monsieur?"

"Hendricks. Nicholas." The swagger of the tone matches his appearance.

"*Enchanté*, monsieur Nicholas." She teases out the name into four syllables. "And what brought you here, may I ask?"

"Adventure, madam. Adventure. I'm a fellow who thrives on stimulation. I pride myself in being among the first, if not *the* first, to sample the city's newest examples of pulchritude and feminine charm."

Their eyes meet. He bows. Adelaide dips into a curtsy that's nearly a full reverence while keeping her eyes fastened on his. "Honored sir," she murmurs, "tonight you shall be our guest. No, no, don't argue. I insist, and my word is always, always obeyed. Cher monsieur Nicholas, I hope you come to know the firmness of my character in days to come. For *ce soir*, I ask only that when you leave my humble house, you sing its praises to those of your acquaintance."

→▸═◁ ◁═▸←

Jervis wends his way homeward. The distance isn't great, but his feet are leaden with self-disgust, and so the journey takes longer than it should, and the public clock is striking midnight by the time he climbs the stairs to the room he shares with his wife and sister-in-law.

Both are awake and dressed and anxious to hear the details of his day. His employment is a boon that neither woman can quite believe. An unknown lady arrives to console the family, and then she offers honest labor in her home; surely, this is God's intervention.

A plate of soup is set upon the table for his supper, but he assures them he has already eaten, and so the food is removed, but the women force him to sit with them and describe every aspect of the house and its mistress, Mrs. Green.

Having begun with a lie, he can't reveal that her name is now Mrs. Anspach or that he surmises it once was something else and will be changed again before too many months elapse. So, he spins out the tale they wish to hear, describing the articles of furniture—though not the fact that they've been hired on credit—the luxuriant carpets, the drapes still stiff with buckram, the gilt picture frames, the double pier glasses in the reception room. Much of this terminology is new to him. Having heard it from his employer, and from the men delivering the furnishings, he uses the language and other grandiose specifics to stave off additional queries. His two ladies are so engrossed in the pictures he paints that they start sighing in wonderment over the impossibly grand domicile in which their breadwinner is now ensconced. It's a given that they'll never be permitted to visit, but it's enough that they can view it through his eyes.

"And the kitchen and larder, Jervis," his wife finally asks. "Tell us about the kitchen. I think your mistress must have one of those new stoves that uses coal instead of wood?"

"A stove with an oven, too," his sister-in-law adds in an awe-filled tone. "So the cook can bake her bread while stirring a pot of turtle soup, or making oyster sauce, or boiling a piece of codfish."

The women have seen such a marvel displayed in a hollowware foundry opposite the nearby dye works, but they also understand they won't ever touch one, much less use it.

"A double oven, perhaps," the wife concludes. "Like the one we noticed— with doors opening on either side of the stove. Now *that* was clever. Imagine inventing a thing like that."

Here Jervis falters, because Adelaide's kitchen is a primitive place and wouldn't even meet the standards of his own poor dwelling. Dining with gleaming silver cutlery isn't what her future clientele will demand, and so there's no long table reserved for elaborate repasts, no buffet covered with crystal bowls. Decanters there are in plenty, but imbibing wines and fortified spirits isn't the equivalent of ingesting a meal. When Adelaide wishes to eat, she sends a boy to purchase (on credit) what she wants from an oyster cellar located on Arch Street.

"In truth, the kitchen isn't complete yet," he tells the women.

"But how can that be, Jervis? Elegant folk must sup, the same as we must."

"I don't have the answer to that question. I can only report what I've seen. In my position, it wouldn't do for me to demand answers on subjects I'm not capable of understanding."

"How like a man," his wife says. "Your Mrs. Green wouldn't keep a home without a serviceable kitchen and larder. She may not have children, and she may be widowed, but she must have friends she'll ask to dine. Surely, she keeps a cook, or have you failed to notice her, too?"

"I'm very tired, my dear" is his reply, "and the morning will come soon enough. I must take myself off to bed." He rises and makes his way to the makeshift bedroom beyond the curtain, but his wife and sister-in-law remain at the table, exclaiming over everything he has told them.

Sleep eludes him as he listens to their excited voices. He has the first real lie to his wife in their life together, and he knows he must continue to deceive her. The burden of this sin is terrible. It tears at his belly and freezes his breath. He wants to howl and curse the circumstances that brought the demonic Adelaide Anspach into his existence.

He thinks of his dead son, and how it would feel if the child were alive and judging his father's cowardice and deceit. *Perhaps the boy is watching,* he thinks, *perhaps he knows my mind fully; and maybe his little ghost is roving about, listening to his mother and aunt while gazing down at me with contempt. He could be anywhere in the room; he could be everywhere at once.*

It takes only a moment for that thought to bring him an even more hideous revelation. What if the boy were alongside him that morning and afternoon and evening? What if he were with him when he answered the door and admitted the gentleman with the fancy cane? At that Jervis shouts aloud, the sound guttural and tortured.

In an instant, the voices on the other side of the curtain are stilled.

"He's been like that ever since the boy's death," the wife whispers at length. "Terrible dreams. And kicking and flailing about like someone possessed. It's the mill that did something evil, not my poor man. But he suffers as if he's the killer, instead of that wicked machine. You're forced to hear him crying out, but I tell you, I live in fear of his fists and legs when those nightmares grip him. He could murder me and not know he's done it."

Her sister nods in sympathy then attempts an encouraging smile, but her poor cracked teeth provide only a ghoulish grimace. "We should be abed. It'll be time to rise again before we know it."

CHAPTER 10

Ella's Mother

"THOMAS, THANK YOU for coming to see me. I apologize for asking you to visit in this suddenly inclement weather, but I know your work doesn't permit you to remain staring out the window while rains inundate the earth, which is how you find me occupying myself." Martha, having risen the moment that Kelman was announced, beams with pleasure as she holds out her hands to draw him into her upstairs parlor. He also smiles, but the expression is polite rather than intimate.

"Your note indicated you wished to speak to me about Ella."

"Yes." Her smile fades. *My dear one*, she wishes to add, but doesn't. Constrained by nothing but hesitation and stubbornness on her part, and pride and stubbornness on his, their natural longings become ensnared by the seemingly irrefutable reasons why they cannot wed. So, their hearts and minds tentatively step forward and withdraw, making them behave like strangers.

"I...I thought it might be helpful for your search if you had a daguerreotype of Ella to take with you. Her mother may resemble her." These statements are only half of what she meant to say, but they're the easier part by far. She moves away from Thomas, to a table beside the settee, and picks up a frame made of mother-of-pearl. It's a costly object, but she handles it with unconcern, as if it were the least important of her possessions. Giving it to him, she waits while he examines it, keeping up a steady stream of conversation to hide her self-consciousness.

"Yes, I realize the pose is stiff, but they always are. You're fortunate you haven't been compelled to sit for a portrait such as this. Five minutes or more frozen in an uncomfortable posture that's anything but natural. The mouth can't move, or the eyes stray. The sitter is even cautioned not to blink! The artist must position his subjects to lean against stationary objects, like the column you see beside Ella, so that they don't shift and mar the image. The science is very exacting." She adds a small laugh, but the effort sounds forced, and so she alters her approach by becoming philosophical: "Thus, Ella's austere expression. She wasn't displaying antagonism toward the process, but there was nothing spontaneous in the pose in which she was placed. I see you're frowning. Do you feel the likeness is too nondescript to be helpful? A girl with fair hair who could be one in a thousand, and her mother equally unremarkable."

"No, the image is a good one. My concern is this handsome frame. Anyone to whom I show it is likely to become too greedy to be trustworthy."

That proposition takes Martha by surprise. She studies the frame as though seeing it for the first time, and through other eyes. "We could remove the picture," she offers in a less assured voice.

"Not without marring the delicate mother-of-pearl. Someone took great pains to create this keepsake."

The opinion pains her, not because she disagrees with it, but because she realizes that her wealth has made her blind. A daguerreotype is rare enough, and few can afford to purchase one; to clothe it in costly garments, and then overlook the price, must seem the height of insolence. Worse, it separates her further from the man she loves. "You're correct. Of course you're correct." Taking back the picture, she replaces it on the table, this time in an insignificant spot, while Thomas interprets her actions as easily as if she were discussing her motives aloud. He yearns to take her in his arms and tell her how unimportant the object is; indeed, how insignificant any mere thing is.

He doesn't, however. Instead, he makes a perfunctory reply that's as restrained as hers. "Perhaps the artist could extricate the image without marring the case. Or, you could commission a new portrait and ask to have it delivered in a plain frame."

"Yes. That's an excellent suggestion."

A long silence ensues; they stand looking not at each other but toward the windows that now rattle with gusts of wind. The sky has grown dark, and the room, for all its glowing vapor lamps, turns gray and dreary, too. What a pleasant place this could become if these two could open their hearts to each other. Instead, they speak of the search for Ella's mother.

"You do comprehend how unpleasant this hunt may become, don't you, Martha?"

She nods, then adds a quiet, "I understand. But what can I do? To deny the girl this opportunity is to lose her."

"You risk the same if you find the mother."

"Yes." As if she can no longer tolerate the predicament in which she finds herself, Martha walks to the settee and flings herself down.

Kelman hesitates before speaking again. "There's another approach, which I considered and then rejected."

"If you rejected it, then…"

"I did so because—well, no matter why. The fact is that you and I can inform Ella that a search was duly conducted and that her parent wasn't discovered."

"But that would be a lie."

"Yes."

"Oh, Thomas, I couldn't enter into a deception like that. I wouldn't be able to live with myself." She pauses, studying his face. In the lamp's glow, only the left half is lit, revealing the scar slicing across his cheek. She thinks back to when they first met and how noble the mark appeared. Having known only her father's friends and acquaintances, all men of affairs who existed in an exclusive terrain of finance and industry, Kelman was her introduction to a realm of honest toil and human-scaled aspirations.

"Why did you reject the idea of presenting Ella with a falsehood?" she asks at length.

His response is equally tardy. "Because I could never deceive *you*. Not in word or deed or private thought." Then, when he feels he has revealed too much, his speech turns professional and brisk. "I must return to the city's business, I'm afraid. A downpour doesn't keep dishonest folk from nefarious deeds."

Martha stands, albeit reluctantly. "I shouldn't have taken so much of your time. Nor did I ask how your investigation into that blaze was proceeding."

"I'm sorry to say, I'm no closer to discovering a motive or perpetrator than I was. Those involved have been understandably reticent." Gazing at her, he seems about to say something more personal. She feels it, and she smiles upward into his face.

Instead, he steps away, adding a practical, "At least the rain will dampen enthusiasm for arson today."

-»=◉ ◉=«-

The storm hasn't prevented Findal Stokes from making his way across the Schuylkill to the Blockley almshouse that was once his home. Having no money to pay for the ferry, he must cross the river by a lengthier route, using the bridge and then wending his way south and west along the dirt lanes that lead to the Darby Road. Walking across the span's wooden slats, he can see the currents churning beneath him; denuded tree limbs and trunks are thrust upward by the waves and then sink below at a dizzying pace. The objects remind him of people drowning.

He lifts his eyes from his contemplation of the river and focuses on the bridge, but the bursts of wind make the elevated space seem no safer than the torrent. He imagines being swept off his feet, tossed into the waves, and then sucked under as if he were no more than a tree branch. "A chapel, a medical library, an apothecary," he mutters, hoping the words will banish the image; "washhouses and cookhouses for fourteen hundred residents, one hundred fifty syphilitics, twenty lunatics, and more than twenty epileptics." The statistics, drummed daily into Blockley's residents, continue to make him feel browbeaten and humiliated, which he believes must have been the trustees' intention: to prove the paupers' lack of gratitude when so much beneficence was theirs. "A chapel," he adds, "an obstetrics ward, a ward for boys, and one for men, others for women and girls…"

At length, the bridge is past, and he begins the trek along the mud-thick road. The rains have no intention of abating and, though they make his journey arduous, they provide an unanticipated boon. Drenched, he can present himself to the warders and, with any luck, fool them into believing he's simply a traveler seeking answers about a woman (a relative, he'll say) who may or may not have been an inmate. This conclusion made, his pace increases. There's something like arrogance in his step. Having once fled the place, he's about to return not as an impoverished inhabitant but as a free man, albeit a very poor one.

As he attains the buildings, though, his courage dwindles. He sees the same tall porticos, the same broad lawns, and the same imposing aspect as if this were a castle rather than a refuge for the outcast. The "finest architect in all Philadelphia" was engaged to design it, so it should appear "appropriately august," which is another fact the inmates were forced to memorize. Findal stops. He feels as if he's a small child again, fearful of the warders, fearful of his father, frightened of all the evil rumors that circulated around the place: how the dead inmates were sold to medical students before they could be buried, or worse, far worse.

Skirting the main entrance with its wide veranda, he trudges across the squelching grass toward the wards. He's tempted to start with the boys' residence, because he's certain to find a few who'll remember Findal Stokes kindly—younger boys who revered him because he was older—but he warns himself that he can't risk being identified. The guards might decide to nab him again. In their minds, he's probably still a fugitive.

Hoping to avoid detection, he jams his tall hat down over his prominent ears and squares his broadening shoulders till he's convinced there's no resemblance to the scrawny lad who once roamed Blockley's grounds. Coming to the women's ward, he knocks at the portal, though the door is wide open, exposing the interior to the elements. Within he hears a hum of querulous voices. Confined by the weather and prevented from working in the fields, the inmates turn their energies from wrestling with the soil to fighting one another.

A warder appears, a giant of a woman with a face as wide as a slab of meat. "You want the men's not the women's residence" is all she says before she turns her back on him.

"I'm not an inmate," Findal tells her, though anxiety makes the words warble in his throat. "I'm looking for someone: a woman who's my mother's sister. My mother's no longer living," he adds in anticipation that the guard will demand why a nephew should come in search of his aunt rather than his mother.

"That's not much help. None at all, in point of fact. Age, height, coloring: those are details you should provide, not some feeble excuse at parentage."

Findal receives the critique in silence then makes a stab at an age, naming twenty-five as a good number, after which he approximates Ella's height. He concludes, "and very fair hair, and pretty, too."

"No pretty women wash up here," the warder tells him. "If they have looks, they can earn a living by lying on their backs." Again, she starts to leave but stops and peers into his face, which causes Findal to back away from the door's overhang and out into the rain.

"Don't you doff your hat to your elders and betters?" she demands while scrutinizing his features.

"Not in the rain, madam. I'm sorry to look and act such a sad sight. But I daren't get wetter than I already am."

Her eyes, which have narrowed into suspicious slits, don't leave off their inspection. "You remind me of someone who was once here. An evil man, he was, and a drunkard even when incarcerated, as well as a cheat, liar, and thief."

"I'm looking for a female relative, madam, not a male."

"Too bad. I could have told you all about him. Stokes was his name, and I heard he met a fitting end to his wicked existence. Knocked down and killed by a wagon in the street. He had a boy, as I recall. Well, no matter." Her steady perusal continues. "You're not fair-haired," she says.

"No, madam. Neither was my mother. But my aunt had yellow hair."

"And pretty, you say?"

Thinking of Ella, Findal's reply is more enthusiastic than called for. "Very."

"You're certain about that, at any rate. Blond and comely. Now that I'm re-membering back to when that villainous Stokes dwelled among us, I do recall a young woman…hair so pale it was almost white. She looked like a country lass, not a scar or mark or pox upon her, and healthy limbs—"

"Yes?" Again, his eagerness gets the better of him. The warder could be describing Ella.

"Why are you searching for her? Is there money in it?"

"Oh, no, madam. I don't come from wealthy folk, which doubtless you can see. I'd like to find her because she's my last living relative."

"Hmmm. No legacy, then?"

"No, madam."

"Then I wouldn't waste your time." Again, the woman makes to leave. It's all Findal can do not to lay his wet hand on her sleeve.

"My mother made me promise when she was dying," he lies. "If it was the last thing I did, I was to hunt without ceasing for my lost aunt."

"And you're certain there's no legacy?"

"I'm telling you the truth. I swear it."

"Something's queer in all this. Why would a boy who's all of what—sixteen or seventeen or eighteen—go a-hunting for a woman who might be better off lost? Maybe she doesn't want to be found; did you think of that? Maybe she humiliated herself, or had a bastard child—"

The speech ceases with a suddenness that leaves the warder panting. "I'm a wonder, I am. I should be earning my living telling gypsy fortunes. I have the second sight. I always did. When you presented yourself at the door, I asked myself what you were up to, because I sensed something odd and mysterious. Well, you'll need look no more for your aunt, my boy, because that blond relation of yours drowned herself. Walked into the river and sank like an iron ball. She had a wee one with her, a bastard child, I presume. So both souls are lost to all eternity."

Findal gasps, though the deliverer of these tidings could never guess the cause of his distress. *Yes*, he thinks, *the suicide my comrades and I witnessed. The woman who carried her baby into the Schuylkill; she didn't even try to float. How could I have not have remembered her?*

Then the worst of all memories returns, for Findal had led his friends in tormenting the woman. They stood on the embankment and described demons dwelling in the waterway that dragged unwary creatures into their lairs. When it became obvious that she meant to take her life, they screamed that she and her baby would go to Hell. They'd even thrown clods of earth down upon her head. She could never have been Ella's mother. That much is sure.

Lost in the past, he doesn't realize that the warder has prodded him with her finger.

"That's all the information I can supply. Now let me return to my work. You make me feel drowned just looking at you."

CHAPTER 11

An Unexpected Disclosure

TWO DAYS FOLLOWING Findal's excursion to Blockley, Kelman crosses to the west side of the Schuylkill River to present himself to the institution's director. The purpose of the visit is the same as Findal's, though, of course, Kelman is unaware of the boy's mission. With him he carries the daguerreotype image of Ella. During the time that's elapsed since his conversation with Martha, the costly frame has been replaced with an ordinary one, making the sitter seem humbler; curiously, her beauty, which had been reflected and augmented by the glowing mother-of-pearl, appears lesser, too. Kelman doesn't hold out much hope of success, but he must start somewhere, and the almshouse, being confined and manageable, will provide a greater opportunity for interviews than walking from one tenement home to another asking strangers if they've ever seen a woman who resembles the girl in the portrait.

Because of the aftermath of the storm, the Schuylkill is now in flood, its banks overflowing with detritus from upriver. The air is rank with rotting vegetation and the carcasses of creatures caught up in the surging waters. The stench will worsen as the days pass, but it's bad enough for now. Boarding the ferry, Kelman wishes he'd chosen the High Street Bridge and so had been elevated above the reeking embankments. The boat is quicker, however, and it will enable him to complete his business efficiently.

Hidden Stream, he thinks as the lines are cast off and the short journey commences; the phrase is a translation of *Schuylkill*, the early Dutch settlers' name for the river. Today the waterway looks not so much hidden as engorged, and dangerous at that. In fact, with so many objects hurtling south to where the Schuylkill joins the Delaware, he's surprised the captain deemed it wise to risk his vessel rather than wait for the inundation to subside. But money must be made, and a man who owns a business that's dependent upon the weather must take risks or cease operation.

Arriving at Blockley's entrance, Kelman is told to wait until it can be ascertained whether or not the director has time to spare for an interview. The interview being granted, he's escorted upstairs to the man's reception chamber, a place furnished as handsomely as a banker's or barrister's. A new Turkey carpet graces the floor; the chairs are upholstered in velvet and plush; draperies frame a view that encompasses wide lawns and the riverfront glistening in the distance. Nowhere in the room is a hint that the establishment might serve as a refuge to the poor. Kelman finds himself growing increasingly irritable over the director's complacency and his obvious indifference to those in his care.

A cigar is offered. Kelman declines, his manner too abrupt to be polite. He wants to vacate the dandified space as soon as possible. "Sir," he begins, "I'm here at the behest of Miss Martha Beale—"

The director interrupts with an ingratiating, "Indeed? Miss Beale! A fine name and a fair fortune. The institute would be delighted to have her as a patron."

"I'm here at her behest," Kelman continues, as if the man hadn't spoken, "because she wishes to find the mother of a girl she adopted. A poor child she rescued from the streets."

"Indeed," the director repeats, though the word now drips with condescension. "Whyever would Miss Beale want to do that? Better to let sleeping dogs lie, I should say. Or, as they say, 'Lie down with dogs, wake up with fleas.' Besides, what does that foolhardy scheme have to do with me?"

Bristling at the man's fatuousness, Kelman replies with a cool, "Miss Beale's motives are known to her alone. I'm merely the messenger."

"Naturally." Puffing on his cigar, the director examines his visitor, noting the somber clothes and an undefined yet evident lack of refinement. A grocer's son, he decides, or worse—maybe a shopkeeper's assistant or even a common laborer. A person who got himself an education but lacks—and always will lack—the delicacies of people to the manner born. "I hope Miss Beale understands the jar of worms she'll open if she proceeds with the course of action she's proposed.

Before her efforts are done, her adoptive daughter could have a hundred darling mamas all clambering to be recognized."

"Miss Beale is aware of the hazards she may encounter."

"I wouldn't risk it, and I'd advise her to do the same. Take my advice as a gentleman who knows whereof he speaks: The poor can't be trusted. It's as simple as that. And no amount of solicitude, or turning a blind eye, will change the fact. They lie to you for the sake of lying; they cheat you blind; they're lazy as the day is long, and idiots, to boot, as well as morally corrupt. Why else would they be here at Blockley?"

"Probably because they've been cheated by factory owners and bankers," Kelman says, the words so deceptively calm that the almshouse director at first believes he didn't hear them aright. When he does apprehend their meaning, he puts down the cigar and sits straighter in his chair, leveling a superior gaze on his guest.

"That's an odd position for one in public office to espouse, sir. It's industrialists and financiers who run the city, not the—"

"I'm aware of politics and policies," Kelman interrupts. "I'm not here to argue with you." Which statement isn't true, because he'd like very much to challenge the man's accusations.

The director glares. Were it not for the magical name of Beale, he'd order the impertinent fellow to leave. No, not a laborer's son, he tells himself. The man was probably born into squalor, just like my charges here. Thus the chip on his shoulder, and the critique of the metropolis's leading citizens. "My time, Mr. Kelman, is at a premium, as I'm sure you realize. I'm happy to serve Miss Beale, but I fail to understand what you wish from me."

Placing the picture of Ella on the man's desk, Kelman can scarcely restrain his ire. "This is the girl. I'm hoping the mother, if she's still living, may resemble her."

The director scarcely glances at the image. "That's a very large 'if,' sir."

"Yes, I understand."

"Let me supply a few more hypotheses for you to consider: *If* she hasn't consumed so much gin as to be unrecognizable, and *if* she hasn't disfigured herself by disease from selling her body, and *if* her wits haven't started wandering—which is how a lot of them go—and *if* the girl took after her ma instead of her pa, then I'll wager you have a chance of finding the woman, *if* you know where to look."

"That's why I'm here, sir. *If* there's a possibility the woman was an inmate here at one time in her life, then my search will have a starting point." Kelman moves the portrait closer to the director, who doesn't give it another glance. "You've guided this institution for a considerable period. Do you see any resemblance to inmates past or present?"

"Not a bit. Not a bit."

"Please examine the picture, sir. Take as long as you need. I'm in no hurry."

"But I am," says the impatient host, pushing the image back toward Kelman. "I have a large asylum to run and decisions to make. How am I supposed to differentiate this girl from countless others? *Years* of others like her. You can inquire in the women's wards, if you want, though I doubt you'll learn anything. The male and female wardens are as dull witted as cattle. I suggest you don't mention Miss Beale's name, however, or your official capacity in the city's governance. Our inmates don't think well of the police."

"I didn't intend to mention either. The information concerning Miss Beale was for you alone."

Kelman rises. The director does the same and then plasters an artificial smile on his face. "Be certain to give Miss Beale my regards, and please express my hope that her search achieves its purpose, even though I hold reservations about the wisdom of embarking on such a mission. If I were advising her, I'd tell her so in the strongest of terms." He's about to proffer his hand but, noting that Kelman's own hand remains at his side, he withdraws the gesture. The smile turns into a sickening grin. "If, at some future period, Miss Beale wishes a tour of the premises, I'd be happy to provide one. A patroness of her standing would be laudable. I can promise she wouldn't be forced to witness anything unseemly, or converse with inmates not of my specific choosing. One cannot be too careful when there are ladies present."

"I assure you, I'll convey to her all that has passed between us."

⋆⇥ ⇤⋆

Kelman's jaw is clenched in fury as he quits the director's chambers, but he realizes he must achieve a semblance of calm before he approaches the women's wards. This is no time to give vent to his indignation. Walking outside, he stands in the May sunshine, looking away from Blockley's main building and toward the fields and river. The rains have rinsed the outbuildings of grime; the stone and brick look spanking new, while the trees and shrubberies are so emerald-bright they seem as though they had been placed there purposely to impress the visitor with the asylum's orderliness.

Philadelphia lies in a hazy distance, the bustle and commotion of its streets silenced, the good or ill passing between its citizens invisible. Church spires rise above all other structures, but they appear ephemeral and illusory, as though the scene were part of a dreamscape rather than one filled with real people, noise and toil, passions and sorrows. For the residents of Blockley, Kelman thinks, the city must seem like an unattainable world; although they remember the streets and alleyways where they once dwelled, the collective whole, glimpsed from their captivity, must appear finer than any place they'd be worthy to inhabit again.

Curtailing this reverie, he turns toward the first of the women's wards to resume his work.

⇢⟩⟩ ⟨⟨⇠

"What's this picture thing called?" the warder asks as she examines the image of Ella. "It's not a drawing, I think, because the artist wouldn't have made the girl look so grim. He would have given her a smile, maybe. And put some color into those wan cheeks. That's what I'd have done, though I'm no artist and never will be. I've seen hand-tinted pictures. They're lovely to look at." Her hands, which are as broad as a man's, turn the object sideways; her eyes peer nearsightedly through the glass covering the image. "The man should have made the girl look healthy, too, because she doesn't. Not at all. A consumptive, I would have said, and I've known my share of women suffering from the disease. Incurable, that's what they are. We get them here, you know. Some only last a couple of days. Some linger, but it's not a pleasant kind of lingering."

"The picture is known as a daguerreotype," Kelman tells her when it's obvious her brief soliloquy has ceased. "It's a new process for making portraits."

"Must be pricey, then."

"I wouldn't know," he lies. "The image was supplied to aid my search."

"Fancy that" is all she says while she turns the portrait round and round in her meaty fists. She's of such a formidable size and so lumbering and careless that Kelman fears she may break the object. "A picture instead of words."

"Yes," he interjects. "I'm hoping that you can recognize a similarity between this girl and perhaps a resident of the asylum. The girl in the picture is fourteen and fair-haired, and full of health."

The woman nods, her focus wholly on the daguerreotype. "Someone likes her well enough to spend hard-earned money on her portrait. Is she a well-heeled gent's mistress? I know some like them young."

"No. The girl has a legitimate patron: a lady who adopted her. So, madam, I ask again. Can you think back to anyone who might have resembled the person in this picture? Blond? Of medium build, or perhaps shorter. Very fair-skinned—"

"What's a lady doing adopting a big girl like her? Babies are the usual. Is she a widow, then, who needs companionship? Or did you forget to mention her husband?"

"There is no husband," Kelman says.

"Ah, so it is companionship. Well, tell her from me that she should marry. A woman without a man is thin porridge. I should know. I was wed for eighteen years. I may be unlovely to look at, but my mate didn't mind. A finer man you couldn't find; he made me into his equal. Now I'm a widow who must make my way as best I can."

Although he has conducted countless interviews like this, he finds his impatience reaching an intolerable level. Every reference to Martha grates, as do this woman's comments on her marriage. "I'll take back the picture, madam, and I thank you for your time. Perhaps another warder, or even an inmate, might be able to aid me. Then again, perhaps the girl's mother was never here."

"I liked the lad's description better than the one you've given me. He said she was a beauty. That's not this lass you're showing me. And as for being a blonde, well, this picture could be of a gray-haired crone for all I know."

Kelman's so astonished that he almost misses the remainder of her speech. "The lad?"

"Or maybe you two aren't looking for the same person. I can't imagine why you would be, an ill-clad nobody like him and a fine gent such as yourself."

"What lad?" Kelman demands, which causes the warder to stiffen in response. Her size provides an element of danger as if she were capable of knocking to the ground anyone who crossed her. He ignores the belligerent attitude. "What lad?"

"I won't be addressed in that tone. Nor bullied, neither. You may be a gentleman and decide I'm no lady, but you must treat me proper." Handing him the daguerreotype, she bobs a surly, abbreviated curtsy. "Good day to you."

"You say a boy is looking for the same woman I am?"

"I said nothing of the kind."

"Madam, you did. You mentioned an 'ill-clad' youth."

"So what if I did?" Folding her huge arms across her chest, she's the picture of defiance. "There's no law in talking to whomsoever a body chooses to speak with. I'm gabbing with you, aren't I? Though not for long. I repeat: good day to you, sir." So saying, she turns her back on him.

"Madam, a minute more—"

Spinning around with surprising speed for a person of her heft, she wags her finger in his face. "Not a minute, nor a second, neither. I know nothing about the woman you're hunting for. Now, will you leave me be? Or must I summon one of the male guards?"

"The asylum director gave me permission to interview anyone I chose—"

"Well, go back and talk with him, then. Doesn't he know everyone who's passed in and out of the asylum's doors? Go chat with him instead of bothering busy people. And while you're at it, ask his lordship when us lawful wage earners will get our pay, because I don't fancy forfeiting another month's salary."

⤜⊙ ⊙⤛

The remainder of Kelman's time at Blockley uncovers no further information. Perhaps those he meets intuit that he's part of Philadelphia's constabulary, and therefore turn mute at his approach, or maybe they have no facts to share. Whatever the cause, he learns nothing more than the single warder's reference to *the lad*. That revelation is sufficient, however, and sufficiently worrisome, too. He ponders the woman's remarks as he crosses the river again and begins to walk east toward his offices.

An omnibus would be faster, but he wants time to think, and the distance from the Schuylkill to the Delaware's nearby streets provides opportunity for reflection. *An ill-clad nobody* who's also hunting for Ella's mother. Kelman has a strong suspicion the boy may be Findal Stokes. Whether true or not—though, who else could the lad be—how will he share that news with Martha?

⟶▉ ◉▉◀⟵

Reaching Congress Hall, where the city's governmental offices are housed, he mounts the stairs to his chambers. The questions concerning Ella, Findal, and Martha remain unresolved, and he finds himself resenting the girl and her heritage, as well as young Stokes, for the grief they'll visit on the woman he loves. It's of little use for him to remind himself that he must maintain a professional distance during the investigation. Nor does it help to remember that he offered his services and he understood the emotional price of his involvement. So he's left wishing Martha had never encountered Ella—or Cai, either, for that matter—but then recognizes that it was her generosity of spirit that first attracted him. Martha Beale, miserly in deed or affection, wouldn't be the Martha he adores.

"A message for you, Mr. Kelman, sir," his chief constable tells him the moment he reaches the second-floor landing. "I heard it was you walking up," he adds when he notes the quizzical expression on his master's face. "I didn't know where you'd gone, or I would have followed you, because I knew you'd want to receive this communication immediately."

The man is loyalty itself, but he has a habit of believing that all his reports are of vital importance. Ordinarily Kelman humors him, though today he finds himself too distracted to do so. "What's the nature of the message?"

"I couldn't say, sir. I didn't read the letter. I'd never presume to open a communication addressed to you."

Kelman ignores the urge to ask how the constable was able to discern the letter's importance if he didn't read it.

"It's on your desk, sir, waiting for you," the constable tells him as the two pass along the corridor. "It's from Baltimore." A weighty pause follows this disclosure, during which time Kelman disregards considerations of Ella and her birth mother and begins to ponder other current investigations. A connection to the city of Baltimore remains elusive.

"From the chief of the constabulary, sir. I made so bold as to read the envelope."

By now, they've reached the room where Kelman transacts his business; the constable unlocks the door with a great jangling of keys and a showy flourish, as if he were opening a vault filled with silver and gold. "There you are, sir. In the very center of your desk."

Slitting open the envelope, Kelman scans a wordy missive that would do his chief constable proud. Distilled to its essence, the message reveals that a Mrs. Celestine Lampley did arrive in the city of Baltimore via paddle steamer from Philadelphia, and that it's believed that her intended destination—via the customary route of public coach and canal barge—was Pittsburgh. Simply because the female in question purchased a ticket for travel to that city, however, doesn't mean she couldn't have disembarked at another stop along the way.

"I told you it was probably important, sir," the constable says while Kelman returns the letter to its envelope.

Telling the man what he knows, he dictates letters to be sent to the chief of the constabulary in Pittsburgh and all other towns along the western route. But the delay incurred in posting and receiving communications could mean that Lampley has already vanished.

CHAPTER 12

What Mischief Are You Planning

"AH, CHÉRIE, I am entranced to welcome you to my humble abode. How delightful that I should encounter you perambulating in that pretty garden square just now. It's far too early in the morning for a proper call, but no matter, no matter. I establish my own regulations, and so I promise that we shall have an intimate visit, whatever the hour." Adelaide makes a show of examining the pendant watch that loops low across her bodice. "Dear me, only a quarter after ten. You must rise with the songbirds."

While her new friend maintains this stream of lively conversation, Ella allows herself to be escorted out of a hired carriage and up the steps to the residence on Wood Street.

"I hope your dear maman won't fret about you. Perhaps we should send a message informing her of your unexpected sojourn." Noticing the girl's frown, Adelaide adds a smiling, "Or perhaps we should keep our *amitié*—pardon me, I must learn to speak only English—our mutual attachment, a lovely secret?" Laughing, she opens the door and ushers Ella inside.

"And you must help me master your language. I appoint you to correct every flaw you notice. Be ruthless with me, Mistress Ella. I wish to sound like an American lady, and at all times. Oh, and you must call me Adelaide, which is my new and very American-styled name, n'est-ce pas? Excuse me! *Isn't it?* Those are the words I should use."

"Yes" is Ella's quiet reply, so overwhelmed is she by her hostess's vivacity, and the surroundings, too, which are unlike anything she's seen before. The foyer and the parlor into which Adelaide leads her make Martha's home seem dowdy in comparison. Here all is bright and new, every surface bedecked with glittering objects. Understandably, Ella mistakes the golden paint for the genuine article and the colored glass inlaid in the boxes for precious stones. A princess, even one who insists she wants to become an ordinary American, wouldn't possess anything less than ornaments fit for a palace. The fact that Ella has been singled out for special attention by this exotic, gracious woman is like a dream come true. How envious Mademoiselle Hédé and Cai would be if they could see her now, and her adoptive mother, too.

"Yes, dearest Adelaide" is the murmured correction.

Ella has never been asked to call one of Martha Beale's acquaintances by her first name. She blushes in confusion. "Yes, dearest Adelaide."

"Ah, how charming. Innocent youth with pretty pink cheeks. I'll tell you something in confidence, my dearest Ella. Soon, I intend to create an exclusive school for young ladies like you. A seminary, as you refer to them in this country. My students will live with me, and we'll sing songs and laugh and take tea, and dine well. And sometimes we'll even study! But never too much in one day to be taxing. Doesn't that sound delightful? But you mustn't ask your mama to let you attend yet, because I'm not yet ready to receive scholars. Another wondrous secret between us two!"

Squeezing the girl's hand, Adelaide gazes into her eyes, then leads her on a promenade of the room, extolling her deportment and grace. "You will soon be a beauty unlike any other," she declares as she encircles the girl's waist with her arm.

Ella doesn't even notice that the French accent has vanished; if she did, she'd tell herself that royalty must be better students of language than common folk.

Pausing at the bellpull, her hostess announces an excited, "We must have refreshments to celebrate your arrival. Cakes and maybe a little negus. Not too strong, of course, because doubtless your mama would disapprove of you imbibing spirits, but a girl your age...well, you're no longer a child, are you, my dear?"

Before Jervis can appear, for this is whom Adelaide intended to summon, Solange enters the room. Because it's too soon for customers, she's dishabille, though, in truth, this is how she always dresses until evening approaches. She

stops and stares at the newcomer, while Ella, who's surprised to find another resident in Adelaide's home, stares back. Neither looks happy to discover the other.

"Solange, my dear, come meet the captivating Ella. A formal curtsy to each
other, ladies, if you please."

Doing as she's commanded, Solange then looks to Adelaide for a clue as
to the girl's identity and potential position in the house, but the older woman's
expression is inscrutable.

Ella also glances at Adelaide, her face full of childish hurt. When she returns
her scrutiny to Solange, jealousy and betrayal pinch at her eyes.

None of this behavior is lost on Adelaide. She takes the hands of both,
pulling them with her and then seating herself on the settee between the two.
"Solange will become something like the mistress of our little school, I think.
Don't you agree, my dearest one? She's very wise, and also very spirited. What
do you say, Solange, will you use your experience to train some younger girls?"

"If that's what you want" is the sour reply.

Adelaide laughs. "It's not what I wish, but what you desire. And you, my
lovely Ella, will you put your confidence in my Solange? Above all else, I yearn
to have you and she become friends, even if one of you is assigned the role of
teacher and the other of student."

"Yes," Ella tells her, though the assent is reluctantly given. She sends Solange
another sidelong glance while she makes her promise. The look is met by haughty
indifference, making it clear that Ella's proposed teacher will never be her friend.

"Brava! But, of course, I'm premature in my schemes. Today, our newest
companion must return home to her loving mama, while Solange and I remain
here alone. But we shall miss you, my little chick. I assure you we shall."

Envy roils through Ella's stomach. She glares at Solange's dressing gown,
which looks dirtier than it should, and far from new, despite an apparent effort to freshen its appearance with additional lace and ribbon trimmings. She
wonders why Adelaide, who's so beautifully accoutered, would permit one of her
teachers to clothe herself so poorly.

At the same time, Solange assesses the child who's been brought into the
house, noting the high-buttoned shoes, the under- and overskirts that barely
reach the ankles, and the demure and girlish neckline. Some customers prefer a

virginal appearance, she knows; the thought brings a sneer of contempt that she makes no effort to hide.

In the midst of this silent war, Adelaide glows, then orders a startled Solange to perform the menial task of finding "our lazy footman." Before she can obey, however, the double doors slide open.

"You called, madam?" Jervis starts to say in the ingratiating manner in which he has been taught, then stops and stares at Ella, his expression revealing shock and disbelief.

"Some negus and cake for our guest," Adelaide commands, her tone a warning that he should maintain an appearance of decorum and keep all opinions to himself. "But don't allow the mixture to become too potent for our little blond chick here."

His mistress's admonition goes unnoticed. Jervis continues to stare at the girl, his look one of horror.

"Are you deaf, man?" Adelaide hisses, which causes Ella to turn toward her hostess in surprise, as if she'd never expected a highborn lady capable of vulgarity. "Obey me at once." Which Jervis does, though not without another dismayed glance at Ella.

Realizing she has displayed too much temper, Adelaide beams at her visitor. "I shouldn't become impatient, should I, Mistress Ella? But it's because my heart is so full. I desire only the best for *ma chére petite amie. Pardon*! My dear young friend."

The negus and cakes are produced, the beverage warm and redolent of nutmeg but laced with so much port wine that Ella's head begins to spin. With great care she replaces her glass on the table and then rises unsteadily, thanking Adelaide for entertaining her and insisting that it's time to return home.

"Nonsense," Adelaide says with a laugh. "My small chick has—how do we say, Solange—*ébriété*? Inebriation. We shall put her upstairs for a brief repose before returning her to her darling maman." Anticipating the girl's protests, Adelaide stands, kisses her cheek, and places her hands in Solange's. "Lead her to the bedroom next to yours, dear," she says, silencing another imminent argument by assuring Ella that her home will always be open to her "dearest girl" and that now is as good a time as any to test how sweet her dreams can become when under her "admiring friend's roof."

Adelaide is watching as the two begin mounting the stairs when a knock at the door announces another visitor. Jervis admits a woman shrouded in a veil. Becky Grey has arrived, at Adelaide's request, but doesn't dare risk exposing her identity to those passing in the street; she waits until the door closes behind her before unpinning the lengths of dark French netting.

Solange, ever hopeful for customers, turns back to gaze down into the entryway, but not Ella, who stares at her feet, clinging to the railing and feeling her way with uncertain steps.

Glancing upward, Becky encounters Solange's disappointed stare as well as the tottering posture of her companion, whose unsteadiness, combined with her costume, makes her appear young indeed. Without recognizing Ella, the sight appalls Becky nonetheless.

"What mischief are you planning?" she demands.

Evaluating how intently Becky watches Ella's hunched shoulders and stumbling feet, Adelaide at first fears the girl has been discovered; then she assures herself that such a disaster is impossible. Why would Becky suspect her friend's adoptive daughter was here? No, the house on Wood Street would be the last place she'd expect to encounter the child. Laughing to mask her unease, she also regards Ella and Solange's ungainly progress. A motherly smile slides across her face. "Oh, my dear friend, can't I entertain whom I choose in my own home—"

"Your home!" Becky scoffs. "With a lease signed by me, and a quarter of a year's rent paid in advance—also by me."

"And very grateful I am, too, though I anticipate repaying you in full in the near future. A gentleman who shall remain nameless and was my first customer may be interested in investing. He's a well-born and well-connected gentleman." This is partly a lie, however. Nicholas Hendricks has made no such offer. "And very, very rich. You should be happy for me, Mistress Grey."

Becky pays no attention to the claim of early repayment; instead, she returns her scrutiny to the girl struggling up the stairs. There's something familiar in her posture, but she tells herself she could have passed any number of girls the same age as this one trying to earn their keep by selling their bodies. "I don't approve of your peddling children."

"And who says I am? The young duckling you saw"—for Ella has now disappeared from sight—"is a sister of my resident practitioner. She's here for a brief visit only, and unfortunately she consumed an alcoholic beverage. I should have supervised her better. You're correct to criticize me. I willingly bear the blame for her slight intoxication and assure you it won't happen again."

Becky regards the speaker. She has no reason to accept this declaration as the truth, and she doesn't. "I repeat: I don't approve of peddling children. The young woman looks seasoned, and doubtless is. But subverting the morals of girls is unacceptable. If that's your intention, then I withdraw any promised aid. You can make public our prior connection if you wish, for I won't be blackmailed by a woman who sells children."

"Ah, Becky, so fierce and self-righteous, and so very mistaken as to my intentions. Men desire companionship. Isn't that a natural state? And women like to please them, which is also natural. And isn't the natural world revered? But, come, let us sit down and converse like friends."

"I'm not your friend, Honora."

"What a tigress you are. Can't you trust me for once? I desire no more than you—to earn a living as best I can. Alas, you have gifts and abilities I lack, so I must choose what to some must seem repugnant. Surely, you wouldn't wish me to demean myself by running a boardinghouse?"

Becky makes no answer; she remains standing in the foyer, even though Adelaide has moved toward the drawing room. "Why did you insist I come here this morning?"

"Why, for the pleasure of your company."

"I think not. You're a person who never does anything without a selfish motive."

"You speak about human nature again, and you insist upon altruism, which is mere sentiment. Beasts don't have the instinct for selflessness, and neither do men or women. Or children."

"Tell me what you want. The less I see of you, and of this residence, the better."

"This residence that you boasted of providing for my use not three minutes ago?"

Becky nods but doesn't speak. Instead she drapes the veiling across her arm as if in preparation of replacing it. Her adamant posture has softened, and she seems less willing to confront Adelaide than she was when she arrived.

"Or did I mishear you?"

"You heard me correctly."

"I thought so. Then let me explain a crucial fact: the actress Becky Grey had better not try to cross me, or threaten exposure, or claim I'm using extortion, because her lofty career will come to a swift demise when the public learns she has financed—and is financing—a bawdy house. And one that may, or may not, according to my whims and those of my clients, harbor young, suggestible girls. Now I propose you depart before you can make any additional and unacceptable pronouncements."

CHAPTER 13

Two Homes

MARTHA PACES THE drawing room floor. She simply cannot sit still, and every time she pauses and seems about to stop at Kelman's side, anxiety propels her forward. As for Kelman, he can only bear witness to her distress and wish he could assuage it. The luncheon they shared might as well have been blotting paper served on a series of china plates. Ever since Martha's panicked note arrived at noon at his office, his focus has been on Ella's disappearance.

"Tell me again what you learned at Blockley yesterday," she implores, although she has asked the same question a dozen times before.

"One of the female warders told me that a 'lad' was also searching for Ella's mother."

"The 'lad' whom you surmise is Findal Stokes?"

"Yes."

"Oh, why didn't I put an end to that absurd friendship? I knew she was bringing him food—"

"You did what you did because you're kind, and you want Ella to be good-hearted, too."

Martha's having none of that rationale, however. "Is that who she's with, do you think? Could she have gone somewhere with him? Hunting for her elusive mother, or could she have been..." The words die off.

"Yes, it's possible she's with him, especially as she's been eager to find her mother. She must have revealed her hopes to the boy, which, in turn, led him to the almshouse. I don't imagine it was pleasant for him to return there." Kelman hates exposing Martha to the likelihood of young Stokes's participation in the situation, but what can he do? She must have the truth.

"But where could they be? Where could they have gone?"

"I have men searching for her. Wherever she's taken herself, and whoever is harboring her, she'll be found, I assure you."

"But it's now—what?—nearly three o'clock in the afternoon. Mademoiselle Hédé told me she was acting oddly at breakfast, which means she could have left shortly thereafter. She could have walked out of the house six hours ago. Six hours! Oh, why was I so permissive? Why didn't I force her to remain inside unless in my company or Mademoiselle Hédé's? Or hire a secret-service agent to watch her when she slipped away from home? What mischief has befallen her—and all because of me?"

It's useless for him to argue, because she's been berating herself in this vein ever since he arrived.

"The boy doesn't mean her any harm, of that I'm convinced."

"Oh, harm! What separates hurt and intent in this matter? Nothing but happenstance. Let us say that she is with this Stokes, and hasn't met with some heinous crime—been abducted, or…well, we both know of worse fates. And let's say he's infatuated, as you suggested, and that he wishes only the best for her. Say, too, that she shares his youthful ardor. And then what?"

He starts to answer, but doesn't. It's clear Martha is too overwrought to heed him.

"But what if this boy isn't the honest person you surmise? Or that he's fallen in with a gang of thieves, which is probable, given what you've told me about his history? Then what becomes of Ella when she's attached to such a person? Findal could have taken her to a hiding hole he maintains; perhaps his intentions are honorable, but surely his companions won't share his scruples. They'd learn soon enough that Ella is my adoptive daughter, and then what? Wouldn't they connive to hold her for ransom? And would this Findal—well meaning though he might be—be capable of interceding? No. The answer is no."

Martha curtails her speech, but only for a moment. "Oh, what have I done? I swore that I'd respect her opinions, even those that differed from mine. I wanted her to know what it was like to be loved unrestrainedly. I scoffed at conventional wisdom that decreed how children should be reared, declaring the methods antiquated and cold. In everything I've done, I've made one error after another, and now I've put this child in jeopardy."

"Martha, you're not at fault—"

"I am." She falls silent. There's nothing he can say to convince her otherwise, nor does she want him to attempt to soothe her.

"We'll find her," he says after some additional moments elapse. "By nightfall, I hope."

She gives him a wan smile.

"By nightfall," he repeats.

"You're very certain."

"I am…determined."

When she speaks again, her tone has altered to one of quiet pragmatism. As comforting as it has been to allow her passions to bubble over, she understands that self-rebuke is a waste of time, as well as being self-indulgent. At issue is Ella, not her own history. "I wish I shared your optimism, Thomas. So, what would you have me do?"

"Wait. Even though that's the antithesis of your nature."

She nods, but her expression remains grave. "I'll do as you say. I'll wait. And hope and pray for the best. Now, go. My histrionics have consumed too much time."

"Don't reproach yourself, Martha."

Whom else should I reproach? she wants to ask, but she doesn't.

"Everything you've done has been driven by the best motives."

"I wish I felt comforted by that thought, but I don't. Now go. You have more important work than humoring me."

As he starts to depart, a hired coach pulls to a stop in front of the house. Almost immediately thereafter, the double parlor doors are flung open, and Ella appears. She looks ill and wan but unharmed, though her eyes are downcast and her progress into the room is hesitant.

"Oh, Ella, where have you been?" Martha runs toward the child but then pulls back when she smells the port used in the negus. "Who gave you fortified wine?" she demands, then softens her tone. "You'll tell me everything eventually, I know. For now, I'll give thanks that you're home. And Mr. Kelman, too, for he has had constables and day watchmen searching the city."

Ella hangs her head but doesn't answer while Martha and Thomas share a look of dismay.

"Are you hungry, dear heart? Or thirsty? Or are you simply weary from being gone so long?"

Ella makes no reply. Instead she stands limply, allowing Martha's hands to caress her shoulders.

"I was worried to distraction. Everyone was. And although we didn't want to frighten Cai, he must have sensed something was wrong and kept asking where you were. Promise me not to run away like this again."

"I didn't run away," Ella says in a whisper; then she starts to sob and doesn't utter another word of explanation. Not with Martha holding her close, or helping her upstairs, or undressing her and putting her to bed.

⇥▷◉ ◉◁⇤

Throughout the remainder of the afternoon, while Ella alternately weeps and refuses to speak, Susannah Rause storms up and down through her house.

Marching into her private parlor, she finds it confining and loathsome; her bedchamber is the same, as is the formal sitting room, the dining salon, and the entry foyer. No place provides refuge from her bitter thoughts. Instead, everything and every place inspire contempt. She hates her home, hates her possessions, and hates her life and herself. And her husband, Darius, too, though she's uncertain which of them she abhors most: him for what she's recently discovered about his business practices, or herself for having failed to understand how textile mills operate.

And the two of us regular churchgoers, she rails, *sitting in our pew each Sunday, listening to the Gospel's message, bending heads in prayer, and seeking God's redemption. What a sham! It's a wonder the Almighty doesn't smite us for our deception.* This chastisement is leveled at Darius, but she knows she also deserves admonition. Hasn't she broken the holy bonds of matrimony by being consumed by lust, as well as gluttony for material goods?

In her wrath, she tears at the scalloped flounces that decorate the bodice of her dress. One rips off, then another; the destruction of her costly raiment brings a kind of pleasure. Susannah despises even her clothes. *How many children have been maimed to create my morning and evening attire, my visiting dresses, and my ball gowns? How many, like that boy Darius mentioned? And what's the reparation? A hamper of food that Darius's manager reluctantly agreed to send the bereaved parents. A hamper of food, but no child to enjoy it. But no, Susannah, you mustn't demand better compensation, because if a monetary policy were established in one Philadelphia manufactory, then everyone laboring in every mill throughout the land would be clamoring for aid.*

By now, she has reentered the second-floor hall. The staircase is before her; without further consideration, she hurtles down it, running full tilt into her husband as he walks through the front door. Darius Rause, rotund and magisterial, is not amused.

"Mrs. Rause, what does this conduct mean? This is no way to greet your husband after his daily labors."

She's about to burst out her list of grievances, but the implacability of her husband's countenance silences her. Her expression remains rebellious, however, which causes Darius's thick torso to swell with indignation. The side-whiskers and beard in which he takes such pride bristle with condemnation.

"Let me escort you upstairs. A show if pique is unwise in these public spaces. We must never give the servants cause to gossip." So saying, he takes her elbow, pinching it between his thumb and forefinger until Susannah feels her arm turn numb. "Lift up your skirts, lest you rend them by tripping on the steps. Your costume has seen enough damage already, and you know how particular I am about your appearance. A man in my position must have a wife who's attractively accoutered at all times."

She says nothing throughout this forcible journey, though additional attacks on his cruelty as mill owner whirl through her mind. When he locks the door to her parlor behind him and releases his hold on her elbow with a none-too-gentle push, she spins around to confront him.

"Silence, madam. Let me remind you to lower your voice and to speak in a reasonable tone. And with appropriate dignity—"

"How can I be dignified when you—and I, by default—cause the deaths of innocent children?"

"To which young innocents to you refer?"

"You know perfectly well. The boy who died after being mangled by a loom. Jerson, or something like it."

"Jervis, I believe. A sorry case, but not unexpected. Those who choose to work with steam-powered machinery understand the risks—"

"Choose to! What option does a child have when applying to your factory?"

"All God's children have choices, my dear wife. If the boy didn't want to labor for me, he needn't have applied for employment."

"Then you'd force him to make his family go hungry!"

"He had parents, Susannah."

"Who clearly couldn't earn enough without their son's meager—"

"I warn you; keep that infamous temper of yours in check."

"I won't. I can't. Not when we're condemned to Hell for what you've done. Doesn't Jesus caution us to take care of children?"

Darius Rause's silence is severe. He regards his wife with ill-disguised aversion; she meets this gaze, but his superior power overwhelms her and makes her glance away.

"Do not attempt to tell me how to run my business. Nor will I permit you to act the pious lady with me. You, who have been committing folly after folly."

This time she forces herself to look into his eyes. "Whatever do you mean?"

"Don't play the innocent with me. Don't I know who visits this house?"

Her lips tighten. She lifts her jaw in a semblance of disdain. "I hope you do. I make my acquaintances well known to you. And you approve all guest lists prior to our entertainment evenings."

"Laudably said, madam, but unfortunately untrue. I'm well aware of the ruse you've been attempting to practice with your spurious cartes de visites."

"I've attempted no ruse, Darius."

"Ask your former maid whether you have" is his harsh reply.

Susannah says nothing for several moments. When she speaks again, her tone combines contempt with playful wheedling. "I trust you didn't believe a common woman like her over your lawful wife."

"Who is also Nicholas Hendricks's jade."

"That's not true, Darius."

"Spare me, my dear. I'm too intelligent to be deceived by that preposterous statement. Although, I do admit that I'm heartily sorry for you for wasting your time with a superfluous fellow like Hendricks. And perhaps endangering your health, as well, because I've discovered that he's well known to our metropolis's numerous bawdy houses. But perhaps you're aware of that fact. Maybe, too, you have little choice in your illicit amorous attachments, as you're no longer in the blush of youth."

What can she answer? Continuing her lie is demeaning, admitting infidelity equally humiliating. Instead, she sits, assuming a regal pose that seems the greatest falsehood of all. Then she waits for her husband's wrath to descend upon her.

"I see you expect fulminations, but I'm a rational man, not given to passions and recriminations. You have chosen to live your life immodestly. You have chosen to exist in a state of sin, all the while accusing me of defying God's laws. This seems to me the height of self-deception, not to mention a contradiction. So, madam, don't preach to me about salvation. Don't I supply labor to hundreds of workers? Doesn't my mill provide them with means of sustenance and an honest rather than a dishonest trade? Accidents will happen among the careless or physically or intellectually ill-equipped, but that's the cost of commerce, whether it's a large concern like mine or a single shopkeeper employing one small boy to stock his shelves. Those with determination and resolve win greater rewards than the slothful and slow-witted; this is the way of the world. You wouldn't expect a wolf to spare a lamb, would you? You'd expect the more aggressive animal to feed upon the weaker, thereby strengthening its body, and in turn, strengthening others of its kind. The rule applies to humans, too.

"You choose not to speak, Susannah, which is wise, for there's nothing of importance you can tell me. You have proven yourself to be weak in all respects. You cuckold me for a man who is, in every way, my inferior; and, lest we forget, you're barren and have given me no heir. The single task for which a female is created is the one at which you have failed spectacularly."

Susannah starts at this unexpected attack, but her husband will brook no interruption: "Perhaps if you'd had children, you wouldn't have let your mind stoop to maudlin sentiment by fretting over the death of some hapless lad, or by granting the imbecilic Mr. Hendricks access to your bed."

CHAPTER 14

Fire!

THE NIGHT WATCHMAN is the first to smell smoke. He's patrolling the area known during the city's early days as "the Society's hill" and is keeping himself alert by ruminating on how a Society of Free Traders who were the very antithesis of gentry would view the present denizens of the streets they built and once inhabited. Honest toil exchanged for rich folk squandering legacies. The watchman decides those same Free Traders might rise from their graves in disgust if they knew how changed William Penn's town had become. So, the odor of smoke initially conjures the idea of brimstone and ghostly apparitions. It requires a moment's concentration to realize the smell isn't hallucination but genuine.

"Fire!" he shouts. "Fire! Fire!" Then he clangs the bell beside the outdoor market on Second Street, which at dawn will resemble the shambles it's named for but that now is empty and quiet.

"Fire! Fire!" Following his nose, he courses up Pine Street, then north past Cypress, shouting all the while till he reaches Spruce Street, and, running west till he reaches Fifth Street, confronts a blaze that's growing by the moment.

Two fire brigades arrive, but rather than fight among themselves, they combine forces to battle the blaze. They know the residence's owner; his past generosity ensures every protective measure they can supply. Water is sluiced onto the brick walls; leather buckets and firemen's axes allow more water to pour inside through the shattered windows, but the blaze continues to spread. Soon the second-floor windows glow from within, then the glazing bursts of its own accord and crashes onto the pavement.

"Where's Mr. Rause?" the cry goes up. "Where's his wife? What about the servants?"

Neighboring homeowners, awakened from their slumbers, peer out of upper windows; those nearest to the conflagration deem it prudent to wrap themselves in cloaks and vacate their houses. "Where's Rause?" they ask. "Where's Susannah?"

One of the onlookers persuades a fireman to attempt to enter the building, which the man does, holding his waterproof hat over his face. The heat drives him back before he can take three steps inside. Tomorrow he'll tell his children that he believed he was facing Nebuchadnezzar's fiery furnace. Today he refuses a second attempt. "Anyone who's left in that house is surely dead," he announces, turning down a lucrative offer to breach the house's rear door.

After that there's a shout that several of the servants have been found, safe and unharmed and crowded together in a privy in the home's back garden. Because of where they found shelter, their dignity is wounded and their nightclothes stained, but they're alive. None, however, can account for their master and mistress, because none of them considered alerting the couple before escaping. Dark mutters of "ingrates" and "scoundrels" pass among the gathered householders while, privately, they wonder if the Rauses were hard taskmasters who never garnered their servants' loyalty.

The fire roars on, sending flickers of flame shooting into the night sky, but miraculously the house stands. Everything within must be charred beyond salvaging, but the stout walls survive. The neighbors, transfixed by the battle between man and nature, consider their good fortune in purchasing well-constructed properties and make mental notes to augment their insurance. Their unease increases, however, when the home's owner fails to appear. By now, two hours have elapsed since they began to gather, and the sky in the east is growing purple-gray.

"Can Darius Rause have been killed?" they murmur to one another. "And his wife? Surely not." But the scorched window frames and blackened cornice give testament that their fears may be realized. "A fine gentleman," some add in grave tones, "and his wife was always his greatest pride."

Then a footman, who resides with other male domestics in a rear, unaffected outbuilding, and who has been lending his aid in the bucket brigade, decides belatedly (for which he'll be castigated) to tour that edifice's ground floor to make certain that valuable carriage trimmings haven't been stolen by passing miscreants. He screams in terror; those rushing to help him discover Darius Rause alive but nearly insensate.

After being given water, urged to sit, then to lie down, to speak or remain silent, little is learned about his condition or how he escaped, or whether his wife fled with him. A surgeon arrives on the scene and orders that the man be removed from the vicinity of the noxious fumes. Carried into a neighbor's home, Rause is placed in bed, his head propped up by numerous pillows that the surgeon insists will help free his labored breathing.

It's then that those attending him hear that Rause tried to rescue his wife. Finding the door to her bedchamber locked, he attempted to batter it down. When that effort failed, he called for help, but he soon discovered that the servants had already fled. Running downstairs and out the service door, he shouted their names, then dashed into the outbuilding in hopes of securing a ladder and the help of the men dwelling there. What happened next, Rause doesn't recall. At the conclusion of this speech, the surgeon proclaims that his patient suffered a form of apoplexy, which would be consistent with his size and liberal diet.

He orders a treatment of sal volatile, mustard poultices, leeches, and bleeding. Although greatly weakened, Rause protests, insisting that he should rise and find his wife. The surgeon argues that he must have rest or risk another and potentially lethal fit. Apoplexy in a man of his years can prove fatal, he warns him. Then he assures Rause that Susannah has been rescued and is also recovering but that she needs tranquility as much as her husband does. The others in the room avert their eyes at this lie, but Darius Rause accepts it and falls into an exhausted slumber.

⊷⊨⊙ ⊙⊨⊷

Kelman is unaware that a second fire has ravaged another building. Throughout the night, he has been hunting for Findal Stokes. Without knowing the nature of Ella's degradation, Kelman can only surmise by her speechless sobs that it must have been serious, and he has no one else to suspect but the boy whom she apparently favored.

The search has taken him to the northern and eastern reaches of the city, where the tanneries, docks, and shipwrights, and the alleys, courts, and tenements abutting them, could provide refuge for a person whose object is to hide from those in authority. Having discovered no trace of the boy—despite providing a description of Findal's most prominent feature: his large ears—Kelman begins to wend his way back into the heart of the city. He's convinced that he's been lied to, convinced that someone—or many—are harboring the lad, and convinced that his revelation that young Findal has done grievous wrong to a wealthy young lady (and must pay for his crime) has been met with furtive approval. Some of his listeners, Kelman suspects, probably view the boy as a budding hero, perpetrating on an affluent female the same immoral act poor girls often suffer at the hands of rich gentlemen.

Morning has advanced by the time he reaches his offices. There, he discovers that constables and night watchmen have been scouring the nearby streets looking for him. His absence during the Rause fire could not have been more inopportune, but he's met with equally damning details. A death occurred at the residence. The body of Susannah Rause has been found, not within the locked chamber her husband attempted to open but in the ground-floor parlor. If the fire brigades had been quicker, he's told, she might have been rescued. A few minutes could have made all the difference.

CHAPTER 15

What Martha Beale Hears

DERELICTION IN THE line of duty. Such, noble readers, is the opinion of the citizens with whom this scrivener has spoken. A gentleman whose name is equated with all that is upstanding within our city has been done a gross injustice by our policing force, his majestic residence lost to him, but more grievous than that tragedy was the demise of his wife, who, herself, was a glittering jewel, among the best of Society.

The pages in this journal and numerous others have been devoted for many years to decrying the fact that our fair Philadelphia has grown too populous to be suitably maintained by a system that served its earliest residents and has now become outmoded. We refer, naturally, to the division of our metropolis into boroughs and wards, each with its own constabulary governance and private fire brigades. "Consolidation" is the by-word and rallying cry. Consolidation of these petty fiefdoms is critical in order that our citizenry may avoid fatal conflagrations such as the one that occurred at the Rause abode, and the other damning spectacle not a fortnight past.

Every one of this scribe's readers is fully aware that at present, a criminal can simply skip across a street and into another borough or district, and thereby avoid prosecution for his evil-doings. However, consolidation, or the lack thereof, in no measure excuses Mr. Thomas Kelman for the injustice he visited upon Mr. Darius Rause, whose faithful wife is now deceased through the blundering incompetence of that supposed servant to the populace...

Martha puts down the newspaper containing Freers's screed. The journalist's attack upon Thomas seems engendered by personal enmity rather than rationality, but she's aware that others will take up a similar hue and cry. She yearns to speak with him and commiserate; she considers sending a note to suggest a visit but warns herself that his time is valuable and that she has been demanding too much of it. Folding her hands in her lap, she gives herself over to troubled thoughts. The mystery of Ella's disappearance is no closer to being resolved than it was the evening before. Having been put to bed, the girl finally slept as though deprived of slumber for days. Martha has tiptoed in and out of her room and sat silently at her bedside, but Ella hasn't stirred, and her face appears as tortured as it did when she arrived home. *What horrible thing did she experience?* Martha wonders. *Is Findal the cause of her distress? Or are others to blame? Or is it something altogether unknown?*

Unable to find answers, she rises and crosses to a window, though she doesn't bother looking out at the street. *I should send for a surgeon and describe our predicament. But he'll insist on waking her, which may do more harm than good. No. Better to let her have her repose and awaken naturally. But is this a natural sleep? She was suffering the effects of strong spirits; is it possible she was poisoned, too? Inadvertently or purposefully makes no difference. The results are the same.* Naïve though Martha is in the habits of the city's rogues and ruffians, poisoning is something every householder understands. In its most common form, it's the result of a family consuming spoiled meat or poultry or fish; in its severest, it enables pregnant young servants to commit suicide. Martha considers the antidotes she knows: for laudanum, emetic draughts; for poisonous foods, emetics and castor oil; for alkalis like potash, first soda and ammonia, then oil or milk, then barley water. Were it oil of vitriol or prussic acid, Ella would be dead.

This final acknowledgment impels Martha to take up her pen and request her surgeon to come to the house with all due speed.

⇥ ⇤

Waiting for the man's arrival, she remains in the foyer so no time can be lost between his appearance and Ella's treatment; she herself opens the door the moment the brass knocker drops in place.

"Oh," she says, seeing Becky on the front steps, "I thought you were the surgeon."

"Is someone ill?"

Martha fails to notice Becky's distracted tone while her friend, equally consumed with her private fears, misinterprets the depth of Martha's worries.

"Ella."

"Oh, dear. The health of children is a trial, isn't it? My own little William can bring delight and heartache in a single day."

Although Martha's aware of how practiced the speech sounds, her thoughts are focused on the girl sleeping upstairs. She doesn't question Becky's odd behavior. Nor—and this decision will return to haunt her in future—does she explain the nature of Ella's malady. Instead, she asks a polite: "And how is your young Will?"

"Thriving. Growing. Walking, which is both adventure and trial." Becky pauses long enough in her recitation to examine her friend. "You look anxious. Is anything amiss, other than Ella's well-being?"

"No, no. But please, come inside, and let me send for some refreshment."

"I would enjoy that very much. I realize the hour is early, but I don't believe friends as close as we are need stand on ceremony."

"Of course not." Leading Becky into the parlor and ringing for a maid to bring food and drink, Martha leaves the doors to the foyer open so she can listen for the surgeon's knock.

"I read about your Thomas Kelman in one of the newspapers," Becky states as she sits. "The criticism was unfair, and biased, too. But then most of the critics I've encountered delight in being cruel. It's the nature of the beast. Ask them to perform in a play, and they'd meet with certain disaster."

It takes Martha a moment to realize that Becky is referring to the fire at the Rause abode. How long ago her own perusal of Freers's attack seems!

"Did you know Susannah Rause?" Becky asks.

"By sight, of course, but she and I were very different people. We never became intimates."

"A terrible thing to die as she did."

Her ears trained to the front door, Martha answers with an abstracted, "Yes."

"It's not your Mr. Kelman's fault, however. You must realize that."

"Yes. I hope he recognizes his innocence, as well."

"You must insist upon it. Tell him from me that detractors can be and must be overcome."

"I shall. Certainly."

As if drawing up courage, Becky leans forward. "How shall I say this? I knew Susannah, as a matter of course. And Rause, too, naturally. Husband and wife could not have been more opposite. He is all pomp and bombast and show. She was more…effusive in her emotions."

"Ah…" is Martha's sole response. Intimate details about the Rauses are of no importance to her.

"She had a special friend, a man named Hendricks, who decided to invest in my theater. I always suspected the financing came from her, but I accepted the investment, for which I'm not proud. Hendricks is a reprobate of the first order. I made certain the sum was an insignificant one—not that the fact excuses me. Nor did I permit him to fraternize with the actresses in my employ. Apparently, he informed Susannah of my strictures."

"Ah…" Martha repeats, glancing at the tall-case clock. Nearly thirty minutes have elapsed since she sent for the surgeon! Where can the fellow be? She imagines cataclysms preventing his arrival: the footman knocked down by an omnibus, or the surgeon gone to attend another patient and his servant unable to supply the address. So preoccupied is she that she doesn't hear what Becky next says.

"Apparently, also, she accommodated his caprices. Or so one rumor had it." Becky pauses again. "She was at pains to keep the relationship a secret, however, even from me. She would have succeeded had she not once chided me about my 'rectitude.' Now, I have no evidence except a woman's instincts, but what I've come to suggest is that the husband may be culpable in his wife's demise. If Rause suspected his wife of infidelity, perhaps your Mr. Kelman—"

At this moment, the entry door is finally flung open, and the footman announces the surgeon. Martha leaps from her chair without apologizing to Becky or making any reference to the information she has shared.

⇢⋙◉ ◉⋘⇠

Prior to waking Ella, the surgeon listens to the events of the prior day. He draws a chair close to the girl's bed and watches her eyelids flutter in sleep. "I suspect nervous hysteria," he says at length. "If she'd been poisoned, her symptoms would be different. Her skin would have an ashy pallor or would be unnaturally ruddy, and her breathing would be fitful and labored, rather than measured. What you've described, Miss Beale, is consistent with the signs of hysterics: copious weeping, incoherence when responding to questions, or mutism. Most sufferers of hysteria are women. Ella is only a girl, but it's clear that something momentous has driven her to this state. You tell me this boy cannot be found?"

"That's correct."

The surgeon hesitates before speaking again. "If I were you, Miss Beale, I'd move heaven and earth to find this young fiend. Your adoptive daughter may never be able to reveal what happened to her. Indeed, when she wakes, she may not remember the precipitating event at all. Whatever occurred, he should be punished. At the very least—the very least—he has rendered a young girl insensate."

Martha nods but doesn't otherwise respond.

"With your aid, Miss Beale, I'll awaken her now, but before I do, let me provide my recommendations for her care: A plain diet, no mental or psychic stimulation, and myrrh and aloe pills once daily. I don't recommend bleeding, because the activity in itself can produce anxiety. Don't seek explanations. If she recalls what happened, then she'll reveal it in her own good time. Now, are you ready?"

"Yes."

"The important thing is to remain calm. Whatever happens when this child wakes, she must be greeted with equanimity."

"I understand. I'm prepared to do my part. But I do hope that some of her sorrows have been eased."

Martha bends over Ella's bend, murmuring her name and entreating her to bestir herself, because the day is beautiful and the sun shining brightly. The surgeon assists by covering the girl's bedclothes with a flannel blanket that's been heated in the oven; then he moves out of view so that when Ella opens her eyes, she'll see only Martha's face.

Their efforts meet with success. Ella's eyelids flicker open. Seeing Martha, she smiles as though the past day had never existed. When she spots the surgeon, she asks a worried, "Is Cai ill? Oh, I must get up and help him. Poor little thing. I wish he were stronger than he is."

CHAPTER 16

A Truth Kept Hidden

THE MOON HAS risen as Jervis is making his way home. A luster bathes the streetscape, making everything appear clean and shimmering. The shadows produced by buildings and the few pedestrians stretch along the ground as though it were the sun that had cast them in relief rather than midnight's pall. He marvels at this oddity of nature and wonders if it's an omen. Do the lengthened images mean that dark doings are ahead for him and the two women in his keeping? Or is the glistening white, where no brightness ever shines, a sign of potential blessing? He clings to that ideal for the space of two blocks before deciding that he's too uneducated to guess the answer. His mind warns him that the omen must mean evil times are afoot. His soul, however, swells with hope, and he marches on, focusing on the task before him, and praying, though he rarely darkens the doors of a church, that it goes as well as he has envisioned.

⊷⊷▣ ◉▤⊶⊶

He's in luck in carrying out his plans, for his sister-in-law is still awake and dressed when he enters their shared chamber. His wife is snoring and obviously deep asleep.

"Do you fancy a walk, Lena?" he asks.

"Now?" is the surprised reply. "A walk in the moonlight! To be sure, I would love it. Sister won't waken till morning. I gave her a draught of that calmative elixir to help soothe her mind. I'm not sure she'll ever cease mourning. Or you, probably."

Jervis nods and then smiles in gratitude, not only for his sister-in-law's thoughtfulness but also for her apparent tranquility. He's never certain how he'll find her when he returns, and this state bodes well for the conversation he has prepared.

The two stroll toward the river, Lena commenting on the brilliance of the moon and the city transformed within its glow. Her chatter is animated and verges on becoming giddy when she stretches out her arms and finds the sky's light has turned them a glossy white. "Do I look like an angel to you, Jervis? An angel come to live on earth? I must, I think, because I'm so fair-colored—or used to be. That's what angels look like, isn't it?"

Regarding her, Jervis can see traces of her former beauty. The blanching effect of the unearthly light has eradicated the lost teeth, the scars upon her face, the tremulous, bony frame. "You were a pretty girl, Lena. That's a fact."

"Wasn't I? Oh, wasn't I? My glory, and my misery, too."

"That's also a fact."

"Don't you go scolding me, Jervis. Doesn't Sister do enough carping about my formerly wanton ways for all three of us? And haven't I been on the straight and narrow path since I came to live with you?"

"Have you, Lena?"

"Well, of course I have! Whatever do you mean? You're not questioning me, I hope."

He doesn't answer, and they continue on, but she no longer primps or twirls at his side; instead, she becomes querulous and offended.

"I'd work if I could, Brother. You know I would."

"Yes. Yes, I do."

"Could I help it if one employer after another found fault with me? Well, perhaps I was to blame on occasion. But not always. Not always. And then there was no other recourse…no other recourse but what I done."

He says nothing, but she makes up for his lack of speech by doubling her own.

"And don't you think it haunts me still? I'd be made of stone if it didn't. But I was never as pure or loving as you and Sister."

By now they've reached the water's edge. Between the commercial piers, there's space for fishermen and eelers to ply their trade. Jervis helps Lena descend to the miry beach. Cracked oyster and clam shells crackle underfoot. The smell is none too pleasant: fish innards and the rank weeds that catch all manner of debris. The moon's rays embellish even this scene, however, lighting a broad path over the rippling tide.

Lena gasps in delight. "The water looks like you could walk on it, don't it, Jervis? Like a street paved with golden bricks." She steps straight toward this envisioned lane as if she believes it's real; he must pull her back before she walks into the waves.

"Stop, dear. Your imagination's playing tricks. You'll soak your boots if you keep going."

She yanks away, her happy mood turned bitter. "Maybe it'd be best to let me go. I wouldn't mind drowning. Floating away in the night with the moon showing me the way. That would be nice, wouldn't it? I know I'm nothing but a burden to you and Sister."

"Don't talk nonsense, Lena."

"That's what you always say. You and Sister."

Jervis suppresses a sigh. "I'm sorry you feel that way, dear. You know we want to help you. And always have. You've faced difficult times. Thanks be to God, they're over and gone."

Without answering, she keeps her gaze fixed on the river. "My own little daughter," she murmurs, "and I too terrible a mam to keep her. How many years has it been, Jervis, for I've lost track of time."

"Now, now, dear. Let's not—"

"How many years? How many? How many?"

"Never mind about that now—"

"I asked you a question! And don't pretend I didn't." That quickly, her quiet mood has grown harsh. "What fiend of a woman lets her mate sell her own flesh and blood?" she wails.

Jervis's heart sinks. He was hoping for reason; instead, he's facing the opposite. "Lena, dear friend and sister, desist. You can't change the past. You can only hope to make the future better."

"That's what you always say. You and Sister. Cooing and cooing at me like molting pigeons. You accept every miserable thing that happens to you. Then whisper 'Thank you, God, for sparing a poor sinner like me.' But your boy wasn't a sinner any more than my—"

"Lena. Stop. I didn't come here to—"

"And she's just as dead to me as he is to you."

Jervis grabs her shoulders. "Stop. Now."

"I almost hope my child's dead, too. For what sort of life would she have in that place—"

"No more!"

"Why can't I speak about her?" she cries out. "You and Sister always telling me to quiet my voice and keep my dignity. I'm not made of mud like you and she are. I have a heart in me."

"Be still, Lena. You'll attract attention."

"What do I care? Oh, I wish I were dead. I do. I do."

For a moment, it crosses his mind that he could leave her here and let her do mischief to herself, or else get carted away for disturbing the peace. It wouldn't take long before she'd land back in the lunatic asylum outside the city. Maybe the regimen there would finally cure her, and maybe it wouldn't. But either way, he and his wife would no longer be forced to weather the woman's inner storms.

He banishes the idea, however, and pushes her roughly up the slick stone steps of the jetty. In an instant, she becomes docile again.

"What a pretty night, Jervis. And fancy, you taking me for a saunter out under the stars. Sister would be jealous if she knew, wouldn't she? But mum's the word, my dear brother. Mum's the word."

What can he answer? Certainly not with the speech he'd composed on his way home. Telling Lena that he encountered a girl who looks startlingly like her lost daughter and who shares the same name would enkindle a dangerous state of mental activity. He realizes that he was wrong to have considered the idea. Very wrong. And foolhardy, too. The truth pains him; for he had begun to convince himself that good might finally come of ill. But no. No. He must keep the secret. It will do no good to assure her that the girl—if it truly is her child—is thriving, that her clothing is fine and costly. Nor can he reveal what now seems a preposterous scheme: that if Lena can behave herself, that she might someday serve as cook or laundress on Wood Street, and so eventually encounter her lost daughter.

What nonsense was I inventing? Don't I know how Lena will react, and why her mental state is so precarious? One brute of a man after another, a son burned when he tumbled into the cook fire, the girl taken from her mother's arms and sold. It's no wonder the woman's wits are unhinged. No, I'll make no reference to this Ella. Maybe when Lena shows signs of improvement and stability…but not yet. Or maybe never.

"Yes," he says, "it is a pretty night. But I don't believe my missus would begrudge you taking a stroll with me."

"You're a dark one, Brother," she says with a laugh. "I can sense you're keeping something private. I always know when you and Sister are holding secrets. You can tell me if you fancy me. I won't be shocked. Many gents have over the years. And some I've fancied myself." She titters. Jervis hears trouble in the sound. She's about to enter into another of her unfortunate moods.

"I'm not hiding anything from you. Your sister doesn't, either."

"I don't believe you. In fact, I think you're hiding behind her skirts at this very minute. You don't fool me. You're hungering for me. I know you are." By now they've reached a broader part of the street, and she dances away from him, flipping up her skirts till they expose her knees.

Jervis makes a grab for her but misses. "Behave yourself, Lena."

"No. No. No." She twitches her skirts higher and spins farther away.

"Behave, I tell you."

"Oh, you miserable prig. You and Sister both. Neither of you has enough warm blood between you to keep the winter's cold out of a bed. 'Behave. Behave.' That's what you're forever jeering at me. Well, I won't. I won't."

"Lena. Stop your playacting. You'll have the night watch arresting us."

"What do I care? You and Sister would like it if I were gone from your home. She would, at any rate—"

"Lena. Be reasonable."

"Reason can go to the Devil! And so can you."

Having tried admonition and practicality, he now attempts levity. "The Devil's got other folks he's busy with. Now, will you come home before we're both hauled away for disturbing the peace?"

She hisses at him, backing away till she finds herself in a corner and can go no farther. "I'm brave and you're weak, bold while you two wring your hands and weep 'Woe is me.' If I didn't think you'd fall straight down dead from shock, I'd tell you something marvelous and cunning I did—"

By now, he has moved close to her; he stretches out his hand, the gesture slow and reassuring as if toward an angry dog. "Come home, Lena. It's late. Let's get you home."

"Something you'd never have the heart to do. Not in a million, million years—"

"Come along, Lena. It's late and I must be up early—"

"Then go along home, you wretched coward. Go home to your sniveling wife."

"That's unkind, dear, but I'll overlook it."

"Just like you overlook everything," she screeches.

"Lower your voice, dear. Please." Jervis is cursing his impulsiveness. He's also beginning to wonder if he shouldn't quit his employment. What if Lena were to follow him and accidentally discover Ella's existence? What chaos might then ensue! Mightn't she start insisting that the child was hers? And demanding to be reunited, too? Wouldn't she be incarcerated again? Yes, assuredly. And wouldn't he and his wife be blamed for mismanaging her care? She might even wreak costly physical damage on the Wood Street house, which he'd be forced to repay. Envisioning those potential scenes, he winces, which expression Lena misinterprets.

"Hide your head and weep into your porridge, for all I care. You've never avenged the death of anyone, but that's what I've done. A fiery furnace. No, two. Two, but the first didn't work the way it was supposed to—"

"Fine, dear. We'll tell your sister about your heroics in the morning."

"Are you listening to me?" she roars. "No! You're such a weakling, you don't believe me—"

"Of course I do. Don't your sister and I believe everything you say?" Jervis has finally managed to grasp her arm. He pulls her close in an embrace that's part comfort and part restraint. "Everything you tell us, dear sister."

"You don't. You don't. You think I lie and invent stories."

"Never. Never."

"I told you my boy didn't fall into the fire. His hellish pa pushed him."

"That's right. But it's best to not think about those hard times, dear. You're alive and with your sister and me, and all is well. And maybe I should look for other labor that doesn't keep me away from home for so long."

Lena nods, her passion now waning. "I'm an avenging angel, aren't I, Jervis?" she whispers. "Burning up our enemies—"

"You're any kind of angel you wish, dear."

At this she buries her face against his shoulder and weeps, the noise as unconstrained as a child's. "Don't I know what it's like to lose a little one? Two little ones. The two darlings of their mother's life. My own two lost ones."

⋅→▸═◉ ◉═◂←⋅

Ella wakes with a jolt, the bed jouncing under her as if she'd fallen from a height; her chest constricts with a soundless scream of terror. Her eyes stare into the darkness of the room—her room, the place familiar in every shadowy object and every smell and sound. She frowns as she tries to remember her nightmare, but she can only recall fear and that she was crying. No, not crying: sobbing. Turning her head, she finds the pillow wet with real tears. The bedclothes have been wrenched to one side as if she'd been kicking them. *Or at someone*, she thinks.

It's that last realization that catapults her off the mattress. She stands on the carpet. The woolly texture beneath her toes should be comforting, but it, like the furniture and homey aromas, fail to alleviate her dread. *I must leave this place*, she tells herself. *I must leave before they catch me.* Who *they* are, she doesn't know. Only that she must escape. Her nightmare has overwhelmed all rational thought.

She hurries across the room, dressing with haste, only pausing to question what clothes she can easily carry with her. The horror of her mysterious dream is so palpable that she doesn't dare light the lamp, so she stubs her toes and bangs her shins as she rushes about. At each unanticipated blow, she gasps; she's so beset, she doesn't bother to stifle her groans.

In the adjacent bedroom, Martha's other adoptive child, Cai, also wakes, and with as much fright as Ella, for he believes in ghosts. He lies still, listening to the sounds that he's certain are inhuman grunts and moans. He stifles his whimpers lest the demon on the other side of the door hears him. *What has it done to Ella*, he wonders. *Why didn't she scare it away? Ella's brave. Has the ghost smothered her, or wrapped her up in shrouds like the ones in the book of fairy tales? Is it going to steal her away when it flies up the chimney and howls across the rooftop?*

Terror congeals him, but gradually concern for Ella supersedes his own fright. Making not one sound, he slides out of bed, stands on the floor, and waits, listening. The harsh sounds next door continue. Gathering every piece of courage he can muster, he tiptoes to the door, depresses the latch, and slips into Ella's room.

"Cai! Go back to bed. It's too late for you to be up."

"Where's the demon?" is his whispered response.

"There's no demon. Were you dreaming about one?"

"No. I woke up and heard it. It swooped down the chimney to carry you away." His breaths are as rapid as a panting dog's.

At this, Ella risks lighting the lamp in order to prove how wrong he is, but her own anxiety begins to infect them both.

Cai looks at the jumble of clothes. "Did the monster do that?"

"There are no monsters here. Nor ever will be. I'm responsible for my clothes being in disarray."

"Why?"

"It's not important. Now you go back to bed like a good boy."

"Why? Why did you do that? Mademoiselle will be ever so cross."

She tries to walk him to his room by promising a story to put him to sleep, but he remains steadfast in his belief that something dangerous is at work.

"Why?"

"Don't you want a story?" Desperation is now creeping into her tone.

"I want to know why you threw your clothes on the floor. Did something wicked make you do it? That's what Cook said when I dropped my bowl of porridge yesterday."

"You dropped it because it was too hot, not because you're evil."

"But an evil creature might have made me do it. He might have made me stumble. Or turned the porridge so burning hot I couldn't hold it. Something bad made you put your nice dresses on the floor."

"There aren't any evil creatures in this house, dear heart."

"I can hear them. At night. In the chimney."

"That's only the wind whistling in the flues. Now, you go back to bed."

"No. I want to stay with you."

Frustration gets the better of her. "You can't stay here, because I'm going away."

"Going away! From here? Why?" In his dismay, Cai ceases his careful whispering.

"Hush, or you'll wake Mademoiselle."

"Why? If there aren't any monsters here, then why are you leaving?"

"Hush, now. Hush."

"Why? Why?" By now the boy is almost shrieking, and Ella must clasp a hand across his mouth to keep him quiet. "Shush...please shush."

Try as he might, Cai can't stop whimpering, so she draws him down onto the floor as if preparing to play a game of marbles. "Quiet, dear heart, quiet. See, there are no demons here. Just us being comfortable, and warm and safe. See how nice this is? And nothing to hear but the sound of us talking to each other."

"Don't go, Ella."

"Not yet, I won't."

"No, never! Never!"

What can Ella answer? Certainly not that she also woke in a fearful state, convinced that wicked folk were conniving to snatch her from her home. Nor that this belief impelled her to run away before they could find her. To admit the truth would be to frighten the boy more than he already is. Besides, her motives now seem foolish. Who wakes up from a nightmare and then flees into the dark city? Why not stay tucked safely in bed and wait for morning to dispel the weird fabrications?

Instead of trying to explain her motives, she invents one that will sound soothing: how she intended to go visit a person who has been kind to her, someone who likes to protect her. When Cai interrupts her, demanding a name, Ella tells him it's a secret and promises that, after seeing the mysterious person, she'll return and will never, ever desert him. And that someday he can come visiting with her. And that he'll be protected, too.

Ella murmurs words of consolation until he falls asleep on the bed of jumbled garments. She then blows out the paraffin lamp, stretches out on the floor beside him, and also sleeps.

CHAPTER 17

Ignored Advice

THE NEXT DAY, Ella's nightmare becomes reality. She carries a secret cache of food to Findal but can't find him in any of his nearby haunts. Assuming he's found some type of labor, she's nonetheless disappointed at not being able to share her nightmare with him, as well as her confused memories of the house on Wood Street.

Martha would be horrified if she knew Ella had again slipped out of the rear entry and was wandering about on her own. For no sooner has the girl begun her roving than a cabriolet starts rolling behind her, its horse moving at a leisurely pace as if the driver were enjoying a period of peaceable contemplation. Ella doesn't notice it. Even if she did, she wouldn't question its presence. The city is full of carriages and coaches, all ridden and driven by grown-ups going about grown-up business. Frowning because she would love to speak with Findal, she doesn't see the carriage pull close, or a pair of male arms lunge out to grab her. A handkerchief is thrust over her mouth and nose before she can utter a yelp of surprise. Adelaide whips up the horse and carts off her prize.

→>═◉ ◉═<←

Martha's first reaction is shock after finding Ella gone and her garments strewn. Horror soon follows. The girl must have run away. She tries to convince herself her fears are due to an overwrought imagination, so she searches the house, at first slowly and then with growing apprehension. No one has seen "Miss Ella." Not Mademoiselle Hédé, who has been giving Cai his morning lessons while Ella supposedly was still resting after the prior day's exertions; not the cook, nor the maids, nor the majordomo, all of whom believed her to be upstairs either in her own chamber or in Mademoiselle's classroom. Alone, Martha walks from attic to cellar and back again, murmuring a hopeful, "Wherever you're hiding, do come out. I'm not angry over yesterday. Some time, you'll tell me what happened, but not until you're ready. We'll make no more mention of the situation, and we'll continue as thankful and loving people." The words are carefully chosen. Martha doesn't risk saying "family" or "mother."

Her appeals go unanswered, leaving her standing in the second-floor hall listening for a sound that might indicate Ella's presence. Anxiety grips her. *I should inform Thomas*, she tells herself, but she hates the thought of what she perceives as her continuous wheedling. *No. He has more important problems than helping me control my household. I must face this crisis on my own. Perhaps I'm overreacting. Perhaps Ella will saunter back home any moment, or this afternoon, or this evening.*

Steeling herself, she mounts the stairs, raps on the nursery classroom, and with forced cheer asks Cai if he and Ella had had any exciting conversations the previous day, or at any recent period—which is when the story of Ella's secret friend is revealed. "She's coming back for me," the little boy repeats over and over, "because she'd never leave me alone with the monsters."

Martha sends her footman to Thomas Kelman's office with a request that he come to her house as soon as it's convenient.

⊷⊷⊙ ⊙⊷⊷

"What do you intend to do with her?" Nicholas Hendricks's tone has a mocking air. He indicates Ella's slumbering form. Dosed with laudanum, her body is inert, her face guileless and trusting.

"Perhaps I'll give her to you as a present."

"And have me risk your disfavor? No, thank you. My lady cat can scratch, I think."

"I can do more than scratch."

He laughs. "You're a wicked one. A wicked, wicked woman."

"More than you can guess. And you, sir, have your own devilish traits, or you wouldn't have helped me escort this fair damsel to my home."

"Damsel? I call her a child."

"Children grow."

"So you intend to keep her here until the moth turns into a butterfly?"

"I intend to keep her...for a time."

"Ah, likely the daughter you never had. How poignant. I look forward to witnessing her transformation."

Adelaide's eyes harden, but there's a sorrow lurking there that her anger can't conceal.

Hendricks notes the reaction. "The feline has a heart, after all."

"We all have hearts."

"Forgive my disbelief at that statement, madame." Growing bored, he turns toward the door, but Adelaide lays a restraining hand on his sleeve. Her grip is stronger than it appears.

"I did love once. This girl is my revenge for what is no more."

He shrugs his shoulders while shaking off her importunate grasp. "Then let me wish you well of your little plot. As for me, I'm too lazy a fellow to risk playing for high stakes, whether in sport or in life. Vengeance, ardor, and passion: they're too exhausting to consider. Now, forgive me if I leave you with your little one—"

"So that you can seek out the comforting arms of Solange?"

"Perhaps."

"I can't let you do that."

"Madam, desist" is his trenchant reply. "I've invested in this house. At your tearful request, I might add. I'll bed whom I wish."

"No."

"I tell you I will."

"And I say you will not." She grabs his wrist, drawing blood with her fingernails.

Hendricks looks at the color staining his impeccable cuffs. He tries to yank his arm free, but her nails dig deeper into his flesh.

"Let me go."

"Not until you pledge to help me."

"Help you? Help you do what? Keep this girl for pleasure or ransom? No. The notion is absurd. Someone will soon come looking for her—"

"Not here—"

"This is nonsensical talk. The chase was amusing, yes, as was its climax. But I want no part of whatever stratagem you're envisioning."

"You have a part already, Nicholas."

"Damnation, woman, are you deaf? I refuse to lend additional aid to this folly. Now, unhand me at once—"

"You have a role," she insists. "You were the one who plucked her from the pavement."

--->=== ⊚===<---

"Tell me again what Ella said, Cai." Seated on a low chair, with the boy standing before him, Kelman's voice is soft; his posture and tone are meant to encourage rather than frighten. But Cai is scared already. Ella has not yet returned for him, and soon it will be time for his morning milk and biscuits. When he answers, his speech is jerky, and he often looks to Martha for reassurance, which she silently provides.

"That she…that she was going to come back and…and get me."

"And then what?"

"That she would…that I could meet her friend."

"Who is?" Kelman looks at Martha as he asks this crucial question. Both assume the mystery person to be Findal, but they want to hear the name—not because it will assuage their fears but because they wish those fears confirmed.

"A secret…that's what Ella said."

"Is it a boy, do you think, Cai, or a girl? Or a lady, even?" This last is a ruse; Kelman and Martha are convinced that no adult is involved.

"Maybe…maybe a grown-up…because Ella said her friend wanted to protect her."

"But it could be a big boy, too. Or an older girl?"

"They'd have to be awfully big and brave. Ella doesn't believe in demons or ghosts. But I do. Could a big boy or girl save me from a monster?"

Kelman sidesteps the question with a gentle, "Everyone in this house can protect you, Cai, but there are no wicked creatures anywhere near. If I promise you, will you believe me?" Then he adds a seemingly inconsequential, "Did she say when she was coming back home?"

"No."

"But she did tell you she planned to return for you?"

"Isn't she coming?" is the whimpered response. "Isn't she? Isn't she?"

"Of course she is, dear heart," Martha tells him. "Of course she is." Over the top of the boy's head, she looks at Kelman, who nods his assent at her unspoken query: Cai can be released from his interrogation; they've learned all they can. "Now, you go along with Mademoiselle Hédé and have your morning milk and biscuits. Mr. Kelman will find Ella. Don't you worry."

"Before lunch?"

"I can't promise that, Cai," Kelman answers, while Martha counters with a falsely assured: "Well, he'll certainly try!"

--⇒═◉ ◉═⇐--

Alone, the two regard each other. Martha's so caught up in her worries that she's afraid to give vent to her thoughts lest she weaken. For his own part, he's loath to say what he must.

"Martha…what I'm about to suggest will be difficult for you to hear."

"Not so difficult as what I'm currently experiencing." She steps away from him, straightening her spine, as if bracing for catastrophic news. "I don't wish to sound harsh. Tell me whatever you feel is necessary."

He pauses before starting. "Experience tells me that if Ella had been abducted for ransom, you would have received a message from the perpetrators by now. You have not."

Again, he hesitates. Martha watches him, her silence urging him to continue.

"I will make an assumption, therefore, that the choice to desert your house was her own, and that she's with this Findal." Kelman's about to say "damnable young Stokes," but he doesn't.

"Isn't that what we feared before?"

"Not precisely. We surmised that mischief might have been at work. I now feel that her absence may be none other than rebellion. That's not to excuse her actions." He pauses, waiting for her reaction. When none is forthcoming, he resumes his analysis of the situation. "As I say, I'm not justifying her choices, especially in light of the pain she's causing you, but my theory runs thus: Misguided though she is, she has gotten into the habit of seeking consolation and support from this boy. She feels they're kindred spirits, and may take comfort in the fact that he shares her lowly birth. She may even take pride in helping him. That sense of worthiness could imbue her with a feeling of power that she's never experienced before."

Reflecting on his words, Martha nods her head. She says, "But no good can come of this…I won't call it a romance. This is no Juliet and her Romeo—"

"But what if Ella feels it is?"

"She's too young to know those sensations, Thomas."

"Is she? Plenty of girls in the class to which she was born are mothers already."

Martha doesn't immediately reply. Instead, she takes another step away from him. "Yes, that's true enough. But, if what you posit is correct, then I remain concerned that Ella may be in danger, which is what I felt before. Perhaps she and Findal share a youthful exuberance—and naïveté—but they don't exist in a vacuum."

"No. Which is why I want to make the following suggestion: place a notice in the newspapers." She begins to protest, but he pushes forward. "Hear me out. As you're aware, it's customary to publish private messages such as breaches of contract, and requests for information on missing persons, and so forth. Worded carefully, no one but Ella would—"

"But who's to say she'd see this appeal, let alone read it? If she's in some secret hidey-hole, where would she find a—"

"Wait for a moment, and let me to finish. *If* she's run away, as I believe she has, and *if* she's closeted away in some inferior place, then I imagine she may be beginning to have conflicting thoughts about her decision, which could now seem to her to be ill considered. She may be looking for an excuse to return home. You'd provide her with that rationale. She's more mature than I think you realize. Doesn't she look at the daily newspapers with you?"

"For educational purposes, yes."

"And doesn't she notice the personal messages?"

Martha shakes her head. "Perhaps. I don't know."

"But she might?"

"Possibly."

"In which case, she could be hoping that you—"

"I can't do that, Thomas. I can't. She's my heir. Any nefarious person read-ing my appeal could—"

"Not if the phrasing were ambiguous enough so that only Ella would un-derstand it."

Again, she starts to interrupt; again, he prevents her. "I'm not saying that will be the sole method. I'll have my men searching for her, and you may wish to hire a secret-service agent as well. But a printed appeal—"

"No. The risk is too great. Remember when my father vanished? Remember how I was prey to false information claiming he was still alive? If Ella has run away, as you infer—and let me add that I understand your deductions—then what would prevent people with criminal intent from abducting her? Despite your proposition, I fear we're back where we were yesterday." Martha's voice cracks. "And no secret-service agent, either, Thomas. Your constables and watchmen are good and reliable. I trust them not to gossip about the case. We must pretend to the world that all is well."

"At the risk of contradicting you, this wasn't your approach before."

"We had only supposition then. Now we have proof—in her own words—that she intends to ally herself with young Stokes. Yes, I realize she didn't name him, but who else could this mystery person be?"

He shakes his head, his expression somber. "I'll do as you wish, but let me give you further food for thought and ask you to consider her disappearance from her standpoint. Maybe, without realizing it, she yearns for you to make public your affection. Perhaps she wants to know how desperately she's missed."

Martha hesitates before she speaks. "Everything in me warns against public exposure. You may insist it's my upbringing, and perhaps it is. But I fear this suggestion of yours, Thomas. I do." He attempts to interrupt, but she's insistent. "Let us see what your constables can accomplish before we consider the step you've advanced. If she can be found, and brought safely home with no one aware she's been missing, so much the better. Can we not afford a day or two for a surreptitious search?"

CHAPTER 18

Scandal

A CLANDESTINE HUNT for Ella spreads across the city, the day and night watchmen being supplied a description of the girl—without a name—as well as of the boy, who is identified. It's understood, though never stated, that the girl must come from an upstanding family who doesn't want its reputation sullied by scandal, but neither Martha Beale nor any other member of the elite is mentioned. To the watchmen and constables, Kelman adds a group of men who are dressed in ordinary clothes rather than uniforms. They're instructed to penetrate the city's underbelly and to seek information on young Stokes and any colleagues he may have. Kelman advises these men not to bother with scruples. Their task isn't to arrest miscreants: it's to befriend them.

His plan in place, Kelman can only pray it works, though his faith in the project is scant. Findal has proven adept at hiding before, and, if it's true that he has now taken on the role of Ella's protector, then he'll be that much more difficult to unearth.

Martha prays, too, then also roves the streets, hoping against hope that her adoptive daughter will magically appear. Toward evening, she returns home, only to realize that tonight is the opening of *The School for Scandal*, in which Becky Grey will star. As it's the first play her new company in the Southwark Theatre has mounted, and as Martha is determined to maintain an equable appearance, she writes to Thomas, asking him if he'd care to accompany her; he, preoccupied and reluctant, agrees. As they set out, she looks at him with a rueful air and says that this public appearance is a test of their ability to dissemble, to which he can only nod in assent.

–•═❯ ❮═•–

The buzz of conversation of those entering the auditorium sounds like one extended gasp of wonderment. Limelight, recently employed for the first time in London's Covent Garden, has made its way across the Atlantic to provide the Southwark stage with a sheen that bathes the space in light so incandescent it seems supernatural. The more prosaic among the patrons murmur knowledgably about the effect of oxyhydrogen flames heating cylinders of quicklime, thereby producing an intense glow, but the remainder of the theatergoers simply gawk at the marvel. If this new lighting technique is any indication, Becky Grey and her troupe intend to set Philadelphia ablaze with artistry and novelty. The curtain is late due to the continuous chatter. When it rises, it's to wild, anticipatory applause; then Richard Brinsley Butler Sheridan's comedy detailing the questionable mores of Georgian-era society takes flight.

Or so it does for everyone but Martha and Thomas. Laughter, knowing and uproarious, surrounds them, the bon mots uttered by Sir Benjamin Backbite or Lady Sneerwell—or Sir Oliver Surface, Sir Peter Teazle, or Snake; or Careless, or Charles Surface—winging into each appreciative ear. Guffaws are accompanied by whispered repetitions of favored phrases: "There's no possibility of being witty without a little ill nature; the malice of a good thing is the barb that makes it stick…" Or: "Whenever I hear the current running against the character of my friends, I never think them in such danger as when Candour undertakes their defense…" And: "When an old bachelor marries a young wife, he deserves—no—the crime carries its own punishment along with it." This line is declaimed by Lord Teazle just before the curtain falls on act one and is immediately quoted, and requoted, within the hall.

Then, when Becky appears as Lady Teazle at the start of act two, the crowd rises to its feet in approval. Acknowledging the praise, she curtsies deeply, her gold satin dress billowing upon the floor and her tawny locks catching the light until it looks as though her bowed head is surrounded by a halo. "Brava! Brava!" is heard throughout the house before she has uttered a single word. When she delivers the line, "I know very well that women of fashion in London are accountable to no one after they are married," a stomping of feet is accompanied by hoots of praise. "She's a bold one!" several men concur in loud, admiring tones; one even whoops out the name of Becky's former husband, William Taitt—the name of whom receives a shrill hoot of derision.

Listening to the commotion, Martha wonders whether Becky was wise in choosing a character so dangerously close to her own life's story. She affixes a smile on her face that she hopes appears approving, but the amatory adventures and misadventures of London's "big wigs" seem wholly inconsequential. She casts a miserable glance at Kelman, who responds in kind, but they're in a public place surrounded by prying eyes and must maintain the appearance of formality.

One of those pair of prying eyes belongs to Adelaide, who watches Martha and Kelman, to the exclusion of the action on the stage. When the performers speak, she gauges how the couple receives the message and finds herself outraged at their apparent callowness. *What is the woman doing whiling away her time at the theater when her daughter is missing from her home? And why is Kelman with her instead of hunting for the girl?* Disgust turns her artifice of pleasure into something so sharp that her laughter clatters forth like nails or knives, while Hendricks, seated beside her, marvels at her mirth.

"You're certainly enjoying this, aren't you? I'll introduce you to some of the gents I know afterward, as well as to our star thespian. The theater is a leavening ground: demi and haut monde together in one not-so-chaste space."

The sally receives no answer. Adelaide is still punishing him for his attempt at rebellion.

"I believe you'll approve of Becky Grey," he adds in hopes of soothing her. "Before you arrived in our fair city, she found herself the center of a scandal when her husband was murdered. Apparently, the culprit had held her prisoner. The saga was rather convoluted, but it does add to the woman's intrigue, wouldn't you say?"

"I have no opinion on the matter."

"Madam, dispense with your ill humor."

"Perhaps I'd rather listen to the performance than to you."

Hendricks sighs but says no more, while Adelaide maintains an outward appearance of rapt concentration. When the audience applauds, her gloved fingers slam together in approbation.

⇥ ◉ ◈⇤

Remembering the evening but little about Hendricks's friends or acquaintances, or of Becky's icy greeting upon being "introduced" at the patrons' reception following the performance, Adelaide scans the morning newspaper. She's chosen the one to which Freers contributes, because his gossiping tongue amuses her. In this instance, he's quick to draw similarities between the playwright's louche personal history and Becky's notoriety. The words concerning the actress's ill-fated marriage drip with acidic glee. Adelaide merely skims them; she knows the story nearly as well as Becky. Nor does she pay attention to a reference to "a resplendent mystery lady on the arm of bon vivant Nicholas Hendricks," but she pauses when she comes to Martha's name, whom Freers links with a "certain lackadaisical government official, one Thomas Kelman, who should be investigating the sorrowful death of Mrs. Susanna Rause rather than disporting himself with our city's wealthiest heiress." The reference causes Adelaide's eyes to squint in exultation.

Her gratification is short-lived, for further perusal of the paper reveals no mention of a missing girl, no appeal for aid in discovering her whereabouts, no statement that such person or persons retaining information shall be compensated for shedding light on the matter. *Is it possible the high and mighty Martha Beale doesn't know Ella is gone from her house? Or that she's glad to see a budding female removed from the abode she plans to share with her lover, Kelman?* Adelaide has experience only with the circumstances of her own existence. Jealousy, lust, and hate are the coins of her realm, so Martha's silence is a puzzle she's not equipped to solve.

She crumples the newspaper and stalks from the reception parlor, mounting the stairs with haste and bursting into the room in which Ella has been sequestered. Her intent is to tell the girl that Martha Beale cares nothing for her.

When Adelaide is faced with her prisoner, who drifts in and out of a drugged state, her resolve deserts her. The drowsing girl looks so innocent and so utterly dependent that she can't find it in her heart to harm her. Instead, she stands enervated and perplexed. Without a modicum of maternal inclination, some primitive instinct still prickles, but the unfamiliar emotion creates an internal battle. Adelaide, who can boast of her competence at villainy as others boast of exquisite taste, can only shiver in confusion.

She leaves the room—but silently, so as not to startle her sleeping prisoner—and encounters Solange while turning the key in the lock.

"How long do you intend to keep that one?" she demands.

"What business is it of yours?" Caught off guard by her unanticipated sensitivities, Adelaide fails to take the high ground.

Solange cocks an eyebrow in surprise at this shift in their position and then presses her advantage. "Whose business should it be if not mine? You advertise a girl like her, there'll be no custom for me."

"I don't plan to advertise her."

"Just pass her around to a few choice gents, is that it? Along with their port and cigars? A bonbon after I've provided the meal? No, thank you. If she stays, I go."

"I told you that I have no intention of using her in that fashion. Now get yourself bathed and prepared for the day. You smell none too fresh." Adelaide makes to move past her interlocutor, but Solange prevents her.

"Then she's reserved for fine ladies, is that it? You're planning on creating a female clientele, and leaving me to service all the vulgar gents. Me and whichever other bawds you can attract."

"My business is my own. Now, I suggest you ready yourself. I made numerous contacts last evening. Our trade will soon increase. In fact, I've already put out requests for girls to join you."

Solange laughs; it's a mean, unpleasant sound. Were it not for Ella, Adelaide would ignore her hireling's bold reaction, but she doesn't. Rather, she grows wary; her fingers tighten around the key to Ella's door.

"I work so the princess can idle away in feather-bed repose, is that it?"

"You work so you'll be paid. Now, get yourself dressed."

"What you've done is illegal, Missus. Nabbing a kid off the streets and locking her up—"

"You're one to talk to me about legal and illegal. Now get out of my way and dress yourself, or leave this house. I can have Jervis toss you out bodily if you continue to challenge me."

The two women glare at each other, though Solange is no match for Adelaide and never will be. When she replies, her tone is less defiant; it makes up for the loss by being truculent: "Just so long as you don't use her like I said. You start handing her around like a candied sugarplum, and no one will want Solange. I've been in a place where that happened. An insult, it was. I don't intend to repeat the experience."

"And I don't intend to have a common slut like you dictate my policies."

"Common! You promised me a share of the profits."

"When there are profits—which, so far, have been negligible."

"Is that my fault?"

"Whose else, *Solange*?"

Jervis overhears the whole of this exchange. Padding about in the unobtrusive manner his mistress has dictated, he was on his way from the parlor to the pantry when he heard Solange accost Adelaide. Her combative tone arrested him, and he paused in his labors lest his mistress summon him to come to her aid. The notion of this girl who might be his niece offered up like a sweetmeat becomes more than he can bear. He stands listening while the women conclude their argument; he hears Solange slouch back to her room and Adelaide march off toward her own. Every inner warning tells him that now is the time to act. He must rescue the girl at once. He must. But how? And then what to do with her once he has taken her from the Wood Street house? He can't bring her home; not yet, anyway. And if he returns her to her own abode, who will defend him and say that he's not the criminal who abducted her? His mind spins along a fearful trail of eventualities, each of which leads to wrongful imprisonment. He speculates on the loss of income for his wife, which would induce her and Lena to gradual starvation. The result is that he can't bring himself to move from his spot beneath the stairs.

How long he remains thus immobilized, he doesn't know. It's only an importunate rap upon the front door that rouses him. Opening it, he admits Nicholas Hendricks, informs his mistress that she has a visitor, and finally scurries back to the kitchen. He would bewail his inaction if he could. Instead, he closes his thoughts to Ella in the same manner he'd close his eyes if he saw a careening wagon about to crash into him.

--→►●═ ●═◄·--

While Hendricks converses with Adelaide and allows a mute Jervis to serve him cherry cordial and Franklin cake, Kelman finally has the opportunity to interview Celestine Lampley. Despite her given name, he finds her anything but ethereal; instead, she's phlegmatic and uncommunicative. Rather than bridle at the charges that she quit the scene of a crime and may be implicated in homicide, she shrugs her shoulders then folds her arms across her chest to show she doesn't care one way or another: not that she was apprehended in her flight, nor that she owned a burning building in which an unidentified woman perished. Kelman surmises that the facade is a ruse. He's determined to overcome her seeming indifference; she's equally determined to maintain her pose.

"I don't believe you understand the serious nature of these charges, Mrs. Lampley," Kelman tells her.

"You don't, eh?"

"No, I do not. Leaving Philadelphia as you did makes you appear guilty of arson, and perhaps of the greater crime of murder as well."

"Guilty of arson on my own property! That's laughable. As to murder, I wouldn't harm a fly."

"That's not what your servants have said."

"My servants! I can count on my fingers and toes the times each has lied to me. Each of them! That's sixty lies between 'em. And who knows how many more fibs they told you?"

Kelman stifles his impatience. "I've also been taught mathematics." He alters his approach. "And you can't identify the woman who died in the fire."

"No."

"If she was a client of your establishment, wouldn't it be a matter of examining your books?"

"My books? I don't keep a hotel, Mr. Kelman."

"So you have no idea who the dead female could be?"

Again, she shrugs.

"Please answer me, madam."

"No."

"None whatsoever? Philadelphia isn't a large place, and your house served a select few. Most were repeat customers."

"How do you know that?"

"I make it my business to know such facts."

"Thinking of running a little trade on the side, are you?"

"Madam, I will repeat my previous warning: these are serious charges you're facing."

"Serious to you, but not to me. I repeat: I don't keep a guest register. Even if I had, it would have been burned up. If I knew who was there that night, I'd tell you." She smiles. "Maybe you can tell me, since you claim to be so wise."

Kelman takes a breath. He's tempted to dismiss her and let the reality of her situation penetrate, but he can't bear to be defeated. "Mrs. Lampley, your prospects are grave. Surely you're aware of that fact. You damage any possible leniency a court will provide by continuing to obstruct this investigation."

"Didn't I just state that I don't keep a register?" Her voice rises in frustration.

"I'm asking about your memory, not bogus names written on a page."

"So my memory's in question, is it?"

"Madam, my patience is growing thin. I asked you a question. Be so good as to answer."

Glaring at him, she flings out a defiant, "Well, it wasn't Susannah Rause."

It takes Kelman a second to decipher the response. He sees Celestine Lampley watching for a reaction, but he maintains an inscrutable expression while his thoughts begin piecing together Susannah Rause's connection to the house and, finally, what her husband might or might not have known about it.

"True enough," he says in a noncommittal tone. "She died in a fire at her home."

Lampley makes no reply, but neither does she lean back in her chair. Her eyes remain fixed on Kelman, who senses a change in her emotional state.

"I take it that you were no admirer of Mrs. Rause?"

"I didn't say I was, and I didn't say I wasn't. I only pointed out that she didn't die at my house."

"That's correct, but your tone of voice made your feelings apparent."

"All right, then, Mr. Kelman. I can't say that I did admire her. Women like her feel it's their due to be idolized."

"Am I to assume she was one of your clients?"

"You can assume all you like, but you won't set me a-blabbing."

"Come, madam. Enough of this cat-and-mouse game. Was Susannah Rouse a client of yours? A simple yes or no will do."

Another dismissive shrug is accompanied by a leaden, "Yes."

"Good. A plain answer to a straightforward question. Do you happen to know the identity of the gentleman who was her lover?"

Celestine Lampley's face undergoes a series of minute spasms. Rage leaps from her eyes. She turns away, but Kelman has noted the reaction. "No."

"I think you do."

"I tell you, I don't."

Kelman sits back in his chair. He listens to her altered breathing, hears her fidgeting movements, and waits.

"You won't get anything from Celestine Lampley."

He says nothing.

"I'm telling you, Mister. Celestine Lampley's no blab."

Again, he remains silent.

"Are you deaf, man? I've told you everything I know!"

Kelman waits. She does, too, but her nervous behavior increases; he outlasts her.

"The woman had no business with him," she says, her voice exploding. "None! Him so much younger, and her just an old hag—"

"His name?"

Additional spasms attack her face until she bursts out a choking, "Nicholas Hendricks!"

Kelman registers the identity. He saw the man's name in print just that morning. Apparently, he was in the audience the night before, having accompanied an unnamed female to the theater. It's clear that Susannah Rause's death has had little effect. None of these discoveries are revealed; instead, Kelman continues to scrutinize the woman sitting before him. "You feel strongly about Mr. Hendricks, do you?"

"I didn't say I did, or I didn't. Don't twist my words, Mr. Kelman."

"I don't need to, Mrs. Lampley. Your reactions speak for themselves."

Her mouth clamps shut as though to prevent further utterances from escaping, but she can't help herself. "He said he'd help me out…with money…and other things. Then she got her hooks in him, and he turned his back on me."

"Money? And what 'other things'?"

"Never you mind."

"What 'other things,' Mrs. Lampley?"

"He was going to become my partner in the business, if you must know. That's how Hendricks likes to use his spare change. Investing in bawdy houses. He calls it a 'game,' says it ensures him the 'pick of the litter.' That's what those gents are; it's all a party to them. Folks like me struggle, and the rich think we're playing at parlor tricks. Their lady friends are the same. 'Oh, thank you, Mrs. Lampley,' they tell me after they've taken their fill of an afternoon. Then they slip on their gloves and tie up their bonnet strings, as if they've only come to my property for tea and a bit of a chat instead of doing dirty deeds behind their husbands' backs." With that, she spits out a vehement: "I'm glad Susannah Rause is dead. I am. And I wish she'd perished in my home, instead of…" She says no more.

"Instead of what? What are you telling me, Mrs. Lampley?"

"Nothing. I said I couldn't identify anyone who visited my rooms that night. And I can't."

"Or won't."

Kelman's steady silence would unnerve the steeliest of constitutions. For all her bravado, Celestine Lampley isn't one of those ironclad souls.

"Now, will you let me leave?" she all but begs. "I've given you what information I have."

"No, madam. I've told you that your situation is dire. You'll be returned to prison—"

"You can't do that! Keep me shut up against my will. I had no call to burn down my own house. You'd have to be daft to think I did."

The interruption goes unnoticed: "—where you'll be kept in custody until this case is resolved. I'll also need to question you regarding the Rause fire."

"I wasn't even in the city when that occurred!"

"There are such things as accomplices, Mrs. Lampley."

"Why not blame Darius Rause for murdering his missus? If you think I have a motive, he's got one ten times as large. Fifty times, maybe." By this time, she's nearly screaming.

Kelman ignores her. Rising, he walks to the door, summons a constable, and instructs him that Celestine Lampley is to be housed in Moyamensing Prison until the two recent cases of arson can be successfully investigated.

Chapter 19

The Devil

OBLIVIOUS TO THE fact that he's the subject of a citywide search, Findal Stokes makes his way to Martha Beale's house. By habit cautious, and always aware that danger lurks nearby, he keeps to the shadows, holds his head tucked down, and tries to become as invisible as possible; and he succeeds. No one pays attention to the beggar boy moving silently along. He's not asking for money or employment and therefore is easy to ignore. Easy not to notice, altogether, for who wants to be reminded of destitution in the midst of the nation's most successful industrial city, one whose name would be better translated as the "City of Tenacity, Perseverance, and Wealth" than the "City of Brotherly Love"?

So Findal, for whom so many trained eyes hunt, arrives at his accustomed position across from the house on Chestnut Street without attracting a single glance. This is the second time he has visited the spot in as many days. He has been disappointed in not encountering Ella, though of course he's unaware that she's missing from her home and can only surmise that she must be ill. The thought grieves him. He longs to offer her comfort or to cheer her with one of their little jokes.

Hidden, he sees Cai emerge with Mademoiselle Hédé. Before they can begin their daily saunter, he notices a man—who looks very much like a constable but who's wearing the clothes of an ordinary citizen—scrutinize the pair and then nod to a similarly clad fellow, who begins to follow in the governess's footsteps. Neither she nor Cai is aware of being kept under surveillance, but Findal recognizes the action. *Coppers!* he thinks with natural repugnance, and he wills himself to become smaller and less visible. He can't imagine why they're lurking outside Martha Beale's home, or why one of them is shadowing little Cai and his companion, but he knows trouble when he sees it.

Has someone threatened the family? he wonders. The notion seems probable. Miss Beale is exceedingly wealthy, after all. Even if there were no hint of danger, she'd be wise to have a trained guardian accompany the governess and children. But he knew that no constable or member of the day or night watches could take the job; it would be a secret-service agent who'd fill the role—another species of human Findal finds repellant.

Continuing to study the scene, he grows increasingly perplexed. He toys with the notion of slipping along in the wake of Cai and his governess, then decides that Ella might use their absence to signal him. That conclusion, however, leads to the realization that he won't be able to make his presence known to her. Not with a copper skulking about.

He waits and watches, watches and waits, but Ella doesn't appear. Not at the rear door, nor at any visible window. An hour passes, or so he surmises from the shifting color of the sky, the change in passersby, and the vehicles now crowding the streets. Lunchtime is approaching. Cai and Mademoiselle Hédé will be returning from their stroll in either Franklin or Washington Square, which they do with their unnoticed companion trailing behind.

As the pair reenters the house, the two men resume their sentry positions. Findal creeps as close as he dares.

"Any sign of the girl?" he hears, which makes his heart pound so hard he almost thinks he invented the muttered question. *Ella!* his brain cries out. *Why are they discussing Ella? Where do they think she's gone?* An awful premonition clogs his vision. He forces himself to listen, but blood pounds in his ears.

"Not a one. Nor of that hellish brat, neither. My money tells me those two skipped town. Wouldn't be the first time a girl defied a parent. I think our Mr. Kelman's got it wrong."

"And leave all *that* behind for a street urchin?"

"Love works in mysterious ways."

"If you're crazy in the noggin, maybe."

The exchange is interrupted as a carriage pulls up to the house, and a woman alights and mounts the stairs. "Look sharp. If that's Miss Beale, our instructions are to lay low. She's not supposed to know we're here. Kelman will have our hides if we're discovered."

Falling back, they feign an idle conversation until the woman disappears inside.

"We're safe. It's not the lady of the house. Must be a visitor. Fine time to entertain when your ward has run off with a ne'er-do-well like Findal Stokes."

"The rich are a strange lot, that's certain. I'll tell you one thing, though: when we find that lad, his life won't be worth a copper penny."

⇀⊨◉ ◉⊨↼

Ignorant of this conversation, and of the presence of Kelman's two chief constables keeping watch over her home, Martha receives her unexpected guest: Becky Grey. If the cynical pair maintaining their vigil were to witness the manner with which she greets her visitor, they'd have additional criticism of her behavior, for she affects her most ebullient spirits and acts as though she had no other wish in the world than to idle away an afternoon with a friend.

"You'll stay for luncheon, of course" is the second statement she makes after expressing her surprise and delight at seeing the "city's brightest star." The cost of this dissembling is dear, but what can Martha do? The secret of Ella's disappearance must be maintained. Or so she believes.

So wrapped up is Becky in her success that she doesn't question Martha's effervescence. She assumes her friend must have good news of her own, and she further assumes it involves Thomas Kelman. Perhaps they've reached an understanding, at long last. Perhaps he has finally proposed. Her thoughts travel only that far before circling back to herself:

"I would love to dine with you. In fact, I can't think of anything more splendid. It's been far too long since we've had a tête-à-tête. I don't have to be at the theater until seven this evening, so we can have a leisurely visit."

Martha forces a pleased smile, which encourages Becky to launch into a series of comments and queries regarding her performance, the wisdom of choosing *The School for Scandal*, and how Martha gauged the audience's reaction.

Lunch is served. Martha's first course, a dish of crimped skate with caper sauce, is removed uneaten while Becky cleans her plate while reminiscing with a self-congratulatory: "I realize the choice of Sheridan's play was risky. Lady Teazle can be viewed as an exceedingly shallow creature. Then, too, I feared that the story of my marriage to William Taitt, and the details of his death, might be a detriment to my abilities as an artist. Or, that the audience would conflate that tale with the fictional one. But you say the audience was enthusiastic?"

"You heard them, Becky. And saw them, too. You received an ovation the moment you walked onto the stage."

Croquettes of chicken are placed before the two women. Martha ignores the dish. Becky immediately picks up knife and fork. "Yes, I did. It was intensely gratifying. But I want your opinion of the evening. You're the person upon whom I most rely."

"I'm not certain what to answer...other than to say that you've made your mark on the city. You've established yourself as an actress worthy of renown."

"But you had your doubts."

"I had my...concerns. Philadelphia can be an unforgiving place. Our Quakerish natures are at war with a sophisticated ideal. We want to emulate London and the Continent, while at the same time we decry those excesses."

The chicken croquettes—Martha's untouched and Becky's consumed—are soon replaced by roast fillet of veal garnished with vegetables.

"You have only to consider the arrival here of Joseph Bonaparte," Martha says. "A count and brother to Napoleon: What could have been more indicative of the city's place within a firmament of taste and fashion? Unfortunately, he chose to bring with him a collection of artwork that some deemed downright licentious. In addition, he built a chateau on the Delaware's banks the likes of which Philadelphians had never before seen, and took a mistress—"

"By whom he produced children," Becky adds with a laugh. "I wonder which of his transgressions was worse: The marble statue of the naked lady who was reputed to be his sister, the painting of an equally unclad female, or the notion of the genuine article traipsing around his palatial home?" She dabs at her lips with a napkin. "So, you feared I might be treated with private derision, or publicly ostracized?"

Martha thinks while their dinners are cleared—her veal now congealing in its gravy. After that, raspberry-jam tartlets and ginger cream are offered.

"Yes. That's what I feared."

"But those worries came to naught," Becky all but sings. "My bravery served me well. I acted the part of the scandalous wife accused of infidelity and was subsequently exonerated. In so doing, I became both Lady Teazle and Becky Grey, whom Taitt—I won't speak ill of him, though I think it with regularity—intended to divorce, as he made known publicly. The result of last night's performance is that I triumphed over my detractors. I triumphed over what they intended to be my fate. No one will ever see me again without thinking of Lady Teazle's victory over those who slandered her."

"Not everyone attends the theater" is Martha's sympathetic reply. "There remains a puritanical segment of our society who believes actresses—"

"I'll never win them over, my friend, so I'll leave them to carp and cavil to their hearts' content. If I've gained a group of patrons, then my future is assured, and I'll no longer need to run to you like a waif begging for aid. Ah, what a marvelous meal your cook prepared for us. Pure heaven! But you, my dear, you haven't touched a single morsel." She cocks her head while she examines her friend. "Methinks the lady is protecting a momentous secret."

Surprised that Becky has been able to notice anything beyond her personal sphere, Martha can only gaze across the table in silence.

"Would it concern a certain Thomas Kelman?"

"No," Martha says, but her abrupt tone increases Becky's belief that she's correct.

"You needn't be discreet with me. You know I approve wholeheartedly of a match between you two. The iconoclastic Miss Beale needn't take on airs of acceptable decorum for my sake. So, has he proposed?"

"No, it's nothing like that. Nothing like that at all." Desperate lest she reveal the truth, Martha stares at the embroidered tablecloth, a reaction Becky misinterprets.

"Don't tell me he's dragging his feet. He adores you! Every glance he gives you reveals his passion. You're a lucky woman—"

"Let's not speak of this, Becky. I beg you." She rises, gracing her guest with a stiff smile. "Will you take some tea in the withdrawing room?"

"You don't fool me, my dear. Come. Confess."

"There's nothing to confess." Martha attempts to distract Becky by leading her into the foyer and pointing to a painting she recently acquired: *Portrait of a Girl Reading*, by Thomas Sully. "Isn't it lovely? His work has an ethereal quality, doesn't it?"

"You should have him do your portrait. He's all the rage. Now, don't change the subject. Pray tell me what has happened."

But this is the last thing Martha wishes. She maintains her focus on the picture. "Oh, I'd never approach Mr. Sully. Though I do admit the sitter in this composition has a few qualities similar to mine."

"Hmm...she does have your dark hair. But she's also bookish and too pensive for my taste. Is that how you envision yourself? Because I view you as too hot-blooded to sit still and moon over the pages of a novel. Now, don't try to dissuade me from my queries. Tell me what's happened to make you behave in this singular manner."

Unable to keep up her pretense, Martha turns away, her face pale, her neck taut.

When her friend fails to speak, Becky touches her arm. "Oh, my dear, have you two argued? Is unhappiness rather than joy the cause of your agitation? And here I've been gibbering away like a magpie, and probably saying the most inopportune things. Forgive me. Please do."

Silence greets these remarks. Martha simply can't think what to answer. Every one of Becky's preconceptions is wrong. "Will you take tea?" she asks at length, which causes Becky to turn baleful eyes upon her.

"Oh, Martha! Don't retreat into cold politesse. We know each other better than that. You've helped me in my times of distress, and I hope I've been a loyal confidante to you. Shouldn't we bare our souls instead of sitting down to sip tepid water and engage in equally tepid remarks?"

"Becky," Martha finally says, "there are things I cannot share with you—"

"Can't or won't?" Becky demands, but Martha overlooks the interruption.

"I will in future, but not at present. Now, please, let's discuss this matter no further. You came here to revel in your success. I share your happiness—"

"But you won't let me share in your worries. To my mind, that's not friendship but a form of condescension."

"Becky, let's not quibble. Isn't it enough if I tell you I'll reveal the truth at some future time but cannot do so now?"

"Don't you trust me?" is the nettled reply.

"Of course I do!" Though this is the heart of Martha's dilemma: despite her avowal, she realizes that, fond as she is of Becky Grey, her personality is too volatile to inspire confidence.

Becky, trained to simulate emotions she doesn't feel, recognizes the sham at once. A chasm opens between the two women, with Becky feeling denigrated because of her profession and inferior birth while simultaneously elevating Martha into the realm of the disapproving and unapproachable. "I should return to the theater. Opening nights are heady events, but the reality is that we must perform the same piece again and again."

"I hope I didn't offend in some fashion," Martha says, although in truth she's relieved to be left alone. Lying, even in a necessary circumstance such as this one, is something she loathes.

Becky shakes her head while slipping on her gloves. "Thank you for a superb repast."

"And you for joining me."

"And for your past support, too. Without your early financial aid, I could not have survived."

"It was nothing," Martha begins, and then she notices her friend's posture stiffen. "I'm delighted to be of service whenever and however I can."

⇢▷◉ ◉◁⇠

While Martha's door closes on Becky Grey, Kelman is admitted into Darius Rause's temporary lodgings. The room in which he finds himself is commodious and attractively fitted out. Nothing seems haphazardly positioned or ill chosen; nothing indicates that the pieces are hired, leaving Kelman to wonder whether the accommodations served as a previous refuge for the mill owner. Perhaps he, like his wife, has a secret life.

Half closing his eyes, he lets his glance rove hither and yon as though expecting the place to reveal whatever history it may hold. He knows that inanimate objects often mirror their owners' psyches. A misplaced or hastily moved piece of bric-a-brac speaks as loudly as ones rigidly arrayed. In this instance, what Kelman first notices is the dearth of objects that might have a feminine appeal. True, the lodgings are inhabited by a widower, but he's surprised to find no trace of the deceased wife. No daguerreotype enshrined on a table, no book of verse that might have been her favorite, no little vase she might have cherished. The conflagration could have consumed her possessions, of course, but with a stable behind the house, as well as ample storage, he questions whether this was true.

Rause interrupts the silent scrutiny, watching his visitor before Kelman becomes aware of being observed.

Surprisingly stealthy for a large man, is Kelman's note to himself.

"What may I do for you?" Rause says. He indicates a chair, then settles himself and waits. He appears so much at ease that Kelman doubts the veracity of his behavior.

His attire and physical demeanor seem like a fabrication, too: the impeccably fitted mourning costume, the side-whiskers and beard barbered and sprinkled with talcum, the imperious bearing and condescending gaze. *Who was Darius Rause when he was alone with his deceased wife,* Kelman asks himself. *Was she forced to confront this figurehead every morning and evening instead of a real man with genuine emotions?* Continuing his examination of his host, Kelman decides he looks like an actor's interpretation of an industrialist. There's something manufactured in the pose.

"I'll be blunt, Mr. Rause."

"Good. I don't waste my hours in idle talk. I'm glad you don't, either. What do you want?"

The query causes Kelman to shift his approach. He recognizes that Rause has manipulated the start of the interview. "To discuss the fire at your residence, sir."

"About time."

Kelman's eyes flare in irritation, but he responds with a smooth, "And to extend many condolences, sir. Your wife, I've been told, was a remarkable woman and an inspiration to all who knew her."

"She was." No hint of sentiment is betrayed in the statement. Rause might as well be discussing a former chambermaid whose name he doesn't recall.

"You wouldn't happen to have a miniature portrait of Mrs. Rause, sir, or a daguerreotype?"

"Whatever would you want those for? They're not going to bring the culprit who destroyed my house to justice."

"I was informed that your wife was a great beauty, sir. I simply wanted to see her image for myself."

"You'll have to satisfy your curiosity elsewhere. I have no pictures of her."

"Ah, that's a genuine shame, sir. I assume they were lost in the blaze?"

The reply is a curt: "You asked to see me. What do you want? I can discuss everything I recall of the conflagration, but that'll be the extent of our conversation. As to my wife, I'm not accustomed to confiding personal issues to persons not of my class."

This is intended—and delivered—as an insult, but Kelman receives the statement with private amusement. Only the insecure seek to remind others of their superiority.

"If you would be so kind, then, sir, as to describe the events of that tragic night." He pulls a notebook from his pocket and poises a pencil in anticipation of writing while Rause sighs, settles himself deeper in his chair, and prepares to accede to the request.

Before beginning his narrative, however, he issues a caveat: "I'll give you an hour, and that's all. Rather than pestering me, you should be out searching for the fiend who killed my wife by starting that fire."

"I'm hoping your testimony may provide a clue as to the culprit's identity."

"I don't see how. If I knew who did it, I would have said so already."

"There are details you may recall, sir, that, seen through another eye, could prove important. Your career, happily, has not been spent investigating crimes. Mine has. No aspects of the night in question should escape scrutiny, nor previous instances that you may have deemed unusual."

At that Darius Rause launches into his version of the events that culminated in the death of his wife: the discovery of the fire; his desperate attempt to find and rescue her; how smoke drove him from the premises; how he stumbled about in the acrid air until he finally collapsed. The speech is delivered in a staccato manner. Not an ounce of emotion colors it. Kelman warns himself to keep an open mind; grief, he knows, can take numerous forms. Not everyone rends his hair and rages at the heavens. Still, Rause's composure seems exceptional. Worse, the words sound rehearsed.

When it appears that the man has concluded his narration, Kelman closes his notebook and expresses his thanks; then, as if as an afterthought, he asks if there are other, less momentous, details Rause can recall. Were the servants at odds with one another that evening? Was one noticeably disgruntled? Had Mr. or Mrs. Rause cause to release anyone from service during the prior weeks or months? Each query receives a similar reply: his wife managed the servants; as a busy man of affairs, he scarcely knew their names. The answers strike Kelman as disingenuous, but additional probing reveals only that Darius Rause believed those in his employ were "expendable."

Eventually, Kelman asks a seemingly empathetic, "You're a man of considerable means, sir, and the owner of a large manufactory; is it possible—I don't say probable, but possible—that you have an unknown enemy?"

As anticipated, Rause blusters at this suggestion, but before he can issue additional rebukes about the delay in solving the crime, Kelman casually mentions the blaze at Celestine Lampley's establishment and asks if his host was aware of that conflagration.

"I pay no notice to houses of ill repute," Rause says with some warmth. "What kind of a man do you think I am?"

"I meant no disrespect, sir. I'm merely attempting to draw a connection between the two blazes. Perhaps there is none, although both fires could well have been deliberately set, and naturally, that troubles me. As does the timing. Mrs. Lampley left Philadelphia immediately following the tragedy; she has been found and returned to Philadelphia for interrogation." As Kelman speaks, he notices a change in Rause. Rather than regard his guest with haughty indifference, he now appears engaged. It's obvious, however, that he's attempting to conceal his interest.

"Good for you. Maybe you'll learn something, at long last."

"I already have."

Again, Rause tries and fails to feign unconcern.

"Does the name Hendricks mean anything to you, Mr. Rause?"

"Why should it?" The answer is too quick in coming, but this is as Kelman anticipated.

"I thought your paths might have crossed. He's a man about town, I'm told. In fact, he was in the audience of a play I happened to attend last night."

"What's that to me?"

"He was an acquaintance of your wife, so naturally I assumed—"

"Is that what the damned fellow said: 'acquaintance'?"

"I beg your pardon, sir, for mentioning a person you find repellant—"

"Who says I do? Hendricks is a nonentity, a gadabout, and a fop. I have no cause to have dealings with him. If he inferred that Susannah—"

"My information comes from Mrs. Lampley, rather than Nicholas Hendricks, sir."

Rause stifles a gasp, though Kelman hears the harsh intake of breath and the rumbled exhalation. His face has become a dangerous mottled red. Given his size and girth, he looks like a man capable of having an apoplectic attack. Kelman waits for Rause to regain his composure, but he doesn't dare wait long.

"I'm happy to learn that Mrs. Lampley was mistaken in her assertion, sir. Hendricks, as you intimated, might be regarded as a nefarious character. Apparently, he makes a hobby of investing in bawdy houses. He's Lampley's chief backer—"

"The devil he is!" Rause lunges from his chair, swearing mightily and tearing at his cravat. His cheeks and brow are now purple; his eyes bulge. "My man," he says, wheezing. "Get my man." Which Kelman does, hurrying to the door and ordering another servant to send for a surgeon.

By this time, Rause is prone and gasping for breath while he rips the buttons from his tightly fitted jacket. "The devil," he mutters, "the devil. Well, she got what she deserved." With that, he says no more.

CHAPTER 20

Lena

THE DEATH OF Darius Rause receives unprecedented attention from Freers's newspaper. Restraint is customary when wording mortuary notices: a brief paragraph providing the deceased's name and a minimum of particulars. Survivors are never mentioned, nor the location of the funeral; it's a given that only members of the immediate family and close friends will be invited to attend. The spectacle of hearses drawn by black horses with black ostrich plumes affixed to their bridles, of hired mutes outfitted in black capes and tall hats, is for the public eye; in private, mirrors are covered, clocks stopped at the hour of death, and families maintain a tight-lipped seclusion.

Given the rigors of funerary practices, the three-column report of Darius Rause's demise is in the worst possible taste; insult is added to injury, because the article is printed on the front page. In the midst of extolling the industrialist, the journalist finds ample space in which to excoriate Kelman for being the instigator of "the great gentleman's ultimate and final trial"—he quotes Rause's valet on some but not all of the particulars regarding the "fatal visit"—before further castigating Kelman for his continued bungling.

"Doubtless," Freers writes, "the husband's health was in a precarious state due to his overwhelming grief. Is this, then, the proper or fitting occasion for a government employee to waylay those who mourn? No! A thousand times, no! Our conviction in this instance remains firm. Thomas Kelman is a menace. He should be relieved of his duties before he can slay more innocent people."

Kelman becomes aware of Freers's latest attack when he overhears a constable discussing it with one of the day watchmen. Upon querying them, the pair grows sheepish. "None of our business, is it, sir?" they say.

Then one of the men ventures: "You should stand up for yourself, though. That fellow will have you hounded from the city otherwise."

Kelman makes no answer. Instead, he walks to Christ Church, where Rause's funeral is to be held. Standing in an inconspicuous position where he can survey all who enter the brick-paved churchyard, he waits. He realizes that this may be a fool's errand. Susannah Rause is dead, either by accident or intent; her husband is also; with him, any clues to the cause of her demise are also gone. Kelman has only the vindictive gossip of Celestine Lampley to suggest a jealous husband might be to blame.

Pondering, he studies the passersby, who turn west on Church Alley and stroll either north or south on Second. None glance at the brick-faced edifice that commands the view. None look up toward the spire, or pause to study the tall Palladian window fronting the street. God's sanctuary is ignored, but then he considers the changes in this area known as the Northern Liberties; industry now crowds close on all sides; textile mills like Rause's, as well as sugar refineries, tanneries, white-lead producers, and ironworks, are mere blocks distant. The worship of lucre has supplanted a reverence for the holy.

At length, the hearse arrives in showy panoply. Two mutes descend from the driver's box and place themselves at the head and foot of the coffin as it's conveyed into the church. No relatives accompany the casket. To Kelman's trained eye, the only attendees are hired men dressed in hired garb; doubtless, the undertaker paid them for their labors. No one from Rause's place of business appears, nor does anyone from the vaunted social circle that made him feel superior to Kelman. In death, the man has been left alone.

Reflecting upon the cause—and tragedy—of a life unmourned, Kelman notices an oddly clad woman staring at the hearse. Arrayed in two shawls—one dark, one a dirty blue—and a lumpy bonnet hiding her face, she has a hectic air that makes him instinctively mistrust her motives.

He moves closer, lest she intend mischief to either the carriage or the horses, and hears her talking to herself. The words are mumbled, the cadence singsongy and petulant. Apparently, either Rause or some other mill owner has done her an injustice, for she repeats "Looms, throstle frames, mule spinners, carding rooms" in an aggrieved manner, as if the terms had lodged in her throat and she was spitting them out. She appears to be unaware that she's attracting the ire of the carriage driver, for she sidles up to the lead horse and strokes its flanks.

This earns her an order to "Move off," which the woman either doesn't hear or ignores. Were Kelman not curious about the type of people Rause's funeral might attract, he'd aid the coachman and tell her to desist, adding that a skittish horse is dangerous and that her ministrations are unwelcome. Instead he watches.

"Move off, you!"

This command, like the other, receives no reaction. "I'm telling you to begone. Can't you see that my beasts don't like beggar women touching them?"

"I'm no beggar," she counters, lifting her head to glare at the coachman. Kelman has a sense of having seen her face before, but he cannot place the memory. He tells himself that he's interviewed or interrogated hundreds of people; how could he remember each one? The imperfection of his recollection rankles, however.

"Well, you look like one to me, so move away. The service will be over shortly, and the mourners don't want dirty—"

"Mourners! No one weeps over that skinflint. A regular demon, that's what he was—"

"Get back, or I'll summon a member of the watch—"

"—who shouldn't be buried in hallowed ground."

"Be off, you hag!"

"Demon, demon! Ask anyone who worked for him," she screams; Kelman then realizes he must intervene.

He strides across the street, intending to draw her away and question her accusation, but the driver decides to take matters into his own hands. At the risk of startling his already-anxious horses, he raises his whip and lashes out at the woman, who shrieks and leaps backward.

"Ask anyone! Anyone!"

"Be off, you madwoman." Another lash rains down upon her head, knocking her bonnet off and sending unpinned and greasy blond hair tumbling over her shoulders.

"Him and his wife both!"

"Get back, you damned pauper—"

"Devils with horns and snaky tails for anyone with eyes as keen as mine to see. So, you don't scare me, Mister! Not a bit of it!"

By now, the horses are snorting and pawing the ground. Kelman moves between them and the furious woman. "Hold your whip!" he orders the coachman. Then he tells her to remain where she is.

"Devils: the two of them!" she shrieks before taking to her heels and fleeing. Kelman starts after her, but she disappears from sight, either melding into the crowd or flattening herself in the recesses of an alley. She might as well have vanished in thin air.

When he returns to the funeral coach, the mutes are approaching it. Deranged though the woman may be, she's correct: no one but hirelings will mourn Darius Rause.

⇢⟫══◉ ◉══⟪⇠

In the house on Wood Street, Ella attempts to stand and walk to the cheval mirror in the middle of the room. Someone has dressed her, but she can't recall that person's identity. Nor does she recognize the finery. There's a good deal of lace. As she wobbles forward, she watches the gauzy stuff pool on the floor. *I don't own a lace robe*, she thinks, but her thoughts drift away like miniature clouds. She can only concentrate on the rose and leaf-green colors of the carpet, and on her slippered foot moving forward. The shoe isn't hers, either. She frowns and then immediately forgets what had disturbed her.

She reaches the looking glass and must hold the frame for support. Waves of dizziness attack her; the room spins, then settles, while she sways and worries that she's about to vomit. A great weariness comes over her, pressing her shoulders down and making her head droop till her chin nearly touches her chest. *I'll sit on the bed again*, she tells herself, but halfway there, she can't remember where she's going.

It's at this moment when the door opens, and Adelaide and Nicholas Hendricks enter. Ella hears the noise, although the effort of looking up and seeing who has stepped into the room is too difficult to manage. Her eyes remain fixed on the floral carpet and those disconcerting puddles of lace.

"Well, Nicholas? She's yours, if you want her."

"Pah! What's that stench? Did she soil herself?"

"The room is close. I can't risk opening the windows for fear she'll either fall or call out; regrettably the elixir has not agreed with her digestion. She vomited, that's all, but the reaction has now passed."

Ella takes heart at this last statement. *So I'm not going to be sick*, she thinks. Her surroundings continue to whirl about, however, making her wonder whether the woman speaking is wrong. For a split second the woman has a name—*Adelaide*—but it vanishes.

"I washed her myself. She's my gift to you. My thanks, if you will, for your financial interest in this venture. You may maintain her in my establishment, or ensconce her elsewhere. If you do install her in another locale, I would suggest a steady dose of laudanum. That is, until she's thoroughly accustomed to her new life."

"'Thoroughly accustomed'? Prettily put, my dear, but I'm curious about your change of heart. You told me you intended to keep her here."

"Can't I have my caprices? This is one of them."

"Your 'caprices' make she-wolves seem docile. What happens when you alter your decision?"

"I won't."

"I don't trust that declaration—"

"Oh, trust! The dreary staple in the lives of burghers and their wives. Desist from that craven reference. Here is my *cadeau*, my gift for your exclusive pleasure."

Ella listens as feet march across the floor. Her chin is wrenched upward, which startles and hurts her. Her eyes stare into a man's face. Then the face and body spin away, leaving her to resume her dreamy perusal of her dress's hem.

"I don't want her."

"Wait for a bit, *mon chér*. You may change your mind."

"I won't. I don't fancy lovemaking with a corpse."

Laughter greets this opinion. It's so raucous it hurts Ella's ears. She winces.

"She'll be more lively in time. And she'll be a beauty, too. If you wish, I can remove her attire. Once you see this virginal flesh—"

"Send her back, Adelaide. She's no use as she is."

"Never. Besides, there are men who enjoy corpses." The laugh rings out again. "Ah, well, since I cannot tempt you today, we'll leave our fair seductress alone."

"Listen to reason. Let her go before you're charged with abduction."

"Never. Besides, it's too late for that. And who's to know her history except the two of us?" The tone begins to cajole. "Because you're my special pet, I'll allow you a week to decide. After that, she goes on the open market. You may not take pleasure in listless girls, but there are patrons who will—not in Philadelphia, naturally, but moving her is easily done. No, say no more, but remember, *mon amour*, it won't be only me who faces charges if our little game is revealed."

"This is no game."

"You've lost your sense of adventure. Too bad."

"Listen to me—"

"You're the one who grabbed her from the street. I was only acting on your orders—poor, misguided female that I am."

The door again opens and closes. Ella hears a key twist in the lock. She imagines rattling the latch, shouting aloud, and pounding her fists on the wall, but none of this occurs. Instead, her transitory rebellion fades.

She straggles back to the bed and sits on a mattress that crackles under her weight. Testing it, she jounces once, then twice, then remains lopsided and still, fingering the flounces of her garment.

CHAPTER 21

Two Conversations

"MARTHA, WE CAN'T wait any longer. It's clear that she's run off with Findal Stokes. If she'd been abducted, you would have received a ransom note long before this."

"I can't believe she'd do such a thing, Thomas. I can't."

"Yet such events occur every day."

"But not to Ella. Not with all she has here."

Kelman takes Martha's hands and leads her back to the settee, where she'd been perched when her footman announced a visitor. He sits beside her, while she searches his face. "You've provided admirably for her. More than admirably. You've created a wondrous life for her and Cai, but Ella was accustomed to starvation and misery at one time. It's possible, although difficult for you to comprehend, that she may be more comfortable with deprivation than with abundance—"

"No one can feel that way. Hunger, cold, and physical blows are enemies everyone abhors." She shakes her head. "To run away from my home after all the affection I've showered on her." She pauses. "That statement sounds self-serving, as if I expected to be repaid for my kindness. But Ella was grateful, and happy."

"But if her feelings for the boy—"

"Puppy love, and nothing more."

"She's fourteen."

Martha makes no reply for several moments. "I would have helped him, if she'd asked. Educated him. Found him a family with whom to dwell."

"Would you have?"

She looks away. "No. I hoped he'd disappear." Removing her hands from his, she sighs. "Why can't your men find this miserable boy?"

"My opinion is that they must have left the city."

"Then what good are appeals printed in the newspapers? If they've escaped to West Chester or Newcastle—"

"*If*, dearest. If *not*, then, with any luck, they'll recognize your grief and make an effort to relieve it."

"But they might not. Given what's occurred—"

"That's correct. They may not respond."

"And then what? Oh, Thomas, I feel so powerless! I am powerless."

"No. Not powerless. You and I both, we're simply at a loss for answers. They will come. I'm convinced of it."

"But when?"

This time, he's the one who maintains silence. Eventually he speaks. "I understand your feelings of frustration. I share them. My solutions are practical ones, but they can't alleviate the pain of uncertainty. If your appeals continue to meet with silence, then you may choose to offer a reward. But let's not discuss that possibility yet. As you know, doing so brings its own difficulties and heartache."

Hearing this proposal, she shuts her eyes but makes no other response.

He also retreats into rumination before embarking on another subject. His voice changes, becoming resolute rather than introspective. "Martha…there's something I must tell you."

She waits, perplexed at his altered tone and posture, for he is now sitting tense and erect. For a moment, she considers that he may be about to propose marriage, but she banishes the notion as being both ill-timed and absurd.

"Yes?"

"A confession, if you will. Against your wishes, and without informing you, I stationed two men outside your home in case Stokes might appear—"

"Oh!"

"I understand if you feel upset."

"I'm perturbed, yes. Not only for your…secrecy, but also…" Her speech falters. "What if Ella hasn't run away with the boy but has been abducted, and her captives spotted the trap?"

"No one could possibly have noticed my men. You were unaware of their presence."

"Oh, Thomas." Having anticipated other words, though which ones she hardly knows, she struggles to comprehend the significance of this revelation. "I wasn't looking for them, so how can you be certain—"

"Even if you had been, I promise you wouldn't have seen them. In fact, you didn't. Neither did anyone else in your household. For their part, they reported nothing of a suspicious nature. I can supply a detailed description of their observations, if you'd like."

"No. No, that's not necessary."

"I ask your forgiveness. I needed to make certain the situation was what I surmised it to be. Surveillance of your home was a means to an end."

"I wish you'd confided in me."

"If I had, you might have unintentionally revealed the stratagem. You must understand that it's not a matter of trust, but of practicality."

"But still…my home, and all of us in it, under observation…" Her words trail away.

"I deemed it necessary."

"Yes, obviously, you did."

More silent moments pass. Although she recognizes the validity of the decision, she feels belittled. Her rational self argues against the reaction, but her emotional self rebels.

"I realize you may feel a sense of betrayal, but I thought the circumstances warranted additional care."

"I wish you'd had confidence in my ability to be discreet."

"I do."

"Not in this, apparently."

Hearing her irritation, he retreats, which augments their estrangement.

At length, she stands and walks to her desk. "I'll do as you've suggested," she says with her back is to him, her pose formal rather than affectionate.

"Martha—"

"And let myself be guided in this matter."

"My intentions were for the best."

"Yes, I understand."

"Trust me in this, I beg you."

"I do."

"Martha—"

"I do trust you. I do."

Despite her avowal and his remorseful tone, when they part, neither is happy nor at peace.

Less than three hours following this conversation, the situation alters when Findal Stokes is found. A day watchman happens upon him, holding a horse's reins while its owner visits the tenant of a building he owns. The property is in the vicinity of Cramp and Sons, Shipbuilders, an area of hastily built ropewalks and warehouses and of small, ancient stone structures that are the remnants of the city's once-outlying farms. Only the stone buildings have an air of permanence, but they're begrimed and saggy with age.

Findal assumed the location would provide anonymity, because it's overcrowded and inhabited by people of many races and many languages. But it's also an area frequented by thieves who prey upon the newly emigrated, which, in turn, inspires more vigilance among the constabulary. The watchman's assumption when he spots a well-groomed horse in the hands of a pauper is that the boy stole the animal and is waiting to fence or sell it. He doesn't ask himself whether someone hired the boy to perform the service; he is about to grab the reins when he notices Findal's telltale bat-like ears.

"You, boy," he orders, laying restraining hands on Findal's shoulders. "You're wanted for questioning by the police." The watchman ignores the niceties of which agency has jurisdiction in this particular borough. Kelman's wishes were plain: wherever he is, find him and bring him to me.

"I don't know where she is. Indeed I don't, sir. I told you before. And I'll tell you again. If I knew, I wouldn't keep it secret." Findal has been nearly reduced to tears by his interrogation. It's not that he minds Kelman's anger and accusations; it's the thought of Ella in danger—which his interlocutor insists is "very grave."

"I've been looking for her, too. Ever since I spotted your men guarding Miss Beale's—"

"You what?" Kelman says, his equanimity deserting him. He clenches and unclenches his hands on the desktop separating him from Findal as if he'd like to throttle the boy—an action that doesn't go unnoticed. Findal's eyes flicker back and forth between Kelman's fingers and his furious face.

"Saw your men—"

"Spotted them, did you, you miserable—" Kelman curbs his rage, but just barely. "And where were you when you made that estimable discovery, Master Stokes?"

"Across the street, sir. Where I make a habit of watching for Ella."

Kelman curses inwardly. His most senior men outwitted by a mere boy. His hands turn into fists.

"One of them made a signal to the other, and then he followed the governess. The other fellow stayed put."

Worse and worse, Kelman thinks. He's so angry he can't allow himself to speak. Then his fury turns to fear. If Findal noticed the house was under surveillance, wouldn't a practiced criminal have also? Kelman's fists uncoil, but the hands remain rigid. "So, you noticed two men—"

"Yes, sir. 'Coppers,' I said to myself. Which I thought was clever, because Miss Beale's a rich woman, and—"

"How did you realize they were 'coppers'?"

Findal gazes at him as though the man has gone daft in the head. "*How*, sir?"

"Yes. That was my question. How? You do understand the word, don't you?"

Findal nods but continues to look perplexed by the query. "Well, sir, they just were."

"Damnation, boy! Don't talk nonsense. By what means did you determine they were members of the constabulary? They were dressed in ordinary, workaday garb—"

"Just like you are, sir. Though your jacket and trousers are finer." Findal intends this as a compliment, but Kelman glowers.

"Do I look like a *copper* to you?"

"Yes, sir. Of course, sir. That's what you are, isn't it?"

Kelman groans, but he forsakes this line of questioning. Perhaps, at some future time, Findal Stokes will prove useful in providing his constables with better wardrobe choices, but for now, he has more important issues to attend to. "So…you also observed the house, but you witnessed nothing untoward—"

"Begging your pardon, sir, 'untoward'?"

"Illicit, criminal, of a questionable nature."

"Ah…un-toward." Findal appears to stow the word away for later use. "No, sir. All looked right as rain. The same delivery men who always bring the milk and eggs and meat and whatnot; the scullery maid washing down the rear steps; another maid polishing the front brasses; the usual bustle inside: draperies opening and closing; and like that. Except, of course, Ella was nowhere to be seen." He screws his eyes up tight. He's afraid he's about to start crying.

Observing this display of emotion, Kelman can't help but feel pity. The boy has made every effort at appearing presentable, but each article of clothing is either too large or too small, besides being poorly patched and darned. He is a scrawny, ill-nourished chap who has grown tall despite a scarcity of food; his new height makes him appear thinner and less healthy than when Kelman initially encountered him several years prior. He wonders what Ella finds to admire in this unfortunate specimen. That assessment leads him to the conclusion that their friendship has been doomed from the start. Ella is Ella Beale; in time, she'll take her place among the city's elite. This boy is nothing, not even a common laborer. Surely he, if not she, must understand the insurmountable obstacles dividing them. Despite his empathy, Kelman's next words are stern.

"You're guilty, young Stokes, of misleading a young, impressionable girl. You shouldn't have haunted her house, nor had any conversation with her. I won't go as far as to say that it's your fault she has disappeared, but you certainly encouraged her recklessness."

"No, sir, I did not. I'd never harm Miss Ella, nor Miss Beale, neither."

"Your heedlessness and selfishness did the job very well, however."

At this, Findal begins to weep. Misery causes him to hunker down into himself while the tears roll unabated. It's the reaction of a child, and it makes him appear smaller and younger than his sixteen years.

Kelman's heart twists at the sight, but what is he to do? Encourage this sorry youth in some adolescent fantasy? No, the boy must learn where he stands in the eyes of the world. When Ella's found, which eventuality has become disturbingly uncertain, she and Stokes must never be permitted to converse again.

"Can I help in the search, sir?" Findal gulps back his sobs and wipes his streaky face. His expression has gone from despair to a kind of frantic hope. "Search for Miss Ella, that is? I've got sharp eyes, and I know my way around. I could—"

"No, you may not," Kelman all but shouts. "You'll do nothing of the kind. It's high time you recognized the impossibility of your so-called friendship. You and Ella Beale have nothing in common, and never will. What made you presume to imagine you could overcome the class distinctions by which society is governed? You, a child from Blockley?"

"But Miss Ella, sir, she wasn't born—"

"Enough! This conversation is concluded." With that, Kelman calls for a constable and orders that the boy be taken to Moyamensing.

"Not prison, sir! I've committed no crime."

"Where else am I to put you, Master Stokes? Free, you'll continue interfering with this investigation. Sent to Blockley, you'll escape again, just like you did before. Until Ella Beale is returned safely to her home, you'll remain under lock and key. Thereafter, you and she will have no contact whatsoever."

With Findal dispatched, Kelman quits his office and walks toward Martha's home. His footsteps match the heaviness of his soul, for he knows that the accusations about class and society that he leveled at Findal are the same ones separating him from Martha. Trudging on, he ponders the unwelcome similarities in four disparate lives, as well as the disturbing news he's about to share. Duty alone carries him forward.

CHAPTER 22

Can There Be a Connection?

WHEN KELMAN'S USHERED toward Martha's second-floor parlor, he finds that she's already hurried to the door to greet him. Seeing his grave expression, she blanches and takes a step backward.

"Tell me" is all she says, which Kelman does, stating the salient facts in a succinct manner. He makes no mention of his overwrought reaction, nor of Findal's discovery that the Beale home was under surveillance. He's aware that the omissions are cowardly, but he counters by trying to assure himself that they're unnecessary to his narrative—an assertion he doesn't believe. When he finishes, her face has turned a slick and shiny white.

"Sit, my dear one. I fear you're about to faint." He moves to her side, but she shakes her head. She's made of sterner stuff than even he realizes.

"I'm quite well, thank you. Albeit stunned. This is my worst fear, but I shan't give way to feminine weakness." She takes a steadying breath. Her pallor remains, although her expression is fixed.

He hesitates. "We can at least sit while we discuss the situation."

"No. I prefer to stand. Nor do I wish to detain you. Truly, I'm fully recovered. I've mastered that sudden unease."

Again, he hesitates.

"I require no attention; I assure you. There's nothing further to discuss, is there? Haven't you told me everything I need to know?"

He nods. He'd rather supply comfort than facts, but her demeanor has become too stoic to admit to weakness or to the need for emotional or physical support. "I'm hesitant to leave you in this state."

"And I'm not hesitant to say that I'm myself again. Now go. I have a house-ful of people to aid me should I need it—which I don't. And, Thomas, when you continue your search, I agree to your scheme of hiring secret-service men. The expense is immaterial, as are any scruples I may have expressed in the past." She pauses. "What about the notices I sent to the newspapers? Should I reword them?"

"No," he tells her after a moment's consideration. "Request that the appeals be withdrawn. Printing them may harm our cause. In cases of abduction, it's necessary to allow the criminals to make the initial approach."

"But they haven't—"

"Yes, I know."

⤜▦◉ ◉▦⤛

Leaving Martha, Kelman returns to his offices in order to interview Nicholas Hendricks regarding Celestine Lampley and her accusations. He has no stomach for the meeting, which seems to him immaterial and a misuse of his time. He should be overseeing the hunt for Ella, or combing the streets himself, instead of palavering with an inconsequential fop like Hendricks. The Rause conflagration must be addressed, however, if only to silence the carping pen of Freers. Perhaps Hendricks started the blaze out of mischief or malice? The notion is outlandish, but odder things have occurred.

"Mr. Hendricks," he says upon entering his chambers, for the man is al-ready there, waiting in the anteroom. That he's early for the appointment strikes Kelman as unusual, for gentlemen of his upbringing seldom arrive on schedule. But there's no cause for suspicion if someone behaves in a timely manner, so he ascribes it to a private foible.

"What's this all about?" Hendricks's tone has a combative edge that Kelman registers; he also recognizes that the man has reason to be perturbed at finding himself interrogated.

He indicates that his guest take a seat and places himself at the desk where he conducted the interview with Findal Stokes. It's a shabby piece of furniture that the visitor's eyes quickly assess as being ugly, as well as unfashionable. "You're acquainted with Mrs. Celestine Lampley."

An emotion that looks like relief floods Hendricks's face but is quickly replaced by wary uncertainty. "I am."

"And also enjoyed the...the kind regard of Mrs. Susannah Rause."

Hendricks frowns. When he replies, his voice has assumed a facetious air. "At one time, yes."

"Presumably, you do no longer, sir, as the lady is deceased."

"I don't believe in maligning the dead, Mr. Kelman. Mrs. Rause was a charming lady. That's all I'll say on the subject."

"Who was also your mistress."

"We enjoyed each another's company."

"At Mrs. Lampley's establishment."

"If you will." Hendricks crosses one perfectly tailored knee against the other. The creases in his trouser legs appear permanently engineered, as if the buff-colored cloth never sags or stains. Kelman finds himself taking offense at the man's ensemble, as well as the man.

"I have Mrs. Lampley's statement to that effect, sir. You may not be aware that she has been returned to the city and is now in custody."

Again, there's a curious reaction to this news, as if Hendricks were attempting what to make of it, or what benefit might accrue because of it. "May I ask on what charge?"

"You may."

Hendricks waits, but Kelman doesn't supply the answer.

"Ah, I understand. So we're to play a guessing game, are we?"

"If that's your definition of this interview, yes, we are."

Hendricks smiles and relaxes in his chair. His boots, new and made of glossy patent leather, squeak. With effort, Kelman keeps his eyes trained on the man's visage rather than on his irritating garments.

"Was Darius Rause aware of his wife's liaison with you?"

"I wouldn't know."

"Can you venture a guess?"

"Mr. Kelman, at the risk of being impertinent, may I ask if you've ever been wed?"

The question, and the easy manner in which it's delivered, startle. Without thinking, Kelman answers a subdued, "No."

"Neither have I. So I couldn't possibly surmise what conversations the Rauses shared. She may have revealed all; she may have kept a lock on her privacy. It really was no concern of mine."

"No? You never worried about Rause's displeasure?"

"I can't say that I did."

"Then I must differ with you, Mr. Hendricks. I believe it mattered a good deal. Mr. Rause was a powerful man, with powerful friends—"

"And I'm nothing but a bon vivant. Is that your inference?"

Kelman lets the question hang in the air until Hendricks becomes weary waiting for a reply: "Very well, yes. Husbands don't enjoy being cuckolded; it can make them vindictive. I warned Susannah to take precautions."

"And did she?" Although Kelman knows the answer from his interview with Rause, he decides to extend this phase of his interrogation. Something is niggling at his brain, warning him that the man's apparent imperturbability may be a subterfuge. To what end, he can't determine.

"I don't know. I never hid myself in her boudoir and listened to her discussions with Darius, if that's what you think. An uncovered love affair can add a frisson to a marriage, or so I'm told. Now, you indicated you wished to discuss Celestine Lampley."

Kelman, though, isn't finished discussing Darius Rause. "Did he kill his wife?"

"Oh, come, Mr. Kelman! That's altogether beyond the range of my understanding or conjecture. Was he capable of the physical act? In reply, I'd have to refer to his size and girth and answer in the affirmative. Did he have a motive? There again, that depends on how sacred he believed his marriage vows were. Besides, didn't she die in the fire?"

"Or was killed first."

"Well, it wasn't me that done the foul deed." Hendricks laughs, affecting a stage villain's crafty accent.

Kelman regards the man. The distaste for his lackadaisical manner is so strong it burns in his throat. He wishes he could dismiss him, for Hendricks, with his odious "investments," now seems wholly unreliable in supplying evidence, or anything else. Instead, he asks a cool, "You have a fondness of the theater, don't you, Mr. Hendricks? I saw you at the opening of *The School for Scandal*, in the company of a very attractive woman. You appeared to be taking the death of Susannah Rause in stride."

All color leaves Hendricks's face; his cheek muscles go slack; his mouth and mustachios droop. For the life of him, Kelman can't fathom the changes wrought in the man. "Surely, you didn't imagine your presence at the play would go unremarked, did you, sir? After all, you're a well-known gentleman about town."

"No…yes…that is, I gave the event little consideration."

"Your companion seemed fully engaged, however."

Again, the look of panic, which doesn't disappear when he next speaks. "Yes…well, women are more susceptible than men to playacting."

"You don't consider Miss Grey an artiste?"

"Yes…no…I don't know. Look, didn't you want to ask me about Celestine Lampley? Well, I wish you'd do so, because I've other engagements I must attend to."

Kelman says nothing while his eyes try to penetrate the mind of the man seated in front of him. References to his erstwhile mistresses have been cast off as unimportant, but the mention of the mystery female in his company has produced a reaction that Kelman can only categorize as fear. But of what? "Is your companion of the other evening also an owner of a bawdy house?"

"Don't tell me you consider it a crime to sit beside a pretty lady, Mr. Kelman. As to her position in life, as a gentleman, naturally, I would show discretion. You should ask her, if you wish enlightenment regarding her situation."

"A difficult task without knowing the lady's name."

"True."

Kelman doesn't bother to respond, although his face darkens. He feels he's wasting time in ineffectual banter when he should be searching for Ella. Glaring at Hendricks, he waits, but the man has regained his composure and is now regarding him with a patronizing stare.

"You may remain silent as long as you wish, Mr. Kelman. A gentleman never reveals the names of his female acquaintances. I don't intend to break with hallowed tradition."

Tamping down his anger, Kelman alters his approach by asking questions that he suspects will reveal little worth knowing. Clearly, Hendricks has made a lifetime habit of disingenuous conversation. Listening to the pat answers, his brain repeats: *Susannah Rause…an unknown woman dead in the fire at Lampley's establishment…arson in both instances…a new female companion for Hendricks—who may or may not operate a bawdy house, but who obviously inspires strong and perhaps fearful reactions. Can there be a connection? And if so, what?*

Dismissing the man at the conclusion of this futile interview, Kelman summons his most senior constable and orders him to follow Hendricks, while keeping himself invisible. If it's necessary to elicit aid from local watchmen or other constables, he should do so, Kelman explains, for the man must be unaware that he's under surveillance. Given the recent poor performance of this activity, he restates the importance of covert action. Young Stokes has a natural affinity for detecting those whom he perceives to be enemies. Hendricks may lack those intuitive skills, but he's clearly a man with a secret worth keeping.

Having delivered his directives, Kelman insists that no communication from the subject, whether of a verbal or nonverbal nature, be considered insignificant. If the man pauses to purchase a newspaper, or tips his hat, or enters a shop, the moment should be recorded; and when he returns to his lodgings, a watch should be established, and any people entering or leaving the premises be described in full.

That done, he takes a circuitous route to the spot where Findal Stokes was apprehended. He believes that either instinct or knowledge of the criminal class led the boy there. His unwillingness to reveal his connection to the area is difficult to explain, however. Didn't young Stokes offer to aid the search for Ella? If he had the slightest intuition of her location, wouldn't he have already revealed it?

CHAPTER 23

A Person of Deep Compassion

KELMAN HAD LITTLE need to issue cautionary instructions when telling his constable how to follow Nicholas Hendricks, for the man no sooner departs the area surrounding Congress Hall than he hails a hansom cab and rushes to Adelaide Anspach's house. The constable does likewise, arriving in time to see Hendricks hurry up the front stairs. He looks like a person pursued by dogs patrolling a vacant property. The constable's not given to invention, so his description is based upon personal experience. Hendricks has no fence to vault over in order to reach safety, but terror clearly nips at his heels.

The constable writes this in his report, then waits in the shadows to see what next transpires. If the fellow plans on indulging in additional journeys in hansom cabs, the "handsome" stipend Kelman has provided for this duty will soon be depleted. This sally he also pens. He's famed for his wit, if not his flights of fancy.

Of course, the constable can't possibly understand what transpires within Adelaide's abode. All he can do is stand and count the minutes as they elapse. While he does, he describes a building that has no remarkable details to set it apart from its neighbors. He also notes that the windows are devoid of any sign of residents or serving persons. If Hendricks were not within, he'd suspect the place was uninhabited. "The street," he writes, "is a good one, and looks like it's populated by upstanding folk. Not gentry, but rising merchants with decent incomes."

"You must release her, Adelaide. I insist upon it. This eccentric escapade of yours must cease. A girl wrongfully, no, criminally, detained—"

"I won't do it." Although her lips form a thin smile, there's ice in the expression.

"Why the devil not? The man was asking questions. I had the impression— strong impression—that he felt there was mischief afoot."

"Which there is. How astute of him and of you. Will you take some cherry cordial, Nicholas, or something stronger? I'll ring for the footman." Jervis has been elevated in rank from "my man" to "footman," although there's been no attendant elevation in pay. In fact, he hasn't yet received the salary due him.

"Damn it! Listen to me." Grabbing her shoulders, he prevents her from pulling the service bellpull.

She shakes him off with a furious, "Never touch me like that again. Never."

"I can do what I like. Aren't I paying the lion's share of this house's upkeep?" The words have a bravado his tone lacks, a fact she immediately recognizes.

"So what if you are? Don't you expect to be repaid when I turn a profit?"

"The future isn't what's at issue. You must let her go—"

"No." With her eyes hooded and inscrutable, she again grabs the bell rope. "My footman will show you out, Mr. Hendricks. I'll be happy to entertain you when you're in a more sanguine mood."

Batting away her hand, he glares at her, and the two square off: he, barely keeping his temper; she, ready to let hers fly. She looks as though she's about to strike him, which inspires an involuntary wince.

"You weakling. Are you afraid of a mere woman, or of marring your pretty complexion with a slap across your face?"

"Listen to reason!" is the pleading response. "Let her go. Better yet, I'll incur the initial risk and take her home in a cab myself. You need only bundle her up, and I'll deposit her outside her door. We'll wait until night. Or toward dawn. No one will see us. And, as you once so cleverly noted, she'll never remember where she's been."

"Oh, she'll remember. You can be certain of that."

"How? Given the amount of laudanum she's consumed—"

"Because I've been careful to tell her precisely where she is, and with whom."

"The devil, Adelaide! Why the deuce did you do that?"

"Because it pleased me."

"Pleased you!"

"Well, I didn't do it to please you."

"Tell me you're jesting."

"I never jest."

"Damn your eyes. What on earth were you thinking?" When she doesn't answer, he suppresses his anger and continues in a quieter vein. Fear is still apparent, however. "Let us be rational, and conceive of an end to this nonsense. If you don't allow me to cart her home tonight, you'll have to take her out of state. Tonight, or tomorrow at the latest. She can't remain here."

"Why not?"

"Because that bloodhound, Kelman, will find her. Don't you comprehend the danger you're in? You'll be arrested for abduction."

"Not if she's no longer in Philadelphia."

"Good. Finally, you're beginning to make sense. So what is it to be? Either I take her home, or you spirit her out of the city and state. You can lie if she claims to have been here. You're good at that. No. No, better yet, leave her in a derelict neighborhood, so it appears as though her abductors bolted. A few well-placed bruises and torn clothes, and in her drugged state, she'll—"

"No."

"Why not?"

"Because I don't wish it."

"Be reasonable—"

"You're forgetting that the girl will still name me, whether dragged home or elsewhere. When the laudanum wears off, she'll tell all she knows."

Hendricks's mouth works as he considers the significance of this single word "me," behavior she's quick to notice.

"And I will implicate you by stating that you forced me to do the dire deed, and that you intended to keep the girl prisoner for your own purposes. I doubt you have friends or acquaintances who'd come forward to vouch for your upstanding character."

His mouth opens and shuts. Terror races across his face.

"You don't reply, Nicholas. Good. We'll let this matter rest. And, since you'll take no refreshments, I'll request that you leave. Our conversation has grown tedious, and I must prepare for two new clients—who come from your kind recommendation."

"Release her, damn it. You have no idea what kind of fire you're playing with. An heiress's adoptive daughter, and that heiress with special influence—"

"I know very well who the girl is, and who she represents."

"Then let her go."

"No."

"Damnation, woman! Can't you understand?"

"The girl remains in my possession until I decide what use to make of her, either here or elsewhere. Or until she succumbs from the effects of the—"

"Succumbs! Do you know what you're saying?"

"Yes."

"The devil you do! You're telling me you'll kill her."

"Mr. Hendricks, I must ask you to refrain from raising your voice."

"What are you planning?" As if his hand belongs to another person, it flies out, striking her face.

Stunned at this show of violence, neither move. True to her temperament, she's the first to recover her composure. Her eyes glint with malice. "The footman will show you out."

"Listen to me—"

"Good day, Mr. Hendricks."

"I implore you—"

"Good day, sir."

"You don't know what you're doing!"

"You're mistaken. I know perfectly well what I'm doing. She stays here until I decide to move her elsewhere. *If* I so decide."

"I won't permit myself to be implicated in this folly—"

"You already are. Now, will you leave peacefully, or must a third party witness your distress?"

→⟩▬⊙ ⊙▬⟨←

"I didn't think a gentleman could run that fast, sir," Kelman's told three hours later when he returns from his ineffectual hunt for Ella. "He fairly flew into another cab, then hied it to his lodgings. I've got a watchman on the case, keeping a lookout. Though, from the expression on the gent's face, I don't think he intends to go out of doors for a good long while. Whatever happened in that Wood Street building scared him plenty. I don't believe in ghosts, sir, or any of that hocus-pocus, but the phrase fits. The fellow's skin was whiter than his shirt collar."

Kelman half listens to the conclusion of the report. His mind keeps wandering back to his search, and to the fact that Martha's ward has apparently vanished without a trace. *Why isn't there a ransom request?* he asks himself over and over, while at the same time avoiding the most evident answer: *because Ella's no longer alive.* It's only the constable's question about returning to Wood Street that pulls him back into the present.

"No," he says. "I'll go there myself." With that Kelman stands, although his pose remains irresolute. Nicholas Hendricks can go to the Devil, for all he cares. "Maintain your surveillance on the fellow's lodgings. If and when he leaves, follow him as you did before."

"No other instructions, Mr. K?"

"None yet."

Relief mingled with concern is evident in the constable's reaction. "You be careful, sir. Like I said, I don't believe in evil spirits or what have you, but something's not right in that place."

⊷⊶⊙ ⊙⊷⊶

Jervis opens the door to Kelman. Like Findal, he's attuned to spotting members of the constabulary. His first thought is that his sister-in-law has been arrested again, and that he's being summoned to conduct her back to their shared lodgings, or permit her to be committed to the asylum. Then he wonders if some accident has befallen his wife. That worry also disappears when he reminds himself that no one at home knows the address of his employment. Wood Street houses many similar buildings. How would anyone find him? When Kelman asks if the owner is at home, thanksgiving floods Jervis's face. He gapes and stares but utters no sound. The unexpected reaction makes Kelman decide the man must be either a mute or an imbecilic, or both. He slowly repeats his request.

"That would be Mrs. Anspach you want," Jervis bursts out. "I'll take you to her. No. Wait. I'm supposed to ask you to sit here, and then speak to her first. Your name, sir? She'll want your name."

"I'd rather not supply it."

"Can I tell the lady those are your instructions?"

"If you wish."

Jervis hesitates, for another notion has now crossed his mind. Could this person be looking for Ella? If that's true, how can he reveal her presence without provoking his employer's ire and risking financial ruin? A plan flashes into his brain, causing him to nod as if agreeing with himself. Making a show of looking upward to the landing, he goggles his eyes and nods vigorously again. Kelman, however, regards this exaggerated pantomime as the act of a simpleton. In embarrassment, he looks away. Recognizing his failure, Jervis redoubles the effort, while Kelman continues to overlook the peculiar mannerisms. He studies the room instead.

"Will you tell me your business, maybe, sir? The missus, she'll want to know." He gazes upstairs again, but Kelman ignores the glance.

"I'll tell your mistress when I meet her."

"But, sir, the missus—Mrs. Anspach—she'll ask me what you're about. I'd like to give the lady your name, too," he all but whimpers. For a fourth time, he looks upstairs, jerking his head as if to indicate something of importance. Again, Kelman misinterprets the activity.

"I'll supply it when she and I meet."

"Will you wait, at least, sir?"

"No. I've changed my mind. I'll accompany you. Lead on."

"Oh, but, sir—"

"Lead on."

Conveyed into the parlor by the agitated Jervis, Kelman is surprised to find Hendricks's theater companion. She recognizes her guest immediately but treats him as she does other anonymous male visitors, asking whether he'd enjoy some light refreshments and instructing the "footman" to take the gentleman's hat. Kelman declines both suggestions, but he plays the role he has surmised he should: that of a prospective client. He surveys the furnishings as if measuring what kind of establishment they represent; then he gives Adelaide the same scrutiny.

In response, she affixes a compliant smile, but oh, what glee envelopes her. Thomas Kelman in the flesh, at long last! The person who hounded her lover to his death. The person who destroyed every spark of joy she once possessed. Reveling in her loathing, she gazes at him with an expression of such calculated innocence that he recognizes it for a fabrication. But because he can't detect the truth, he creates another narrative. The faint red mark left on her cheek by Hendricks's blow becomes part of that erroneous supposition. Adelaide is cast as victim and Nicholas as miscreant, a man so base he'd brutalize a woman.

And what does she feel while she pretends to entertain him? Does she worry that he has discovered her abduction of Ella? No. If he had, the police would be now searching the property. Does she then ask herself what brought him here, or consider that her past crimes have finally surfaced? No. It's enough that he has entered her web: Kelman in person, and at her command.

When she deems he's had sufficient time to study her and her house, she speaks. "You'll find us a small establishment as yet, sir. But we're expanding, and if the solitary girl I now have in my employ doesn't suit, by week's end, I anticipate hiring two to join her. Shall I summon Solange so you may examine her?"

Kelman, considering how best to play the game, decides on honesty rather than continued subterfuge. "Mrs. Anspach, you've mistaken my intent. My name is Thomas Kelman, and I'm investigating a certain Nicholas Hendricks. I have reason to believe that you're an acquaintance of his."

She flutters her eyelashes as if perturbed at the mention of the name, which maneuver corroborates Kelman's erroneous theory. Then she raises her hand to cover the mark on her cheek, but she immediately drops her fingers to her side. The effect is of a woman attempting to protect her lover. "Has Nicholas done anything wrong?" she whispers, adding Kelman's name in a hesitant manner as though it were unfamiliar to her.

"I cannot say, but I have my suspicions. Is the lady, Susannah Rause, known to you?"

Adelaide pretends to think; a mixture of seeming apprehension and regret creases her brow. "No. Is she an acquaintance of Nicholas's—Mr. Hendricks's?"

"She was, madam. She is no more. Mrs. Rause perished in a fire at her home."

"Oh, how very terrible." A small tear rolls down her cheek. Becky Grey has strong competition in this woman. "I apologize for being unfamiliar with Mrs....Rause. I'm new to Philadelphia, you see." The lie is accompanied by a covert yet steady perusal of Kelman's reaction. Although they've never met, a description of her was circulated throughout Pennsylvania and New York. Adelaide, once Honora and any other number of aliases, has changed the color and styling of her hair, as well as the manner of her dress, but that doesn't mean she's safe. Understanding the risks enhances her daring. The faux tear is replaced by a tremulous smile. "Nicholas—Mr. Hendricks—was so kind as to befriend me, and then to suggest aiding in the establishment of my business. I hope I've committed no offense."

"May I ask if you're aware of a Mrs. Celestine Lampley?"

"No. Is she another friend of Nicholas's?"

Kelman nods, watching her. The woman's naïveté seems at odds with her chosen occupation, but he tells himself to keep an open mind. Manners can mislead, and this may be a professional affectation.

Interpreting his reaction, she adds an apologetic: "You must think me quite the novice, Mr. Kelman. The truth is that I'm new to this trade. My circumstances were greatly reduced due to a series of unfortunate occurrences; and, well, we women must earn our daily bread somehow. Sadly, I have no other craft upon which to rely. I cannot tread the boards like the wondrous performers I recently enjoyed, nor take pen to paper and make my living as an author; nor am I gifted musically. As to laboring in a shop, I've proven quite inept at that type of commerce. I believed I'd found a savior in Mr. Hendricks." She touches her bruised cheek again, turning away as if in an attempt to conceal her physical and psychic pain. "Again, I must ask if I've committed some potentially criminal offense?"

Kelman suppresses an inward groan, which is part sympathy for the woman and part frustration at misusing his time. He's beginning to doubt whether he'll ever learn the identities of the person killed in the Lampley fire. Nor, at this point, does he much care. "No, Mrs. Anspach. Your trade, though regrettable, is legitimate."

You pompous prig! Adelaide thinks, though her demeanor remains ingratiating. *I hope you rot in Hell eternal, and your hateful Martha Beale with you.* "I'm relieved to hear you say so."

"I'll take my leave of you, madam." Picking up the hat he'd left on a chair, Kelman turns to face her. "Before I go, let me caution you against Nicholas Hendricks. I'm aware that he visited you today, because I had him followed—which, in turn, inspired this interview. I note also that your face is bruised and that you've attempted to conceal it from me. In my opinion, Hendricks is capable of inflicting worse damage than that."

"Oh!" Adelaide gasps as she opens the parlor door and allows Kelman to precede her into the foyer.

"I caution you to be on your guard."

"Thank you for your advice."

Jervis is nowhere to be seen, so Adelaide must walk Kelman to the door. Before she can, however, a moan is heard in an upstairs room. Alert at once, she watches her visitor's reaction, then murmurs a despondent: "My daughter. I'm sorry you've been troubled by her. She isn't…healthy in the brain. I'm afraid the relocation here has upset her delicate sensibilities. The surgeon tells me she'll regain her…her composure in time. Alas, the poor child can never be fully…" As if afraid of burdening him with family matters, she changes the subject. "But I'm wasting your time, and I must apologize. My troubles are my own. You were good to come here today, Mr. Kelman. I'll take your warning to heart."

Quitting the house on Wood Street, Kelman reflects on what he perceives as extraordinary bravery: a friendless woman venturing into a city she doesn't know and bringing with her a sickly daughter. No wonder she hired the footman she did. Despite her trade, she must be a person of deep compassion.

CHAPTER 24

A Vigil

COWERING IN THE pantry, Jervis hears the front door close on their latest visitor and Adelaide twist the key in the lock. Unbeknownst to his mistress, he was privy to the conversation between her and Thomas Kelman, and with Hendricks as well. Jervis has become adept at eavesdropping. The grin that Kelman mistook for an idiot's rictus has been supplanted by an expression of dread. Unhealthy in appearance at the best of times, his face has taken on the ghastly gray sheen of a consumptive. His mouth opens and closes in a fishlike manner while his brain whirs, repeating: *I failed to save my son. Now I'll fail this girl, who may be my niece. Those two connivers will murder her, for certain. What can I do? How can an insignificant person like me help? What shall I do?*

The bellpull rings, summoning him to the parlor. He scurries to do his mistress's bidding.

"Never let me hear that damnable girl crying again, you wretched creature. Do you understand me?"

Jervis's lips part and then shut, but no sound comes.

"Answer me."

"I...I..."

"Never. Smother her, if you must. I don't care. Do you understand?"

"But, I—"

"What if that prig of a copper had recognized the whelp's voice? We would have been in dire straits then, I can tell you. Yes, I include you. My manservant. My hireling. You're as aware of what transpires in this house as anyone. And as culpable."

The fact that he hasn't received even a small percentage of his promised salary is a moot point, because Jervis doesn't dare argue. He can hear her voice berating him, recognize the venom in the tone and the threats she repeats, but her face is no more than a mottled-pink blur, her mouth the maw of a snarling dog.

"Speak, man! Do you or do you not understand how guilty you'll appear if the girl is discovered here? Are you not bringing her food? And tidying her room? Well? Answer me, damn you."

He nods.

"Say yes, damn it."

"Yes—"

"'Yes, madam.'"

"Madam."

"Good. Now leave me. And go dose that putrid thing upstairs. I want no more disturbances from her tonight."

Jervis remains inert, his mouth hanging open in speechless protest.

"Damn your eyes. Do as I say. If she dies from an overdose, so be it. She's served my purpose."

When her servant again fails to respond, Adelaide grabs him by the shoulders and shoves him toward the portal. She's a good deal stronger than she appears, and the force in her arms sends him crashing into the wood. The blow reverberates, causing the chandelier to jitter and dance and the crystal pendants to jangle together. Given that it's rented (like the other furnishings) and therefore poorly attached to the ceiling, it's a wonder it doesn't plummet to the floor. "Look what you've done, you idiot. Or are you deaf now as well as dumb? Do what I tell you, or leave this house immediately."

⟶⟫ ⟪⟵

Climbing the rear service stairs, Jervis stumbles and sinks to one knee. Tears blind him; unexpressed sobs choke the air from his lungs. He wishes he could fall and strike his head and lose all sensation. Maybe he'd even die. The feeble hope propels him onward. Death would be better than abetting a crime. Even his wife's despair at losing her mate, and Lena's inability to protect her sister or herself, seem inconsequential. He climbs another step, then another. He hates his life.

Reaching Ella's chamber, he unlocks the door and finds her in a semi-recumbent position and whimpering softly. Vomit stains the sheets. She has retched up her latest dose of laudanum, which is the cause of her wakefulness. For the first time, she gazes into his face; he finds this more troubling than the glassy stare that ordinarily slides over him, or her uneasy snoring.

"Ella," he says. He has never before uttered her name. Doing so produces an unwelcome stream of memories, and he turns away as though he could avoid examining them.

"I'm going to help you," he adds after several minutes. "But you must be quiet." He has no plan, nor even the foundation of a plan. In fact, until he spoke, he was unaware that he'd made a decision. But such is bravery. Seeming to arrive by happenstance, it's been lurking within our hearts all the while.

She looks at him, her eyes focusing for a moment before reverting to a dull, uncomprehending stare. She breathes out a sound, but there's no meaning in it.

"Hush, Ella. Hush."

Again, the eyes focus. Again, she tries to speak.

Jervis's fear intensifies. He puts his hand across her mouth, and her eyes widen, not in fright but in something that looks to him like comprehension. He nods in hopes that she'll understand that she can trust him, while Ella, in her drugged and hazy state, experiences a flicker of recognition: *This man is...is...*

The connection vanishes, and the more her brain attempts to recall it, the more elusive it becomes. *Do I know him?* her sluggish thoughts demand. *From some other time? From...*

Although the question weaves away unanswered, she's left with a sensation of kindness, and even of love. Then that, too, fades.

"Pretend to sleep now, like a good girl," Jervis whispers. "And tonight—"

At that moment, the door opens, and Adelaide appears. "Get out," she says.

→═● ●═←

When Jervis fails to return home that night, Lena becomes frightened. Ever since her sister and brother-in-law took her into their lodgings, he's been a model of dependability. Yes, his moralistic ways can rankle, but deprived of them, even for an evening, she starts to experience an apprehension so acute that her hands and body start to tremble. She drops a cup that shatters, then spills the soup she prepared for supper. When she tries to swallow a gulp of water, it spews out of her mouth, and no amount of concentration can help the liquid slide down her throat. She's soon parched. Thirst intensifies her fear, and the sense of impending doom transfers itself to her sister.

"Where's my husband?" she demands. "What's keeping him so late? What time is it?"

This last question is repeated over and over as the minutes wear on. Lena listens to the night watch proclaim the hour and conveys the information to her sister, who promptly forgets and soon asks again.

"He hasn't deserted us, has he?" is next added to the litany. "I haven't been the best of wives in recent days. He deserves better. He's a good man, Jervis is, and he likes me to be more cheerful. I should be, shouldn't I? For Jervis's sake. Shouldn't I? Tell me he hasn't deserted us."

"No," Lena recites, though her voice sounds increasingly unsure.

"We'll starve if he does."

"Now, don't you worry. He's been delayed, is all."

"I don't trust that female he started working for. She's got her eye on him, I'm certain."

"Hush now, dear. He'll be home soon."

"We'll starve if he abandons us."

"No, we won't. Can't I work as hard as any woman?"

"You?" is the bitter retort. "You! You've never been good at anything but having babies and abandoning them."

Lena's mouth falls open. The attack is so unexpected, it takes several moments for her to formulate a defense. "Oh, Sister, how can you say such a thing? Don't you remember how I—"

"He'd be here if it weren't for you. You and your wicked ways. Your wicked, wicked ways. You've driven him off, you have. Haven't you?"

"Sister, don't talk that way—"

"Why not? It's the truth, isn't it? Good for nothing girl—which you always were. Even as a wee lass. Doubtless, you've been eyeing Jervis—"

"No, Sister—"

"Sister, sister, sister. You don't fool me with your simpering. 'Sister, may I fetch you some soup? Sister, be brave. Don't weep, dear; your boy's with his Maker. Don't weep, dear; it hurts your husband.' Well, what do you know about my child's Maker, or his father's pain? Or mine? What do you know except your own selfish desires? I wish we'd never rescued you. And now you've made my husband run away."

"Sister, don't—"

"Don't what? Don't say what's true? You've tried to bewitch my husband. You made him quit his home."

"No!"

"I wish you'd never been born. Never. Neither you nor me."

At this, Lena, trembling all over and panting with thirst, struggles out of their lodgings and into the street. She knows she should try to find her brother-in-law and warn him that his wife has taken a turn for the worse, but she has only the name of the street to guide her. Besides, her body has begun shaking so violently she has difficulty keeping to the pavement. *Why doesn't he come home?* she thinks. *Why doesn't he come home?*

Throughout the long night, Kelman sits beside Martha in her upstairs parlor. A single paraffin lamp burns, flickering forth slim beams of light while creating larger and denser shadows that move around the room in a cumbrous manner like giants confined in a small space.

By now, the moon has risen and set; the stars have flamed across the sky, then been diminished by cloud cover. The only alteration in the pair seated hand in hand is a change in breathing as they shift positions. Neither speaks. Their fingers clasp or slacken; heads rest on the settee back, or pull upward, suddenly alert to an unfamiliar noise in the street below. Then the sound passes, and they resume their listless poses.

Thomas caresses Martha's palm; she squeezes his fingers. The unspoken exchange:

All will be well, I promise you.

How can you be certain?

Trust me in this.

I do. I will. I'm trying to.

All will be well. You'll see.

If only I could believe it.

The minutes tick on. The sky forsakes its funereal black for purple gray; that color then turns a lusterless pewter. No sun will appear today. Instead, a morning mist sifts upward past the windows, moving in airy ranks like the souls of the departed.

CHAPTER 25

An Unorthodox Strategy

I know where the girl is...

THE LETTER DELIVERED to Martha's door during the night while she and Thomas sat in silent consolation contains only these brief words. The handwriting is jerky, as if the author were in a hurry or couldn't risk divulging additional facts. The paper on with the communication is penned is inferior, as is the ink; the nub that formed the letters a shoddy one that scratched the flimsy material. Rag paper wouldn't rip so easily, nor would a well-fashioned pen inflict damage.

Kelman examines the message, holding it under the lamp's glare, then against the light, in case the paper has splotches or eradicated efforts his eye can't easily detect. The sheet of paper, folded and refolded and crumpled, too, has seen multiple uses. He curses himself for being closeted with Martha when the thing arrived, and also curses himself for not insisting that one of his constables keep watch inside the house. He could have stationed the man downstairs, where he'd be concealed while maintaining surveillance of the street. How the two watchmen outside the residence failed to notice the bearer of the missive, he doesn't know, but an inquiry and resultant accusations must wait. In truth, he's very angry, both at his subordinates and at what he believes is his own negligence.

Next to him, Martha holds her breath, then inhales a series of rapid gulps of air. She sounds like someone exhausted by sobbing, although she hasn't shed a tear. "At last...the note we've been waiting for."

Kelman nods but doesn't speak. He has misgivings about the communication. A ransom note should contain a demand of some kind; this letter simply states a fact. Nor is Ella named. Is caution the motive? Or is it possible that the writer is an ally rather than a foe? Someone who's prepared to betray the abductor? A disgruntled cohort, perhaps? Or a neighbor unwilling to risk being identified? Or could the thing be a sham?

Turning over the letter, he examines it upside down and sideways as he attempts to ascertain what type of person would have penned the words. At first glance, the handwriting looks barely literate; the strokes are deep and unsteady; pressure that looks inspired by uncertainty has torn the page. Or is the writer creating a ruse? The spelling is assured. No letters have been scratched out, or inadvertently begun.

"You say nothing, Thomas. Why? Don't you believe this is a legitimate communication from the person who abducted Ella?"

"I don't know. Something strikes me as false, but, as yet, I can't identify my qualms."

"The wording seems simple enough."

"It is. Therein lies my concern." With that, he explains his conflicting hypotheses, at the end of which Martha releases a disheartened sigh but makes no comment. "I also admit that I'm disturbed—and dismayed—that my men stationed outside failed to notice whoever delivered this."

"I imagine they must have been as tired as we were."

"That's no excuse. They were instructed to watch the house. Their dereliction hampers our work."

"So we're no closer to finding Ella."

"Not yet. Or perhaps we are. This slip of paper reveals too little to be of aid." In his vexation, he reverts to his criticism of his watchmen. "Those were two of my best men. I can't understand their carelessness. If they'd performed their duty, we would at least have had a description of whoever left this message."

Unable to supply an excuse for the blunder, Martha takes the slip of paper. Her silence makes Kelman recognize that his frustration is having an adverse reaction. "We should take heart, however, that someone, whoever this person is, has begun to communicate. We can only hope that a subsequent missive will reveal more."

"If this is genuine."

"Yes. If."

"And, if not…"

"I plan to act on the assumption that the message is authentic. And that the writer will approach you again."

"Oh, Thomas, this uncertainty is unendurable."

"I know. Powerlessness and fear make the situation difficult to bear."

"More than difficult—well-nigh impossible."

Her head droops; Kelman can see her strength is nearly spent. He wraps his arms around her. "Be brave, my dear one. For a little longer. Whoever delivered the letter wishes to say more."

"I'd pay anything to have her home."

"I realize that." He doesn't add that it's reactions like hers that draw would-be abductors to their trade.

"I know it's useless to blame myself."

"Yes, it is. No matter how much attention you've given to guarding Ella and Cai, some people will put equal effort into thwarting your good intentions."

She sighs, extricating herself from his embrace, and squares her shoulders. "Tell me what to do."

"Be patient. As impossible as that recommendation sounds—"

"I have no other choice, do I?"

"You could vent your anger, as I've done."

She tries to smile but fails.

"And let me position a constable in your house. Actually, two men on a rotating basis, so that the street is continually under surveillance. They won't be detected by any passerby, I assure you."

Leaning forward, her back now straight and her feet planted as though she intends to stand, she thinks. "But the maids and Cook will know they're here."

"You trust your servants, don't you?"

"Yes, of course. But delivery boys and so forth—"

"My men will be discreet."

"Won't the team outside the house have a better opportunity for observation?"

Kelman answers this question with an oblique, "I'd rather rely on four men than two."

"Oh, Thomas, those two who've drawn your wrath probably fell into a momentary doze."

"Which is unacceptable."

Again, Martha considers his suggestions. "Your men won't follow the messenger, will they?"

"It would be advantageous if they could."

"What if they're noticed?"

It's at that moment when Kelman makes a decision. The plan seems to come from thin air, but as he ponders it, the more likely success appears. "Martha, I need your permission to embark on an unorthodox stratagem. If you disagree, so be it, although I hope you won't. I believe we have the means of following the messenger while remaining undetected." Then, reluctantly, because his chagrin is fresh, he details Findal Stokes's private surveillance of her home and how the boy had stood there unnoticed. He concludes by advising that Findal, who is as anxious to find Ella as anyone, be enlisted for that duty.

As anticipated, Martha is appalled by the notion. "I don't want that horrid boy ever coming into contact with Ella again."

"I understand, but hear me out."

Her posture remains rigid, but she listens while he gradually persuades her of the merit in his suggestion. "Stokes has an uncanny ability to disappear from sight. Besides, who'd suspect a ragtag fellow like him of working for the police? Just the opposite would be true."

She shakes her head in apprehension. "Can you trust him not to divulge his mission? Wouldn't someone of his background sell his services to the highest bidder?"

Kelman thinks before responding. Martha's query has struck a chord. "Being poor doesn't make him dishonest. My parents were far from rich; in fact, they were closer to Findal's sphere than I'd like to admit." He pauses. "I've interviewed the boy, and I can tell you he has admirable qualities. Society hasn't been kind to him; he's needed sharp elbows and an instinct for survival that are at odds with the genteel folk with whom you associate. At his core, though, he's honest, and loyal. Extremely so. I believe he'd let himself be killed if it meant saving Ella."

She walks across the room, pausing at the window as she ponders his words. Early morning is fast becoming midmorning, and the city is buzzing with life, each carriage rider, cart driver, omnibus passenger, and pedestrian heedless of the emotions buffeting the parlor overlooking Chestnut Street. Or so it seems. Then that impression is replaced with another; perhaps the bland faces she sees mask worries as burdensome as her own. The revelation provides a kind of strength.

"Will you send for him, Thomas?"

"No. Instead, I'll ask you to accompany me to Moyamensing Prison, where he's temporarily housed. It's not a pleasant place, but such is prison life, and I believe you have the necessary fortitude. Following the interview, if I have your permission, I'll explain his duties and release him. No one will be aware of the connection between you."

"The wardens will, though, won't they?"

"They'll know that the boy was found loitering near your home and that you decided not to press charges against him for vagrancy. It will be a simple transaction: the gesture of a compassionate woman."

->=◎ ◎=<-

To Moyamensing Prison, then, where Martha is assailed by words that make her wince and an omnipresent reek that turns her stomach. Greater than these discomforts, though, is the sense of doom she experiences as she leaves the sunny byway and enters the broad shadow cast by the building. The place is a hodgepodge of neo-Gothic and ancient Egyptian architecture, its high walls pierced by a single row of tiny windows that seem too small to admit any illumination. After the iron-studded portal clangs shut behind her and Kelman, Martha has a panicky sense of never seeing the light of day again. Reflexively, she grips his arm tighter. He pats her hand in reassurance. Then she nods once to indicate her resolve, and they proceed toward the second floor.

As they climb up to the space where Findal will be interviewed, she has a sensation of rising through layers of dungeon. Lamplight is scarce and stinks of tallow; those areas—and there are many—that have been left in darkness look blacker than night. A cacophony of voices assaults her ears. Passing along a corridor, she can't hear her own footsteps, nor the steady beat of Thomas's boots striking the slate floor. The air, if it can be called that, is so thick with stench it's almost impossible to inhale. To no avail, she holds her handkerchief to her nose while mutely accepting Kelman's lead. On they walk, turning one way, then another. She realizes she couldn't retrace her path if she were left alone.

When they reach the assigned room, it must be unlocked by a hatchet-faced warder. Then a straight-backed chair is brought for her—the only piece of furniture in the space. Kelman stands while Martha sits, knitting her fingers together and holding them motionless in her lap. Beneath the kidskin, her hands are clammy and cold.

The door closes. When it opens again, Findal and another warder enter. At a sign from Kelman, the man withdraws, though his expression makes it clear he doesn't agree with this radical decision to leave a prisoner with only a single guardian when a visitor is in attendance.

"Remember to be on your best behavior, Stokes," Kelman says as soon as the door shuts. "There's a lady present."

"Yes, sir." As he answers, a wounded looks passes across the boy's pale face. Seeing it, Martha correctly interprets the reaction. Findal doesn't believe he deserves or requires the warning. He's already made himself as presentable as possible; his shirt may be gray with dirt, his trousers rumpled from sleeping in them, but he's brushed off the straw from the pallet that serves as his bed and has combed his hair with his fingers. If he had a hat, she knows, he'd be holding it in his hands. Her heart softens.

Feeling her scrutiny, the boy turns to gaze at her, his eyes now brimming with adulation. He doesn't speak, but his glance encompasses his entire history as if he were watching it unfold anew: his first encounter with Ella, their growing affection, and his private devotion to the woman seated before him because of her kindness toward her ward.

As if those images were transmitted to Martha, she sees them, too, although the pictures undergo an alteration. She envisions a young boy starved for affection as well as physical sustenance and observes Ella respond to his admiration and then resolve to help him. She intuits Findal's pride and ambivalence at receiving the girl's aid and finally his desire to prove his self-worth. She follows him as he hunts in vain for his missing companion. His sleepless nights curled in doorways or empty pavements, the pennies earned or not, and his despair, bravado, and loneliness enter her psyche. She lowers her eyes, shamed by her lack of charity.

Then she turns to Kelman, her decision made, and utters a quiet, "Yes."

With that simple agreement, he explains the task he expects Findal to perform. The boy pays close attention, though his eyes remain fixed on Martha, whose gaze has returned to her hands.

In conclusion, Kelman demands, "Do you understand what's required of you, Stokes? You told me you wanted to help. This is your chance. If you fail, you risk doing serious harm to the young lady. I cannot overstate the peril."

The harshness of the tone startles Martha, who glances at Thomas in silent appeal.

Findal also looks at him, his expression full of resolution. "I understand, sir. I'd do anything to help Miss Beale and her daughter."

CHAPTER 26

For Good or Ill

HAVING ESCORTED MARTHA to a hansom cab that will convey her home, Kelman returns to the room where Findal waits to receive further instructions. The strategy of utilizing this uneducated street urchin for complex police work gives him momentary pause; at stake is Ella's safety and perhaps her life. There's also the lesser concern about the criticism he'll face when news of the ploy reaches the mayor's office. Even if the plan is successful, Kelman understands he'll be rebuked for his dearth of professionalism. There are those whom he commands who'll turn against him, because they'll be unwilling to admit their defeat at the hands of a boy; their wounded self-esteem will find an easy target upon which to vent their anger and resentment. *It won't be the first time I've been attacked*, he thinks as he motions the warder to open the door. *Nor will it be the last—if I'm able to keep my employment.* That single *if* creates a large uncertainty; he's not at all assured of a favorable result.

After Findal is dispatched from the prison entrance, with a warder's credible curses and imprecations to keep his "dirty self" out of trouble in future or face "worse consequences," Kelman orders Celestine Lampley conveyed to the room. Then he sits in the chair that Martha vacated and ponders the lack of a ransom note.

Close to an hour passes, but he's so deep in thought that he doesn't notice the lapse in time until he becomes aware of anxious voices in the corridor. When the door opens, he's surprised to see two warders rather than one—and no Celestine Lampley.

"Her cousin said you'd told him she was free to leave," one of the men stammers.

"What cousin?" Kelman's face darkens in disbelief.

"The gentleman, sir. The gentleman who came last night. I thought the hour was too late to release her, but I know you like to do things in unusual ways, and the gent promised me—"

Kelman's shocked gaze squelches the remainder of the speech. He turns to the other warder. "Give me this so-called cousin's name—"

"Wasn't it the lady's relation, sir?" is the first warder's nervous question.

"—and description."

"Middling height and well proportioned, sir," Lampley's warder states. He looks to his mate for encouragement rather than at Kelman as he speaks, but he receives only a professional stare, which, in turn, increases his anxiety. "Pricey garments, too. A true gent. He apologized for 'inconveniencing' me. That was the word he used. You could see he was an educated man."

"Name?"

The warder produces and searches an official list detailing the previous night's occurrences. "Norris Hutchinson, sir. There it is, right on this line. I remember he had a handkerchief with his monogram, *N. H.*, in a large script. Like a lady might use. He showed it to Mrs. Lampley. She was right pleased to see him, I can tell you. She must be a poor relation, but she's a lucky woman to have such a thoughtful gent to aid her."

Kelman's disbelief has become exasperation. "You let a prisoner walk away in the middle of the night?"

"It did seem odd, sir, like I said, but the gent said those were your instructions—"

"And no one thought to confirm the order by asking me?"

"We did, sir. Yes, we did. And we tried, too. I can swear to that. But you weren't at your home. Nor your office, neither. The night watch at Congress Hall didn't know where you'd gone."

Kelman groans, the sound like thunder in the small space. "Damnation!" he shouts, which causes the poor warders to jump, but the critique is meant for himself. *If I hadn't been at Martha's house...if I'd paid attention to duty instead of my emotions...or followed protocol, and told my sergeant where he could find me, this debacle wouldn't have occurred.* "Wasn't there anyone else you could have consulted?"

The question is perfunctory, however. Kelman knows the Lampley investigation is his responsibility, and that his unconventional methods are proving his undoing.

"Well, sir, I did inquire of the constable who followed the gent here. He said you'd directed him to keep the fellow under tight surveillance, but, as the gentleman's request seemed legitimate, and as he was so polite and mannerly, insisting the idea was yours—well, what could I do? I didn't want to give offense to a person of his superior situation. The constable didn't agree with me, but Mr. Hutchinson assured him that he'd had a note from you."

"Did you ask to see it?"

"No, sir. I thought it rude not to take the gentleman on his honor."

Kelman groans again, this time in silence. Nicholas Hendricks—for that's who he assumes Hutchinson is—successfully employed the division between the classes to carry out his plan. If he'd been deterred, he would have stated that he merely wished to see a woman who'd been a family dependent, and about whom he was especially concerned. As to the bogus note, he would have manufactured a reason for not sharing it.

"That will be all," Kelman says at length.

"I did wrong, sir, didn't I?" the warder asks.

"No. Not you. The fault was mine. I should have left an address where I could be found."

"I can't think a gentleman like him means harm, sir," is the ingratiating reply. "He seemed genuinely worried about the lady."

And himself, Kelman thinks but doesn't say.

→→▸◄ ◗═◄←

No sooner has Martha arrived home than Becky Grey is announced. In typical fashion, she rushes into the parlor on the footman's heels, giving Martha no opportunity for lying and claiming she isn't at home, or is indisposed, or cannot receive visitors. It requires all her effort to smile and then send the footman for refreshments. The last thing on earth she wishes to do at this moment is idle away time in airy chatter.

"Oh, Martha, I'm very glad to find you at home. Well, perhaps 'find' isn't the correct term, because I've been waiting for you. Out on the street, patrolling back and forth like a woman of, well, the streets, until you returned. I could have asked to remain inside like a civilized person, but I was too full of anxiety. I've come to make a confession."

Martha forces another smile, this one more difficult to affix than the previous attempt. Becky's histrionics are more than she can tolerate at the moment, and she imagines the disclosure will be mere theatrics dressed up to seem important. "Do sit," she tells her guest, for she's suddenly found herself so weary she's afraid of collapsing. Slumping in a chair, she watches Becky arrange herself where the natural light from the window is at its most flattering. Even this small piece of posturing is irksome. "A confession. Yes."

"Martha, my dear, you look exhausted!" is the surprising response. "Whatever has happened?"

The reply takes a minute or two to formulate. Martha weighs truth against fabrication, then realizes she's no longer capable of pretense. Thomas has warned her to tell no one about the abduction, but surely he didn't mean to hide the fact from her friend. "Ella has been abducted."

Becky's hand flies to her mouth. "Oh, my dear God. How? When?"

"Four days ago. She left the house alone—against my instructions—and never returned."

"Four days? Four days! Oh, my dear friend, why didn't you tell me? You must be worried unto death." A small cry interrupts this speech. "Four days. Why, that was the opening of my play!"

"Yes."

"You were present. You and—"

"We were."

"And were you then aware—"

"Yes."

"Oh, my dear God! And yet you sat there and pretended…oh, Martha, what a brave creature you are." At this, Becky commences to weep. She reaches out and caresses her friend's hand, while Martha, enervated, leans hear head against her chair and listens to Becky's sorrowful clucking and cooing. Her own eyes remain dry. "Oh, and I came to visit you and rattled on and on about my success…what a thoughtless, foolish friend I've been. You must have simply hated me. I apologize, my dear. I apologize with all my heart. Of course, you'll pay the vile creatures who did this, won't you? Then your girl will be back home, and all will be well."

"There's been no request for money" is the slow reply.

"No request! How can that be? You must be the wealthiest woman in the city."

"I have no answers, I'm afraid. Thomas believes—"

"Oh, of course, your Mr. Kelman will save the day. I shouldn't have reacted in such a panic-stricken fashion. You're in the best and kindest of hands."

Martha doesn't answer. Instead, her mind considers Findal Stokes. The faith she put in Thomas's plan, and the boy's eagerness to help, is beginning to dwindle, if not to border on the preposterous. She can't help but imagine her father's reaction to having a sometime beggar keeping watch over his home. Lemuel Beale may have avoided noisy displays of temper, but his fury would have echoed through every room; young Findal would have found himself in prison again, and Thomas devoid of employment. "The only message I've received states that the writer knows where Ella's being kept."

"That's a good start," Becky states, although she doesn't sound as if she means it. "What will you do next?"

"Wait."

"Oh…how very trying." Becky rises. Even the thought of enforced idleness makes her restive.

"It's the most difficult trial I've faced."

"You're not accustomed to being powerless."

"Not now, perhaps. You didn't know me when my father was alive." Again, she falls silent. She half closes her eyes. She no longer feels capable of thinking, much less keeping up the pretense of hospitality.

As if this silent message had been verbalized, Becky argues an empathetic, "How can I desert you when you're feeling so bereft? No, I must remain and keep you company. My own dilemma, which seemed so monstrous when I waited outside for your return, is insignificant in comparison." She pauses, torn between her desire to be a considerate friend and her need for counsel. "Let me reveal it to you. Your logical mind may take solace from solving a problem that has no connection to your life." With that Becky begins a rambling narrative about the woman she knew as Honora.

"She saved my life," she concludes after some minutes, "so what else could I have done when she reappeared in Philadelphia and demanded my aid? What would *you* have done? Or advised me to do? Yes, she was and is capable of cruelty; and her transformation from persecutor to liberator was astonishing. Her motives, though, were never altruistic. I didn't trust her then. I don't trust her now. But I'm indebted to her. And, of course, she's exploiting that obligation."

Martha understands none of this tale, but then she's been paying scant attention. In her mind's eye, she envisions Findal Stokes: *Findal attending Thomas's orders, and perhaps even now—no*, she reminds herself. *Remain practical. Don't build hope out of air.*

"She no longer uses the name Honora, but that's of little consequence. She's still the same person, and when I argued against the bawdy house she's establishing, she threatened to expose our financial entanglements and make it appear that I'd subsidized her business!"

The fear in Becky's tone at last captures Martha's interest. "What do you intend to do?" she asks.

"About Honora, or about her threats?"

"Both."

"That's just it! I don't know. Her ultimatums are genuine. I told you she was vindictive, and I believe she'd gladly damage my reputation. Joyfully, in fact."

"What would she gain by doing so?" is the perplexed response.

"Pleasure," Becky says at length.

"Pleasure in hurting someone?"

"Yes. I believe that, at the core of her being, she delights in inflicting pain."

"How repellent."

"It's the truth, however. As I told you when I began to describe the history of our association, I experienced her savagery. So what am I to do?"

But Martha has again grown too weary to help her friend extricate herself from her problems. "Tell her that you're severing all ties with her. Then refuse to see her."

"How can I accomplish that? She was at the theater on opening night, and in the company of—"

"I'm not an oracle, Becky. My advice, which you can choose to take or not, is to stand firm—"

"Which your wealth permits you to do. I'm only an actress."

"But one who has garnered considerable success. Ignore the horrid woman. She'll grow tired of her games. Especially when she realizes how little effect they have. By all means, withhold monetary aid, too. Great or small, the amount maintains a connection she desires and you abhor. If she becomes too importunate, you can ask Thomas for advice."

"Oh, after what transpired last year, I'm sure that has—"

"And now," Martha says, interrupting, "I beg you to excuse me. I fear my strength is at an end. May we discuss this…conniving woman on a subsequent occasion?"

⋅⊱⋅≡ ◎ ≡⋅⊰⋅

Lena bangs on the door on Wood Street. This is the ninth house she has approached, and she's become desperate. If Jervis isn't within, she doesn't know what she'll do next. How many similar residences can there be on one street? This place, she now convinces herself, bears the strongest resemblance to the property Jervis described, but even as she makes that assessment, the impression fades. Rejection upon rejection is muddling her memory; each marble entry stairway has begun to resemble its neighbor; each portal looks like a duplicate of another across the street; each upstairs window, too. Her eyes grow wild in consternation. She looks up and down the street, the homes transforming themselves into sepulchers arrayed in rows.

"Jervis! Where are you? Why didn't you come home last night? You've got us badly worried. Jervis! Come out!" She's so loud and determined in her supplications that the neighbors whom she's already queried peer through their lace curtains and consider summoning the police.

"Jervis! It's Lena! Come out! Come out!" She leans her full weight on the wood, slamming against it till the frame shudders. By this time, she's also sobbing. "If you're here, answer me."

An upstairs sash in Adelaide's house is raised, and the owner herself peers down. "Be off with you, you madwoman." Her voice, intended to be a quiet hiss, resounds in a street gone silent.

"I found you, at last—"

"You'll find no one but a prison cell if you keep up that unholy noise." Adelaide starts to lower the sash.

"Missus. Wait. You know me. I want Jervis. My brother-in-law. Your servant."

"I keep no servant of that name."

"Yes, you do, Missus! Don't you recognize me? The little lad's funeral—my nephew. And you offering employment—"

"I have no idea to what you're referring."

"Oh, but you do! You must! I recognize you, even if you don't remember me. Mrs. Adolphus Green. You gave us money. That's who you are."

"I'm telling you that I'm not—"

"You gave us money."

"I did no such thing. Now, leave off your caterwauling and quit this abode, or I'll summon the watch and have you arrested." The sash slides shut. Lena hears the locking pins pushed into place, which causes her to resume her pleas.

Wailing, she stamps her feet and waves her arms until she resembles a person devoid of rational thought—which, in fact, she is at the moment. "I want my brother-in-law. You can't hide him away in there. Bring him out. Bring him out!"

The front door opens a crack. Adelaide thrusts out a fist filled with coins. "Take this and go away. I've told you there's no servant here by that name. It's only my natural compassion that keeps you out of the watchmen's hands."

With a beggar's instinct for snatching whatever's offered, Lena grabs the largesse; then she gazes at the coins as if she doesn't understand from whence they came. By now, her cries have subsided into noisy hiccoughs. "His name is Jervis. You came to our chambers. You said you represented a charitable society—"

"You've mistaken me for someone else. I've never seen you before. Now go away, before I change my mind about being compassionate."

Lena stares. It's true that this lady looks different than she remembered. The other was dressed in dull blue; this one is showily arrayed. Her hair looks different, too, and she sports sparkling gems, while Mrs. Green wore none. "The dead boy," she says in protest, but the words sound feeble and halting.

Like a mesmerist, Adelaide keeps her eyes fixed on Lena's. Her will is stronger; Lena feels her resolve falter. With it, her stamina also melts away. "I'm very hungry."

"Then I suggest you feed yourself. You've got the means in your hand."

Lena glances at the coins piled in her fingers. She'd forgotten they were there. "Maybe I've got the wrong house."

"Yes, you have."

"But I thought this looked—"

"Or the wrong street, most likely.“

"He said it was Wood—"

"There are others of that name."

"Are there?" Lena peers past the woman into the foyer's interior. "He said 'Wood,' I think, and said something about a vestibule—"

"Will you be a good woman and leave? I don't wish to see you in prison. Or in the asylum, because people like you who scream and make baseless accusations usually spend their days in the madhouse."

Lena nods. She knows this fact well enough. Wasn't she incarcerated in the Asylum for Persons Who Have Lost Their Use of Reason? And didn't Jervis free her by promising to take her into his home? She murmurs his name, hoping he'll magically appear like he did on that occasion.

"I've told you that I don't know the man. Now, be off before I lose my temper."

"Maybe another house nearby?"

"I can't answer that, but I can state that my neighbors won't treat you as kindly as I have. You should make certain of an address before making a spectacle of yourself. I suggest another Wood Street, if that's the name you want. I'm done conversing. So be off."

"But only Jervis knows—"

"Get along." The door starts to close.

"And he's not home to tell me."

"Go along and feed yourself."

Adelaide shuts the door and latches it. In the foyer, her eyes burn and her chest heaves. How dare her servant involve his benighted family! Hasn't she problems enough without lunatics assailing her house?

Her neighbors, though, having witnessed the exchange and watched a poor half-witted beggar woman receive kindly attention, reconsider their opinions of Mrs. Anspach. She may appear aloof; she may entertain gentlemen callers at questionable hours and run an establishment that no one dares mention, but it's obvious she has a generous heart. Perhaps she's even pious. After all, didn't Jesus teach that the least among us deserve our care?

As Lena straggles away from the house, dozens of eyes observe her departure. Then drapes are resettled, and the residents return to their tasks. In twenty minutes' time, she and her cries have been forgotten, which is as long as it takes her to reach Callowhill Street, where she pauses, sits on a mounting block, and begins to recount to herself everything Jervis explained about his place of employment. Concentration furrows her brow while her thoughts tunnel inward.

At length, her eyes open wide in discovery. Of course that's the house where he's employed. Doesn't it resemble the place he described—the foyer she glimpsed and the new furnishings? And the carpet and draperies, too? Of course that's the place. And the lady's the very person she was hunting, too, although Lena can't understand why she was now wearing a brightly colored gown instead of her previous garments. Then, in the blink of an eye, she discovers the solution to that conundrum. There must be two women: twin sisters, and one is visiting the other, just as she shares her sister's home. *Yes. Surely that explains everything. If the lady's a new arrival, she might not be familiar with Jervis's name. Nor would she know how he came to his employment.* Light dawns. The mystery is solved.

Lena smiles, then stands, brushing off the oat husks and hay strewn around the mounting block. She must make herself presentable when she returns and states her case. And she must keep her wits about her this time. The elegant lady was generous, but ladies are notorious for losing their patience.

She retraces her steps, at first with determination, but gradually her confidence dissipates and her footfall slackens. What if the lady summons a constable instead of listening to her tale? Didn't she promise to do just that? With the asylum standing ready to receive her, who will rescue her? Not Jervis, unless he can be found. But who will conduct a search if she's chained in a cell? Not Sister, that's certain!

Lena stops in the middle of the thoroughfare, unable to find satisfactory answers. Instead, all is confusion and grief. She turns to leave, spins toward Wood Street once more, then halts again.

Perhaps I should try the rear entry, she thinks. *Maybe I can find a garden gate, or an alleyway. All big houses have second entrances—and Jervis must keep himself at the back of the house. How foolish I was not to remember the fact. No wonder the lady was irritable. Servants don't enter by the front door.*

Her pace quickens until she finds the street she's hunting. Running parallel to Wood, it's fronted by carriage houses and garden entryways. No one is visible in any of the residences; the horses have been stabled, or are out at their masters' bidding, and the coachmen and stable boys are attending to their duties. With surprising ease, she slips into a garden that's rank with overgrown weeds; a few fruit trees fight for life, but they're so strangled with vines, it's doubtful they'll produce a crop. Where once was a path, chokecherry spirals upward as tall as her head.

A reek of dead creature assails her, and she must hold her hand across her nose and mouth to avoid breathing it in. The stink increases as she nears the house, as do swarms of flies that must be feasting on the rotting flesh. With her other hand, she brushes away the buzzing clouds, although her motion is abbreviated. She can't afford to be seen from an upper window.

This close to her destination, fear grips her, and she hesitates. *What if I'm caught trespassing? What if I knock—quietly, of course—and the lady, rather than Jervis, answers?*

Lena knows the answers to both queries. She'll be hauled away and placed in manacles. *No, I dare not continue. Jervis will come home. Maybe his duties have increased, and he's been hired as a full-time servant. He'll send a message to us, describing his change in fortunes. Perhaps he already has, while I've been frittering away the daylight on a useless search. I'll go back to Sister. That's the best thing.*

Turning, she stumbles on something hidden in the undergrowth. She bends down without considering that it might be the carcass fouling the air and pulls aside the weeds. There, next to her boot, is Jervis's hat. She snatches it up in wonderment and gratitude. *Jervis's hat! He must be very near!*

She looks at the house, searching the windows for a sign of him, then all at once spots the woman who ordered her away. Her back is to the window; she hasn't yet noticed someone creeping through the garden. Lena doesn't wait to be discovered in this illegal position. She clasps the hat to her breast and hurries through the tangled greenery until she's safely on the street again.

CHAPTER 27

Everything That Is Bad

LEAVING MOYAMENSING, KELMAN follows a winding route; he has no fixed destination in mind, only a need to spend time in contemplation. The investigations he has embarked upon lie in shambles. Lampley has escaped; the identity of the woman who perished in the house remains unsolved; both Rauses are deceased and, with them, presumably, the impetus for the lethal blaze. Those concerns seem trifling compared to Ella's abduction and Martha's anguish, however. He passes a hand across his eyes, the gesture reflexive, but when his sight is obscured, he finds himself wishing his inner vision could vanish as well. He shades his face, trying to obscure the nightmare images of Ella and her supposed captor.

The pictures remain; he walks on, his soul so heavy it weighs down his entire body. Who has the girl, and why doesn't that person or persons come forward? Is it possible that Ella's dead and that her abductor, having ruined a plan for financial gain, has fled? But why the message stating that someone knows her location? Wouldn't that indicate that she's still alive—and still a valuable commodity? If so, why don't the perpetrators demand ransom?

He's certain that something is missing and that there are questions he hasn't asked, or potential motives he hasn't examined. He wonders whether the crime is an act of vengeance but then can't comprehend who could possibly hate Martha. *Isn't she committed to good works? Didn't her generosity prompt her to rescue two abandoned children? Hasn't she always aided and supported her friends, Becky Grey being the latest to receive her assistance? So not vengeance, then, but what? What?*

A woman appears in his line of vision. Meandering along in the middle of the road, rather than on the brick pathway fronting the butchers' and fishmongers' stalls that line lower High Street, she's sporting a man's hat cocked at a ridiculous angle, as if daring it to fall. She touches the brim every few seconds then snatches her fingers away, twisting her mouth downward in what looks like a silent sob. Kelman realizes he's seen her before. She was the woman who happened upon the Rause funeral and then ran afoul of the undertaker's driver. The madwoman.

Shouts and warnings pursue her. Muleteers and carters pull up their beasts to avoid running into her, but their imprecations have no effect. She lurches forward in her zigzagging path, her face consumed with loss.

Kelman knows he should confront her. She's a danger to herself and others, but he can't bring himself to detain her. Incarceration in an asylum would follow, which it's doubtful she'd escape. Better to let her live out her days in the relative peace produced by her derangement. The fictions her brain conjures are surely preferable to the realities of a house for lunatics. He pretends not to see her, or the havoc she's causing. It will be a blessing if a wagon inadvertently strikes and kills her.

At length, she trundles away from the thoroughfare and onto the walkway, which places her directly in front of him. The precious hat tumbles from her head, but she catches it with unexpected agility and then holds it to her breast as though it were a baby in need of soothing.

The sight fills him with a woe he can't identify. If Martha were at his side, her purse would be open, her hand already pulling out money to give. Kelman reaches into his pocket and proffers the coins he finds there, but the woman refuses the donation. "When he comes home, I'll have no need. When he comes home. When he comes home." The phrases have the singsong sound of being oft repeated.

She wanders on. He lets her go, although he continues to observe her progress, a sorry creature lost in her singular world. What did she call Rause? A devil? Yes, and probably rightly so. Didn't she also recite terms only a textile laborer would know? Darius Rause's mill must have once employed her, or her spouse, or children. Or all of them.

His thoughts now encompass Martha as well as this nameless women and her thousands of destitute and damaged sisters, each in need of kindness and sustenance and shelter. Some overcome the trials they encounter, he knows. Many more do not; many more die without having experienced a single happy day.

He rubs his hand across his eyes again, then turns toward Martha's house. He can comfort her, if he can help no one else.

⊷⊨⊙ ⊙⊨⊷

Walking up Chestnut Street, however, he realizes that he can't risk being seen entering her home. If an abductor is watching the property in anticipation of delivering a ransom notice, his presence could drive that person away. Having disguised the constables stationed within and without, Kelman knows it would be foolhardy to deviate from his plan.

He lingers for a moment, wishing the events separating him from Martha were no more than a dream. Then reality returns, and he proceeds toward his office, reminding himself that he has work to do that requires attention. Once there, though, he finds he's unable to concentrate. Only Martha and her loss have any meaning; beyond that, all else is inconsequential.

Taking pen and paper, he decides to compose a letter to her to explain the reason for his absence.

"My dear Martha," he begins, then stops; what he wishes to express has nothing to do with explanations, or the current situation, or constables, or criminals. *I must ask her to marry me.*

The notion, so well concealed that it takes him by surprise, causes him to drop the pen, spattering ink on the paper. Watching this small act of destruction, he smiles, not because the letter is ruined, but because of the boldness lying within those black splotches. *I must ask her to be my wife. I can't pose the question immediately, of course. But soon. As soon as Ella is safely returned. Don't we love each other? Why should we waste our brief time on earth fretting about propriety, or misunderstandings we mistake for truths? Why should I fear that she'll be spurned for choosing a mate of lowly birth, or damn myself for marrying above my station? Public reaction should have no part of our decision. We have each other. That's all that matters.*

Avoiding all reference to this decision, he writes the letter he intended, describing his regret at not being present to personally console her.

"My dear," he concludes. "I'm with you in spirit, and always will be. Now and forever. Your Thomas."

⊷═⊕ ⊕═⊷

Becky Grey sits in her dressing room, the evening performance long since ended, the other actors gone to late suppers or their homes. She should be home, too, she knows, but instead she remains in the half-darkened room, pondering a single line from the play. Spoken by Sir Peter Teazle to his wife, it's intended as a sly barb within a comedic interchange; and the audience never fails to appreciate its subtle wit. Taken out of context, though, the words are laced with venom: "I believe you capable of everything that is bad."

Glancing at the looking glass, she sees Lady Teazle reflected, for she's still in the costume of a woman of fashion in late-eighteenth-century London. The wig, the décolletage, the beauty mark and paste jewels belong to a fictional person, but the eyes belong to her. Staring into them, Becky watches herself gaze back. She searches her face, attempting to remember the revelation she experienced during this evening's performance when she heard the line delivered; it was as if she'd never understood its underlying message before. "I believe you capable of everything that is bad."

Rising, she peels away her layers of clothes. She has sent her maid home, so her efforts at undressing are slow, but the need for meticulousness suits her reflective mood. Around her, the deserted building creaks and sighs. At another time, she might worry about her safety in the abandoned theater; tonight it affords her space to ruminate. *What is it?* she wonders. *What am I remembering?*

The air smells of face paint and powder, of cloth nearly singed by the limelights, of dust stirred by hasty costume changes, and dust resettled: every odor full of anticipation and movement. Ordinarily, Becky finds them familiar and comforting. After all, the stage has been her home since she was fifteen, and other performers have been surrogate mothers, fathers, sisters, and brothers, while the houses, grand or provincial, lofty or cramped, have been like unconventional family residences.

Her unease persists, however, and her mind returns to Martha and the disappearance of her ward.

"I believe you capable of everything that is bad."

Becky studies her reflection again, her eyes meeting their glass counterparts and then looking through them into her history. Images of the past flicker forward: ten years ago, six, one, a month, a fortnight; each is fully contained as if she were reliving the separate moments.

The answer she's seeking remains elusive, but, having dressed, she decides to pay a late call before returning home.

→≫══◉ ◉══≪←

Shrouded in a black cloak, Becky raps on the door to the Wood Street house for a second time. Inside, all is in darkness, which isn't what she expected. A business like this should be lively at this hour.

She waits and knocks again, the sound now louder. In the silent neighborhood, it echoes with a querulous clang. An upstairs window opens.

"What the devil?"

"Let me in, Honora. I must speak with you."

The window bangs shut, the noise impatient and irritable, but soon enough the door draws open, and the mistress of the house stands wrapped in a dressing gown; a sneer is planted on her face. She holds an oil lamp that gives off an unpleasant odor, then places it on the floor, where its yellow flame flickers among the lifeless roses of the carpet. "Come in. Do. Some people are abed at this hour. You, clearly, are not one of them."

Becky pushes back the hood from her cloak but doesn't remove the garment. "Where's your servant?"

"He was a thief. I was forced to fire him. You find me without domestic assistance."

"Or customers."

"Aren't you shrewd?"

"Your business isn't the success you'd anticipated, then?"

"Another clever assessment, Mistress Grey. Perhaps I should take up acting and learn to feather my nest like you do. This profession doesn't seem to suit me."

Becky regards this woman who saved her life. Although she knows the action was devoid of altruism, the outcome was the same, and she feels gratitude despite wishing she did not. "Honora…" she begins, then stops, frowning into the gloom. There's no sound to be heard except their breathing; the building must house only this single resident.

"What happened to the girl?"

"What girl?" Adelaide demands.

"The woman. Solange—"

"I discharged her, too. No more footman. No more bawd. You find me, Miss Grey, at a low point in my enterprise. In truth, I've become bored with the trade. Perhaps I should return to my earlier calling."

"This is a more stable existence than running counterfeit notes."

"Stability is overrated. Now, what do you want? Because I doubt you ventured here at this hour in order to express concern about my living conditions."

Becky hesitates before speaking. Her thoughts tumble over themselves, trying to make sense of her puzzling premonition. *Can it be that Honora is involved in Ella's abduction? Is that what I've intuited? The woman needs money, and she's ruthless enough to do anything. Martha's received no demand for ransom, however, which leaves no motive.*

"Well, Becky? Speak up, or be on your way. Since you've wakened me, I might as well use the hours to advantage and pack my belongings. Living alone in splendor is a misuse of my diminished resources."

"But I thought Nicholas Hendricks—"

"I've broken with him. He wished more control over me and my fledgling establishment than I was willing to provide. Don't worry, though, I won't come begging at your door again. On the contrary, I plan to quit the city altogether. As you might surmise, it's never been a favorite of mine."

Becky's hopes soar at this piece of news. Honora gone from Philadelphia! The notion brings an involuntary smile.

"I see my revelation pleases you. It will be a relief to have me and my damaging memories gone, won't it? Don't answer. I know what you feel. You imagine me a bad person, maybe even an evil person, but you don't trouble asking your-self who I am or why. Ah, well. No matter. What do you want? I'm tired, and lamp oil costs money."

"Honora—"

"Adelaide, Becky. Adelaide. For another day or so, or longer, maybe. Be so good as to remember."

"A friend of mine has a child—"

"What's that to me?"

"A ward. A girl of fourteen—"

"I repeat: What's that to me?"

"—who's missing from her home."

Adelaide's foot brushes the lamp, which totters. As she swoops down to prevent a fire, her face looks so fierce that Becky takes a step backward. "Do you intend to burn the place down, Mistress Gray?"

"It was you who—"

"If it weren't for you pounding on the door, I wouldn't be standing here with this poor excuse for illumination perched on the carpet. What is it you want from me? Did you come here to accuse me of stealing this…girl? Do you imag-ine that I spirited her away from your bosom companion, and that I'm hiding her somewhere in the upper reaches of this doleful abode? Is that what you think?"

A frown is the answer, at which Adelaide laughs: "Ah, Becky, Becky, for one so customarily eloquent, you've grown strangely tongue-tied. Is it the hour, or your delight in anticipating my removal from your city?"

"Honora—"

"Adelaide! You must learn your lines better. Or perhaps you're not the thespian you're reputed to be." She turns away, regarding the shadowed hall. Becky watches her shoulders droop. When she speaks again, her tone has lost its harsh edge; instead, the words take on a sluggish life-weariness: "I understand that the trade I entered into is repugnant to you, but it doesn't make me a villain. Nor a thief, snatching innocent children from their happy homes. I assume hers is happy. On the other hand, maybe it's like everyone else's: bleak and more bleak. You don't answer. Why not? You're aware that I have no compunction in taking money that's not mine. Do you think I'd do the same with a child?"

"No" is the troubled reply, for Becky has found that this is precisely what her brain has conjured. *Everything that is bad* reverberates through her mind, but, presented with Honora's doleful attitude and reduced circumstances, the idea begins to seem implausible. *If there's been no request for ransom, then what would the woman expect to gain by abducting Martha's ward?*

"No? Or yes? Do you believe me capable of the villainy I described, or not?" Adelaide reaches for the lamp again, thrusting it toward Becky's startled face before placing it on a table. "You've never known desperation, have you? Or poverty. Or terror."

"That's untrue. I'm not here to discuss my history, though. You asked my opinion of your nature. I believe you to be relentless in achieving your goals. I know you can be cruel. As to the other—"

"'As to the other,'" Adelaide parrots. "Let me put your mind to rest and take you on a tour of my hallowed mansion. You can pry into every corner and make certain your friend's precious babe isn't concealed within a cupboard, or beneath one of the unmade beds. Or perhaps you'll find her and turn yourself into the heroine you crave to be. What's the girl's name?"

"Ella."

"Ella. How quaint. And the doting mama?"

"Martha" is the now-tentative reply.

"Another dowdy appellation. I assume this Martha must be a woman of means; otherwise no one would nab her child. And perhaps her husband's a wealthy gent and likes his womenfolk to have dreary names and to sit huddled beside his commodious hearth. Those kind generally get their spice elsewhere."

Becky doesn't speak. Her presence on Wood Street seems increasingly misguided. *What did I believe I'd discover?* she asks herself, but she finds no answer.

"You remain discreet about the identity of the adoring couple. Very careful of you, Mistress Grey. Very wise not to share it with the likes of me. God knows what use I might make of it, eh? Especially since I'm 'relentless' and 'cruel.' Do you wish to hold the lamp while we climb the stairs, or shall I?"

"There's no need to go upstairs."

"No need to examine the premises to make certain that I haven't beguiled a sweet young lady into this den of corruption?"

"No. In truth, I'm not certain why I came."

"To disturb my rest, I assume." Adelaide grabs up the lamp. She appears undecided whether to hold it steady or hurl it to the floor; her eyes glitter as if watching an imaginary flame spread across the new and waxy-smelling carpet.

Becky shrinks back as though from a blaze, a response that earns swift censure. "I don't intend to set fire to the house. Or to myself, or you. I may have reached a troublesome juncture in my sorry journey, but I'm no suicide."

The declaration rings false, but Becky has no cause to counter it. Instead, she decides her visit has been pointless. Pulling up the hood of her cloak, she prepares to leave.

"So soon away, Mistress Grey?"

"It was a mistake to disturb you. I told you my intentions were vague. I won't apologize, because you and I have renounced those niceties in our dealings with each other. Before I leave, though, let me ask you as a favor—"

"Why should I do you any favors?"

"Because I helped you."

"I also helped you."

"As a favor." Becky continues as if there'd been no interruption, "I ask that you report to me if you hear any rumors about the girl."

"Ella, you mean?"

"Yes."

"Why should I hear tales about your friend's child? Or ward, to be accurate."

"Because you've consorted with people who—"

"Commit crimes? Is that your meaning?"

"Yes."

"Then say so outright. Your highborn friends have turned you mealy-mouthed. You're not the woman I remember." She falls silent. In the lamp's primitive glow, the smile stretched across her face is transformed from cunning into exhaustion; her cheeks sag; her mouth droops. Only her eyes remain bright, but the sheen is fevered and sickly.

"I loathe mothers and children. You didn't know that about me, did you? I made an exception in your case, but I won't for your friend. Your dear Martha and her doting, nameless spouse. So I doubt I'll be inclined to report any mischief I hear. *If* I hear any rumors, which will be debatable once I quit the city. I'm sure my reaction doesn't surprise you. Women like me who have foresworn compassion despise those milky Madonnas who feel the need to nurture the poor and oppressed. Girls and boys rescued from the streets. And to what end? I may be a trickster and charlatan; I may be capable of committing murder; but my speech is genuine. Now, shake hands with me. I don't believe we'll see each other again in this life. If I mount to Heaven, perhaps, though that seems improbable."

Becky starts to reply, but Adelaide turns and climbs the stairs. Her rigid form curtails further conversation.

Returned to the street, Becky watches the house go dark again. A faint sound of weeping seeps from an upper window, then all is still.

CHAPTER 28

"Gone"

THROUGHOUT THE NIGHT, Findal watches Martha's house. Sleep should overcome him, for he's very tired, and hungry, too, because Kelman's payment for his labors remains untouched. He doesn't wish to waste a moment of his vigil by consuming food or drink, though. Dedication and adoration are his sustenance and slumber. No one but ordinary passersby come near the house, and those are few and far between, for the city is at rest. The house itself is nearly dark. One room on the second story, which he surmises belongs to Martha Beale, glows. She must be as wakeful and worried as he. He stares at the curtained windows and imagines her pacing back and forth, or perched in nervous contemplation, only to leap up and begin walking to and fro again, which is what he'd like to do.

He forces himself to remain in a seated position, however, huddling his knees beneath his chin and wrapping his arms around his legs. To anyone who might happen to notice him, he would look like a beggar boy too fearful of his fellow vagabonds' conniving ways to allow himself to doze. Most wouldn't detect him, though; his chosen spot is so black it appears one with the brick and stone at his back. In this attitude, he pictures himself transformed into a statue: a hobgoblin with pointy ears and eyes as shiny as coal. Findal has no illusions about his beauty. He waits, a boy-creature about to spring forth and rescue his beloved.

→▸══◉ ◉══◂←

Becky is also wakeful. Peace eludes her as she stretches out upon her bed, and she rises repeatedly to tiptoe into her son's room to gaze at his sleeping form.

How serene he looks, how happy and free from discord and woe. She touches the coverlets but doesn't dare stroke his sweet, small face lest she disturb him. Her heart swells with love. The furious resolve that enabled her to save him from his father seems the attribute of another braver woman, although Becky recalls every moment: her husband's blows and threats, her rebellion, and the careful steps she took to ensure her release, which unfortunately led to Honora.

A woman who hates mothers and their children; how can such a perversion exist? She ponders everything known about Honora's history but still can't justify this aberration. Didn't she possess a passion so selfless she would have traded her life for her lover's? Isn't that the core of devotion, maternal or otherwise? Can it be possible that her declaration was a fabrication, or a form of self-deception? Is she motivated by jealousy for what she's been denied?

Ruminating on the puzzle, she returns to her bed and attempts to sleep again, but her thoughts won't release her, and she drifts back into her child's room, making certain not to alert the nursery maid in the adjoining chamber. Let her enjoy untroubled slumber.

Why did she turn vicious when discussing "Martha and her doting, nameless spouse?" She mentioned the couple several times, each time full of loathing. Does she hate marriage as much as she hates families?

Becky circles and circles through the exchange, recalling every phrase as well as the mercurial expressions that crossed Honora's face. *"I'm no suicide," she insisted, then she told me to look for the "precious babe" within the house. Why? To prove her honesty? Or disprove it? "I may be a trickster and charlatan…but my speech is genuine." Was there a message within all her talk of retribution?*

Then, there, all at once, is the solution to Becky's inquiry, as well as the instinct that took her to the Wood Street house. Revenge. Honora returned to Philadelphia to avenge her lover's death. It's Kelman she intends to destroy; Ella is the means to that goal.

So stunning is the revelation that she gasps; her body goes cold, then flares with heat. *"A girl and boy rescued from the streets"—that's what she said—yet I never revealed Ella's history, so how could she have known? And what about my relationship with Martha? Is Honora aware? Maybe…no, certainly. And I? I've been part of her scheme from the beginning. The bawdy house a ploy, the borrowed capital…Hendricks and his ilk…all of it…each one a segment of her plan.*

She flies back into her room, dressing without bothering about corset and underskirts. A cloak will hide her disarray. She must find Kelman at once.

What else did she say? "I don't believe we'll see each other again in this life." Becky's thoughts travel no further.

⤙═◎ ◎═⤚

Rushing along the night-black street, she can't find a cab. She hears a night watch-man calling out the hour—three in the morning—but that's the only sound and the only evidence of anyone else being awake. She runs toward the man's voice, deciding that he can alert his colleagues. Unable to find him, though, she curses aloud. If only the hour were more advanced, farm wagons would be entering the city and people would be stirring. Where to turn? Where to turn? Desperation grips her, robbing her of action. Then she springs forward again.

Could Kelman be at Martha's home? Wouldn't that be logical if he were expecting a ransom letter? She hurries in that direction, then stops. She can't risk frightening Martha. Not yet. She must speak to Kelman alone. But how? How? Tearing across one road then another and another, she races toward Congress Hall. Shouldn't a member of the watch be on duty there? And wouldn't he go in search of his master? *"I don't believe we'll see each other again in this life"* echoes in Becky's brain.

⤙═◎ ◎═⤚

Twenty minutes later, Kelman has been summoned from his lodgings and a car-riage with a half-dozing horse commandeered. At first, he doesn't credit Becky's story. This can't be the same Adelaide Anspach he interviewed, he argues. But her vehemence sways him, as does her courage. "I'll come with you," she insists when he informs her that he'll have her escorted home. "She may listen to me. It's you and Martha she abhors. You especially. She'd rather harm you than live.

'I don't intend to set fire to the house,' she told me, but I doubted her even then. She nearly upset the lamp when I was there."

How long that journey seems to take; the horse is whipped up to a sluggish canter, but the shadowless pavements appear to stretch on forever, and the darkened houses cluster like trees in an endless forest. Becky would weep with frustration, but she's too tense for tears. Beside her, Kelman and his chief constable say nothing. Nor does the second constable, who rides postilion beside the driver.

Reaching Wood Street, they find the house unlit. Kelman tells Becky to remain in the carriage, but she refuses and leaps to the ground while he instructs his two men to approach the rear of the house. Keeping Becky behind him, though the task isn't easy, he bangs on the front door, ordering a loud "Mrs. Anspach!" as he does.

No one answers. He pounds on the door again, then a third and fourth time. No window sash is raised; the door remains bolted, as if its last resident had departed and barred all entry to her home. Kelman slams his full weight into the portal, which shudders but doesn't budge. He repeats the effort twice more, each time grunting with exertion. The door remains fast, until it miraculously swings open to reveal the two constables who've crept inside using the rear entry. One of them holds a lighted oil lamp, the same with which Adelaide greeted Becky.

"Mrs. Anspach!" Kelman shouts, while Becky calls a more hopeful "Honora!" Not so much as a breath answers; even the floorboards fail to creak. The house is as still as death.

"Honora!" Becky cries out again. "Show yourself, please. It is I, Becky. If you have the girl on these premises, let her go. No good will come of this plan. Leniency awaits you if you release her. Please. The child's done you no harm. Nor has Martha Beale. Honora? Where are you?" Then, brushing past Kelman, she begins to climb the stairs, but he restrains her.

"Stay here, Miss Grey. Let my men and I attend to this matter."

"No."

"I must insist. For your safety. If what you assert is true, the woman is dangerous. Whatever her alias, if this is the same Honora or Leonora you claim she is, she's committed murder in the past. More than once."

With painstaking slowness, Kelman and his men begin a search of the ground-floor rooms, while Becky's eyes peer upward toward the landing and the shuttered doors that face it. "Hurry!" she urges. "Hurry. You won't find her or Ella downstairs. If they're here, they're in the chambers above." *If I mount to Heaven*, Becky hears repeated, then she bolts toward the staircase.

Kelman utters an oath and follows. "Miss Grey, remain below." He orders one of his constables to detain her, but she wrenches free of the man's grasp, pelts up the final steps, and bursts into the first room she encounters.

The space holds a bed stripped of its linens, a carpet and torchère, but nothing else. The draperies are open, allowing the feeble predawn light to envelope the whole in a purplish haze. The smell is of new furniture and neglect; it's clear the room hasn't seen habitation.

The second chamber is the same. The third carries reminders of an occupant: the mattress rests atilt on the bedstead; a chamber pot is in need of emptying.

It's the fourth room where horrors await.

By now, Kelman and one of his constables have outpaced Becky. Throwing open the door, he turns back to shield her from the sight confronting them while reminding the constable to proceed with caution. "She's armed," he says, "and wounded. We mustn't attempt to wrest the knife from her hand." Then he orders Becky to return to the first floor. His expression is obdurate, but so is hers.

"Honora," she begs. "What have you done?"

"Miss Grey, you have no business here," Kelman insists again. "Be so good as to leave us. You put yourself and my men at risk."

Despite Kelman's efforts to prevent her, Becky pushes past him into the room. Honora stands near the far wall, a stab wound pulsing red at her neck. Although she remains upright, her face is blue-gray in the watery light. At her feet is the body of a man; his throat has been cut. Becky recognizes him as Honora's servant, then realizes with a pang of sorrow disproportionate to her discovery that she never knew his name. "You told me you'd fired him," she murmurs, which seems irrelevant to the violence of the scene.

"The girl?" Kelman says, striding forward. "Ella Beale. What have you done with her?" He raises his hands as if to grab her shoulders and shake the answer from her, but he stops midair when Honora jerks up the knife in an attitude of self-defense.

She opens her mouth. She attempts to speak, but no sound comes forth. Ignoring Kelman, she stares at Becky, her eyes full of mute appeal as well as something darker that Becky recognizes as triumph. "Gone."

With that final word, Honora plunges the knife into her breast, the sound of steel piercing bone as loud as a tree limb cracking. She sinks down to one knee, then both; her effort to remain upright is prodigious. She sways, collapsing in a piecemeal fashion while her eyes remain fixed on Becky's, glittering one moment, then fading, then dull and flat. Hope, pain, travail, rancor, and longing: all abandon her. Dead, she curves into herself, her physical presence diminished, as if those passions had molded a larger woman than she.

Becky doesn't stir while the room is examined. They find copious evidence of Ella's presence, but no Ella. Candles are produced, and the attic and cellar investigated. No one speaks. Becky believes that the girl must be dead, as does Kelman, but they don't express their fears.

In utter silence, the hunt continues; every opened cupboard and armoire inspires terror. All four expect that Ella has met the same fate as the footman. When no body is recovered, their relief is great, but their apprehension increases as well. Where can Honora have hidden her captive?

At length, the rear garden comes under scrutiny. By now, dawn has given way to springtime's early morning, although the day is overcast, and a low fog drifts across the ground.

Becky remains inside watching from the kitchen window while the men methodically push aside the undergrowth. Hands quickly cover noses, protecting them from a stench she's unable to detect. She turns away, sick to her soul, and vomits into the dry sink. Her mind's eye pictures their discovery.

But, no, the inspection of the garden produces no trace of the girl. The reek was a dead opossum, shimmering with maggots. Ella has vanished for a second time.

Telling his chief constable to summon the undertaker, Kelman helps Becky into the waiting carriage and escorts her to Martha's home.

CHAPTER 29

In Kensington

DESPITE THE LATE hour, Lena hasn't had the courage to return home. Midnight has come and gone—and three and even four in the morning, as well—the watchmen chanting out each number while she wandered as far afield as possible. Now she's north of the city's center, drifting through Kensington borough in the vicinity of the former commercial piers that served the metropolis in less populous times. The locale, derelict and awaiting refurbishment by the expansion of Birely and Sons, Shipbuilders, suits her. No one will taunt her here, or scream at her, or give her a not-so-covert shove. When dawn comes, it will be necessary to move on, but for the present she's grateful for the solitude.

Jervis's hat, which she alternatively clutches in both hands or sets atop her head, has become talisman and portent. In her heart, she feels that its owner must be dead. How or why this terrible act occurred remains too complex a puzzle for her to solve. She can't face her sister, who will undoubtedly question her and then plague her with appeals to find her husband. Or else blame her for Jervis's absence, like she did before.

As long as the hat remains in her possession, Lena prays a miracle may happen. Perhaps she'll spot him sauntering down a street, touching his head as if wondering why it's bare. Or she'll hear him calling her name and berating her for stealing this important piece of clothing. Or maybe his mistress provided an elegant replacement and he no longer has any use for this relic.

This last consideration gives her pause and causes a scowl to knife across her face. No, the lady was cruelhearted, and her house had a fearsome air, as if nothing good ever happened within its walls. Lena recalls running away from the place and becoming so short-winded with her pell-mell flight that she turned dizzy and was forced to squat in the street and rest. Someone spat on her; another threw a rotting egg, which produced pain as well as a stink when it broke.

As she remembers, she hears a moan. Deciding it's an injured animal hiding beneath the broken wharf, she alters her path to avoid it. She'd intended to stroll along the water's edge, but now she starts to move inland instead. Wounded creatures can be vicious, she knows, and this one, dragging itself so far away from human transactions, must be suffering indeed. When the sound follows her, she takes pity and changes direction again. Maybe she can bring the thing food or water. Wouldn't the hat hold water—at least for a little while?

Squashing it down over her ears, she descends what remain of the precarious wooden steps and moves closer to the whimpers. Because they're very faint, she reconsiders. *Why frighten the thing if it's dying? Or be bitten as a result?* Uncertain, she cowers while peering down into the darkness beneath the pier. *When the tide comes in, won't the thing be swept along with it, and then out into the bay and finally to sea? Wouldn't it be kinder to allow nature to run its course? Don't people and creatures die every day? Perhaps God intended that the thing should end its life here, where the waters will bear it away.* She resolves not to bother the poor creature. She'll say a prayer that its pain will soon end, and then leave.

Instead, she remains. Then the soft mewlings become mumbled words whose meaning she can't decipher.

"A person!" She lurches toward the sound, then just as quickly pulls away. *What sort of human would hide in this dismal spot? If savagery has been committed, it would be wise to hurry past.* Lena can't risk being blamed should wickedness be afoot. If she ran into the street shouting "Murder! Come quick!" who would believe her? No one. Nonetheless, she lingers, staring into the black space where the pier timbers meet the rocky shoreline.

As her eyes become accustomed to the lack of light, she notices a face, and then long, tumbled hair that's as pale as the person's skin. *A girl. A girl in this dismal place, and this dismal condition, too.* "Are you hurt?" she asks, which seems foolish even as she poses the question. *Of course, the girl is hurt. Why else is she whimpering?* "Who did this to you?"

"Ad..." The remainder of the reply is lost. The eyes, which Lena can now see, open and then close.

"Never mind. Don't answer. I'll help as best I can. You keep silent till you're feeling better."

Squeezing in beside the girl, Lena scents the reek of vomit and something medicinal: oily and sweet. "You've been dosing yourself with laudanum. That's not healthy, you know. Or did someone else do the dosing for you? That happened to me once. More than once. But never mind that. What you need is fresh air, and to walk a bit. Are you able to stand?"

The girl makes no reply. She's worse off than Lena anticipated. Dying, perhaps, either by her own hand or someone else's. She tries to banish the idea of suicide, but cannot. Why else is the girl within reach of the river tides, unless she or someone else wished her gone for good? But if she wished to end her life, wouldn't she have filled her pockets with stones and waded into the water? That dilemma leaves only one answer in Lena's mind: someone left the girl here to die. "Come. I'll help you." Circling the girl's waist with her arm, Lena attempts to pull her upright and out of her rank little den. "And you've a pretty gown, too. Don't worry; it can be cleaned."

The light tone elicits no response, but the girl, who's nearly as tall as her would-be rescuer, allows herself to be pulled upright. In that position, however, she sags into a swoon until Lena becomes convinced that she's breathing her last. "Don't you die," she orders her. "You had a mother once. She wouldn't want that."

"M…"

"Yes. A mother who loved you, I've no doubt. Come, and let's take a stroll together."

But the girl's feet refuse to cooperate, and her body remains dependent on Lena's until her weight threatens to topple them both.

"Wake up, now. You're too young to perish. And too pretty." This last statement is mere banter because, from what Lena can see, the girl is dirty, sickly, ashen, and thin enough to be ugly. The fact that she's wearing a costly gown is confusing. This is no factory wench or girl of the streets.

As Lena studies the ailing girl, her frown deepens. *The face looks almost like— but no, such a miracle can't be. Didn't Jervis and Sister tell me my Ella was dead?* She blinks, imagining her fantasies have gotten the better of her, but the girl remains: flesh and blood, if only barely living. *Don't you go conjuring up weird pictures. Sister and Jervis have never, ever lied. To tell the truth, haven't they been more candid than necessary?*

Despite this admonition, she continues to stare. *The shape of the eyes, the nose, the mouth…how similar to…no, that's not possible. My daughter's gone. And better for her, too. Who wants a crazed woman for a mother? And a pauper, at that. Still, the features look… no, you're weaving fairy stories for yourself. Jervis and Sister would laugh their heads off if they could look into your brain.*

"Don't you go dying on me," she repeats in a harsher voice while trying to obliterate her traitorous pipe dreams. "I was a mother once, so I'll speak for your own mam. You must take heart. Nothing's so bad that we females should lose hope. I've known terrible times, so my words come from experience. Come along. Don't drag your feet. Step lively. We'll quit this rocky beach and find smoother footing. We don't want to be trapped on the shore when the waters rise. The Delaware can be swift in this area. And dangerous, I've heard. Climb up with me, before the currents change."

No amount of cajoling helps. The girl's semiconscious state allows her to attempt to follow orders but also makes her incapable of executing them. She groans while Lena bears her away from the shore and up the perilous steps. Several times she nearly drops her burden. "It's no time for dozing. Wake up, dearie. Wake up."

"Mam," the girl mutters, which sends a searing pain of loneliness, guilt, and regret into Lena's sore heart.

She gazes at the girl's face again. The same blond hair, the same heart-shaped face…no. *It's not possible. My mind's playing its usual tricks. The city's full of young women with fair hair and sweet faces. I mustn't listen to those queer voices in my head.*

"That's right, my dear. Your mam would want you to walk with me."

"Mam," the girl murmurs again, and Lena's eyes swell with tears. She'd weep if she didn't have this new responsibility.

"I had a daughter once. A pretty thing, but my man…my man, he…no matter. She's gone to her reward. Her and her baby brother that toppled into the cooking fire. Come now. We're nearly at the street, such as it is in this forgotten area. You'll walk easier here."

"Mam…"

Again, tears threaten to undermine Lena's resolve. She grits her teeth and drags her young charge up the final step. "Call me any name you wish. I'll be your mam for now. And tell you to take courage." *Who left you here?* she wants to demand, but she doesn't. The girl must be made to walk, not talk.

"I'll be your mam for as long as you wish. And you can be my daughter, if you'll promise to be brave and move yourself about. That medicine is wicked stuff. Whoever gave it to you was as evilhearted as the Devil."

"Ad…"

"Don't talk, dear. I had a nephew who died at the hands of wicked folk, so I know about the Devil's scaly ways. He sneaks along beside us every day. God tries to smite him, but that Devil, he's wily as a serpent. He's got minions, too, like those fiendish folk who hurt the boy. I punished them for what they did, because God was busy fighting other sins. He can't always drop what He's doing, can He? We women are powerful creatures, even though they tell us we're not. Don't you heed them when they say you're only a weak female. Walk tall, instead. And proud, too. Take deep breaths, dear. You're nearly safe. Lean on me."

The dirt roadway is reached, but the girl continues to be incapable of self-propulsion; she sags out of Lena's grasp, and the two sprawl earthward. The girl's head slides into the cindery soil; her eyes flutter open and then shut.

"Wake up, dear. This is no time to rest. Wake up and listen to me. You must walk if you wish to be rid of that foul medicine you took—"

"Ad…"

"—or that someone forced upon you."

The girl fails to rise. Speech, or what little there is of it, also deserts her, and her breathing begins to rumble in her lungs.

Not the death rattle, Lena thinks, jumping up. "Help!" she screams. "Save this poor child! She's dying. Dear God, please help."

Not a sound greets her cries; not a candle flickers in a window; not a door bangs open, not a dog nor householder howl in protest. The city might as well be abandoned.

"Help me!"

As she screams, Lena notices that night has departed and that the first lights of dawn are brightening the sky. What was black has become deep gray. Bathed in this somber color, the girl appears dead already. Lena touches her face but finds it still warm, touches her chest, and feels the labored but steady breaths. She sits and places the girl's head in her lap. *So like my Ella,* she thinks. *So like my little girl who was taken away from me.* Stroking the waxen face, Lena hums a lullaby. "I sang that to my nephew who was lost to us. And to my daughter and son. She had blond hair like yours. And she was as beautiful as an angel. Looks isn't everything, though. A stalwart heart is best. That's what Sister and her husband say. I try to learn from them."

She sings again and is relieved to see the ghost of a smile twitch at the girl's mouth, though the eyes remain shut. *Perhaps my music helps. Or perhaps she's already gazing upon the sainted angels. Ranks and ranks of them, lovely and perfect and glowing, and with wings as wide as a church door.* The vision brings a yearning smile to Lena's face.

"Are you viewing heavenly sights, little one? I think you must be. Sister tells me I have peculiar notions. The medical men in the asylum said the same, and I suppose they're right. But, if you're looking at Heaven, will you take a message to God for me?"

Knowing there will be no reply, Lena waits anyway, comforting herself by smoothing the dying girl's hair. The gesture brings solace to both; Lena is gratified to see the ashy face grow peaceful. The sickly body, now nestled close, also relaxes.

"There's no need to fear the other side, little one. I don't. Even though I've done bad things in my life. Murder, even. And that's a mortal sin. The Rause pair, they deserved their fates, though, because of the boy. But don't you worry. You won't encounter those two where you're going. Susannah and Darius: they're in the eternal fires, where they belong. I only wish I'd gotten her the first time I tried, but there it is. Success isn't always ours for the taking. Never forget that. We must try and try and try again. And didn't I succeed in the end? So you won't chance upon them when you reach the Pearly Gates, because the Devil's stabbing them with his pitchfork at this very moment. But you, my dear, you're climbing the stairway to eternal glory."

Closing her eyes, Lena imagines Heaven and all the wonders the girl is probably experiencing: clouds as pink as sunset, and as soft to walk through as fresh-fallen snow; the sun always shining and spreading its warmth. No hunger. No pain. No dread.

"You tell God from me that I know I did wrong," she says, "because vengeance should rightly be His. We mortals aren't supposed to take an eye for an eye. Or covet. Or kill. Or blaspheme. We're supposed to forgive seven times seventy. Or seventy times seventy? I forget which. But God didn't repay those devilish folk, or smite them, or send plagues upon them, so what was I to do? 'Maybe,' I thought, 'He needs my help.' Fancy God wanting me to come to His aid, but He works in mysterious ways, doesn't He? You can ask the saints when you see them. So that's what I did. I laid my plans and used my wiles, and no one caught me. Nor never shall, I'm thinking. Little fires turn big when you set your mind to it, especially if you're a person no one wants to notice. You tell God I'm not contrite like I should be—that I'm proud instead. I've been weak when I should have been strong; I let my dear daughter be stolen from my arms. But I've changed."

Lena stays silent for a bit, stroking the girl's hair and gazing at her face. "You tell God everything I've said. Tell Him I tried to save you, too. And I would have, if you hadn't been so poorly. I'm a better person than I once was. Jervis would agree, but Jervis can't be found."

A spasm then constricts the girl's body. Horrified, Lena pulls away, letting the torso slide onto the road and the head she cradled slip into the mire. In her estimation, the girl is in her death throes; Lena, her courage so erratic and tenuous, panics. "Tell Him I tried," she repeats in a strangled sob, and she almost adds her name to the request before anxiety about being overheard in this compromising circumstance stops her. "Tell Him I tried."

Then the habits of a lifetime overcome resolve and she flees before she and the girl can be found. If they're discovered together, won't she be blamed for the child's demise?

CHAPTER 30

Safe

ELLA IS FOUND alive, though severely depleted by her ordeal. At the advice of the surgeon, who cautions against questioning her until she's physically and psychically prepared, her waking hours consist of healing foods and brief and cheerful conversation. Martha concurs with the regimen; Kelman does as well. The fate of the woman who held her hostage, and of the man she employed, isn't mentioned, not even when Martha and Thomas are alone together. Well-meaning though the servants laboring in the Beale household may be, gossip is something the two daren't risk. No matter how long it takes, Ella must be allowed to mend in body and soul. Besides, Thomas and Martha ask themselves, what is left to learn? The abduction was motivated by revenge; the perpetrator is now dead, and Ella freed.

When the girl asks how she came to be rescued, or frowns in disjointed memory, Martha deflects the queries with a loving, "You've endured a terrible fright. We'll have ample time to discuss what occurred later. For now, let us give thanks that you're home safe and sound."

Stationing herself beside her adoptive daughter's bed, she reads to her for hours on end; even when Ella dozes, Martha's soothing voice continues while she pages through Charles Dickens's *The Adventures of Oliver Twist*. She hopes Ella will take comfort and courage from its plucky hero.

As for another young hero, Findal Stokes is told he must wait until "Miss Ella is well enough to receive company." He receives this formal dictum with an aplomb Martha didn't expect. Her antipathy turns to grudging respect, then judgment evaporates in the face of his equanimity and obvious goodwill. She directs her staff to feed him, but he refuses the largesse, saying he wishes to work for his bread and butter. Then he quits the area before he can become "a charity case," and Martha's respect evolves into admiration.

⇥ ⇤

Eight days pass. Ella is now encouraged to walk about the house. She's not yet permitted to go out of doors, as the physician believes the bustling streetscape will tax her delicate nervous state. The aftereffects of laudanum poisoning have become his chief concern; during his daily visits, he watches her for signs of mental and emotional impairment.

"Jervis," Ella says while she and Martha slowly promenade through the formal receiving room. The girl stops walking as she speaks, her expression doubtful, as if she were seeing another locale transported into the one in which she stands.

"Jervis?"

"Adelaide's servant. He tried to save me. He said he'd bring you to her house because I was too ill to travel."

"Ah," Martha says. "A brave man." She makes no further comment, but understands she must eventually formulate an explanation regarding Jervis's fate.

"He didn't come here, did he?"

"No, dear heart."

"Why not?"

"I can't answer that, I'm afraid. Perhaps he feared he'd lose his position. At any rate, you're here with me now, which is all that matters."

Ella frowns at the reply. To Martha, it looks as though the girl were having a silent conversation with herself. "We must find him, Mother. Adelaide would kill him if she knew."

"We'll write to Mr. Kelman and inform him of your fears." Buying time, Martha sits, takes up pen and paper, and begins to compose a letter. "Is Jervis a first name, or last?"

"And his sister—no, sister-in-law—that's who…" The words trail off; Ella sits suddenly, then huddles into herself and stares unseeing at the floor.

"Let's go back upstairs, dear heart. You mustn't upset yourself. You need repose and peace—"

"She dragged me off the beach, where Adelaide...I could hear the water..." Again, memory fails her.

"Come upstairs. We mustn't worry the surgeon more than he is already." Martha bends down and wraps her arm around Ella's waist, urging her to stand, but the girl doesn't move.

"I recognized her voice, Mother. At least, I think I did. She sang me a lullaby and asked me to take a message to God—"

"If she rescued you from the river's edge, then I imagine you'll remember her forever," Martha says, though she has misgivings about the purported rescuer's intentions. When Ella was found, Kelman assumed she'd been left for dead. The notion of a mysterious guardian angel isn't consistent with that hypothesis. Besides, didn't the physician warn them that Ella might suffer hallucinations as a result of laudanum poisoning?

"And she said she once had a...Why do I remember her voice?"

Martha strokes the girl's forehead and hair, unwittingly mirroring Lena's gestures. "Because she helped you. And someday we'll find her, so we can thank her properly."

"No, it's something else. Some other memory. Oh, why can't I recall it? She sang a lullaby and told me—"

"Come upstairs, dear one. Please. The physician doesn't want you fretting yourself till you're strong. We'll have some warm milk punch, and I'll keep reading about Oliver—"

"She told me she'd killed two people, but she said she'd never be caught because she'd been clever," Ella continues as if Martha hadn't spoken. "She said they'd burn in Hell for what they'd done. Or maybe she didn't say that. Maybe I was dreaming...oh, I had such awful dreams—"

"No more, dear. Not yet."

"And a nephew, I think. Yes. Jervis's son. A little boy who died—"

"Ella, my dearest. Don't, I beg you. The physician said you were to have no stimulation—"

"She told me she had blond hair like mine, but I don't remember how she looked. It was very dark. Or maybe my eyes were closed. Why did she leave me, Mother?"

"I don't know, dearest," Martha lies, for she's beginning to suspect the mystery woman was Adelaide attempting one final deception before she left Ella to die. "Perhaps she went to summon help and got lost."

"No…she asked me to take messages to God. She told me women were more courageous than they realized."

"That seems like admirable advice—"

"I knew her voice, Mother. I did! But I can't remember whose it was."

"Ella, dearest. You mustn't tax yourself. You were very ill when we brought you home. The medication you'd been given had a dire effect. Maybe you imagined you recognized the woman's voice. Or maybe it was the person who abducted you—"

"No. It wasn't. It wasn't."

"Or perhaps, she sounded like someone you thought you recalled. Like one of the maids, or Mademoiselle Hédé—"

"No…"

"Or somebody else then—"

"Who?"

"Well, I don't know, but our minds are capable of inventing both happy and wicked occurrences. Cai is frightened of ghosts, although they don't exist. When I was a little girl, I used to imagine giants in the clouds. Some were good, and some were—"

"I didn't dream her, Mother. She was real. She stroked my hair and my face, just like you're doing, and told me to be brave."

Martha sits on the floor at Ella's feet, pulling the girl's body into her own. "Dear heart, you've suffered many psychic blows. I'm not saying that a kindly stranger didn't come along and pull you out of harm's way, but—"

"She did. Jervis's—"

"Yes," Martha agrees, against her better judgment. "And when you're well enough, we'll talk to Mr. Kelman about trying to find her."

"Do you promise?"

"I do." Martha agrees to this with a heavy heart, for she's certain no such person exists. As to the man who was called Jervis, well, that's another problem for another day. "Now, will you banish these difficult memories for a while and let me take you back upstairs? We want you to get better as quickly as possible. Not just me and Cai and Mademoiselle and Cook and Mr. Kelman, but a young man who's waiting to see you when you're strong enough."

Epilogue

Spring has become summer, the days languid; the sky a high, gilded blue. A kind of somnolence drifts over the city. Street and tree, house, factory, wharf, and garden reflect the lassitude the residents feel. No one is inclined to rush; speech becomes muted; even the horses refuse to react to the carters' whips. *What's the hurry*, their plodding bodies seem to argue, and the drivers respond by giving the animals the freedom of choice. "What's the hurry?" they reply if a merchant berates them for tardiness. "The sun will rise and set, whether the goods are delivered on the exact hour or not."

Martha has quit the metropolis in favor of Beale House, the country estate her father built on the banks of the Schuylkill beyond the river's famous falls. It's a favored retreat for Ella and Cai, and for her, too, because each moment is measured in the infinitesimal. For Cai, it's the manner in which a ladybug climbs a stalk of grass, or how much breath it takes to scatter a dandelion's feathery seedlings; for Ella, it's the scent of honeysuckle and phlox drifting through her open bedroom window, and the sight of the river, azure or silver-white, shimmering beyond. For Martha, the place is a thrush's song at daybreak and a roseate sun slipping though the leaves, or reading aloud on the veranda while the light grows too dim to see. For Thomas, it's perfection.

They picnic on the Schuylkill's banks, after which the "men" (Cai being called "Little Man" by Thomas) fish in the rock-lined pools while the "ladies" stroll the woods or simply woolgather. In the evening, fireflies are caught and imprisoned in glass bowls that winkle through the darkness until Martha takes pity on the creatures and releases them when the children sleep.

Against all decorum, Thomas is accommodated in a guest bedroom during his weekly sojourns. Beale House, the pair decides, is exempt from the prying eyes of Philadelphia. And anyway, they don't care. He holds her hand when they stroll the gardens; she leans against his shoulder.

Ella returns to normalcy as her memories blur into the stuff of nightmare, almost too violent and fantastic to be real. Findal Stokes is part of her healing. He visits for an afternoon every fortnight. Martha has enrolled him in an industrial school for boys, which he resisted mightily at first, until he consoled himself with the notion that he was undergoing the discipline for Ella's sake. He's on his way to becoming a "right young toff," although he doesn't share this sentiment with his benefactress. Ella dispenses with the disparaging remark and tells him he'll make a fine gentleman someday. "Look at Mr. Kelman if you want an example," she says. "He was humbly born, and you couldn't hope for a better person. Mother's going to marry him. Though she doesn't know it yet."

--)==() ()==(--

"Do you believe that Ella's mystery woman exists?" Martha asks one late evening as she and Thomas wander the parterre garden alone. Much as they'd like to, they can't escape the quandaries that continue to haunt them. So preoccupied are they that they haven't noticed the moon, which has now risen and is so bright that their two figures cast long shadows rippling across the grass. The vibrant colors of day have become monochrome; a stone urn appears white; the yellow roses planted in it are as pale as pewter, the leaves a leathery gray. Neither she nor Kelman remark on the singular effect, which has made the landscape look like an apparition rather than a living place. "Do you?" she repeats.

"The information about the instances of arson had to come from someone," he responds after a moment. "Given the circumstances, however, it's hard to know what's truth, and what was fabricated by Ella's abductor. Her mental state at the time she encountered her anonymous heroine was tenuous at best."

"'Abductors' plural," Martha reminds him.

"Yes, but Hendricks was quick enough to accuse his cohort of masterminding the plan."

"That doesn't make him innocent."

"No. Prison will be his home for a good long while. Not even Celestine Lampley mourned his loss; she never reappeared to serve as a witness to his dubious character. Doubtless, she has reinvented herself elsewhere. My guess would be as far from Philadelphia as possible."

"Another person whose absence the city won't regret." She says no more. Nor does he. Minutes pass in this meditative fashion while they stroll here and there, pondering questions without answers.

"Poor Jervis," she says at length. "And his wife. The combined loss of her child and husband...and that vile woman withholding his wages."

"She'll survive, thanks to your generosity."

Martha shakes her head. "Survival isn't merely having food and a roof to keep out the rain and cold. I can't imagine the mental blows she has endured, or how I'd manage to weather something so heinous. To be left alone when she had a loving spouse and son...Jervis was a brave man."

"He was."

"I wonder if the outcome would have been different if we'd apprehended him when he left that abortive message." She sighs, and then adds a despondent, "Perhaps he wouldn't have been slain."

"Perhaps. But remember, dear one, that the woman who called herself Adelaide Anspach was of a deranged temperament. She had no cause to kill him when she did. Nor in the manner she chose."

"Yes. I know. Still, the consequences are difficult to consider. What might have been, as opposed to what occurred."

"Yes."

She grows quiet again, and the two continue their ramble, their footfalls hushed on the spongy turf. Martha's skirts brush across the grass, the sound like miniature waves washing over a beach. She wants to talk about anything other than this subject. So does he, but neither of them is capable of avoiding it. "The uncertainty about the supposed sister-in-law still bothers me," she muses. "Something seems amiss in the wife's denial of a sibling. I can't identify the root of my skepticism. Maybe it's merely wishful thinking. I want to believe what Ella told us. I want a conclusion to this tale."

"As do I. But the wife has been adamant that she has no sister."

"Aren't there others to query? Neighbors living in the building, or on the same street? Or shopkeepers who had dealings with the family?"

"They've been of no help. Two people initially mentioned another woman as being part of the household; the others insisted the couple lived alone. When interrogated again, all denied a third party's existence. Except for the boy, of course."

"Why would that be?"

"Fear of unnecessary entanglement with the law. After all, Jervis was murdered. In my experience, homicide can silence even the most honest of citizens."

"You're suggesting the people you interviewed might be lying?"

"I don't know. They could be. Or they could simply wish to distance themselves from a potentially precarious situation."

"You're not implying criminal histories, are you?"

"I'm simply mentioning what I've surmised, which is that secrets are being kept. How large or small, I've yet to determine."

Martha pauses before speaking. "And yet, Ella's convinced her unknown benefactor is related to Jervis, and that she made a kind of confession."

"*If* this benefactor exists, and isn't a fantasy inspired by Adelaide, or by the laudanum Ella was fed."

"Yes. *If.* If not, then your investigations remain unsolved, and Ella's savior vanishes."

"For the time being."

Again, she lapses into silence.

"I don't intend to allow two instances of arson to go unpunished. However long it takes, the truth will out. Or I will force it into the light. And if there's a heroine to the tale, I'll find her, too."

The vigor of his tone elicits a brief smile as she turns to face him. "Becky's convinced that Darius Rause set fire to his own house and thereby killed his unfaithful wife."

"Yes, she told me. And vigorously, at that."

"Did she also explain that she suspects Susannah Rause was the primary target in the Lampley fire, because she and Hendricks were regular patrons? Thus the fact that it was her lady's maid who perished in the blaze. A woman who was only doing the job for which she was employed. Becky assumes Susanna found the woman's death advantageous, because she was in a position to blackmail her mistress. If so, that would explain the fact that her disappearance wasn't reported."

"Ah, so it's blackmail, too, to add to Mistress Grey's plot" is Kelman's wry response.

"In Becky's reckoning."

"I see. Has she convicted Darius Rause of committing both crimes, or does she have another culprit in mind?"

"No. She believes Rause was guilty of setting the two fires. Or someone he hired."

"Who mysteriously cannot be traced—"

"Because Rause paid a sufficient amount to purchase his silence. 'For life,' Becky said."

"Time for me to resign and let the sleuth-thespian hold sway."

Martha laughs, albeit briefly. "She parsed out the man's character as though studying it for a drama. 'Vindictive and jealous,' she told me, but 'incapable of risk-taking—a merchant to the bone who required assured outcomes before making any decision.' Those were her exact words."

"According to her reasoning, did Rause purposely killed his wife's lady's maid, too?"

"No. An 'ancillary crime,' she called it. I made her cease her recitation before she could add further nefarious deeds to the case. Becky does exist in the realm of invention, after all."

Kelman also laughs, although the sound reveals a weariness at odds with the pleasant evening. "I'll remember to consult with her in future." Then his voice turns serious. "So far, all I have are theories. None can be proven. Intuition and experience tell me the instances are related, but I lack evidence. It's only luck that revealed the maid's identity. If she hadn't had a family with whom she shared her wages, her demise would have gone unremarked, as so many others have before her and will again."

"But you just told me that 'the truth will out.' Was that bravado, or were you in earnest?" Without waiting for a reply, she sighs, leaning closer to him. "It's time you quit your employment, Thomas. You experience only the worst of human nature."

"And let criminals win, and the critics prevail? No. I'll redouble my efforts instead."

"You'll never win over those particular critics. Naysayers don't wish to be proven wrong. Complaining is their bread and butter."

"I'm not motivated by their judgments and whims. I work so that the unscrupulous are punished, so that wrongs are righted. Besides," he adds in a lighter vein, "haven't you also repudiated the gossips and slanderers?"

"As social arbiters, yes. But those genteel folk have nothing to do with cases of murder."

"Don't they? Weren't the Rauses supposedly genteel? From what you've told me, Darius and Susannah and their ilk rule the fates of us commoners, who dare to challenge the strongholds of polite society."

"I think you're granting them more power than they deserve."

"But not more than they imagine they have."

"Very cynical, sir. Be careful, or you'll become one of the dandified elite."

"Never."

"Good. Make sure that you don't."

"You have my promise."

"And you have my…heart." Looking up at him, her face is luminous in the light.

He touches her cheek, then her lips, then bends to kiss her. In the sleepy night, they stand entwined and still. It's in his mind to ask her to marry him, but a kind of shyness overwhelms him, and he keeps silent.

Eventually, they walk on. Without speech, they become aware of the rustle of small, night-driven creatures. An owl cries, the sound startlingly near; they glance upward to catch sight of it, pale and ghostlike as it lofts from tree to tree, all the while seeming to gaze down in near-human condemnation. Martha shades her eyes against the moon's glare as she watches it depart, winging toward a less populous part of the property. "She—or he—must have believed the sound we made was the work of field mice."

"Or else expected our footsteps would force one or two to forsake their shelters and run into the open."

"I'm glad we weren't responsible for those tiny deaths."

"Owls must eat."

"And mother mice must nurture their young."

"Mice and rats also creep into corn cribs, infuriating farmers who would dispatch legions of owls to pounce upon them if they could."

She nods, her countenance becoming grave. "Legions of..." She pauses. "Do you believe in Satan, Thomas?"

"As a living being prowling the world, do you mean?"

"Not quite as medieval as a horned creature with a serpent's tail, but as a palpable presence, yes."

"Are you talking about Ella's Adelaide?" he asks.

"In part. Though my query is broader than that. The owl wants to eat. Its motive is simple. Revenge, or lust for power, or hate aren't emotions it comprehends, whereas we humans, who are supposedly made in God's image, are riven with a potential for brutality that has nothing to do with survival."

He doesn't answer. He looks at her hand tucked safely into the crook of his arm and then into her thoughtful gray eyes. "I believe that cruelty is omnipresent, no matter how hard we work to obliterate it."

"Isn't that the Devil taking human form?"

"I suppose that's what the church fathers would tell us. Maybe, though, it's not the Devil at work but we humans acting on an impulse we already possess."

"What or who put it there? An owl doesn't hunt because it enjoys killing, or because it relishes the cries of its victims, but we do. Why?"

"I don't have the answer to that. I can only attest to our propensity for violence."

She frowns. "Here we are on this beautiful night, walking and talking, all troubles behind us. But somewhere else, right now, while we stroll about in sheltered comfort, a child is being whipped or starved. Isn't that Satan at work?"

"I've never been much of a churchgoer, Martha, so my notions of accepted theology are shaky at best."

"I'm not sure 'accepted theology' helps to resolve the issue," she says with a small smile before continuing in her reflective tone. "Perhaps our human imaginations can't comprehend emotions that are infinitely benevolent and infinitely barbaric. Instead, we turn God and the Devil into platitudes. The Devil is viewed as merely mean-spirited, a creature bent on mischief because God banished him from Heaven, while God is equally diminished and transformed into an aging man with a flowing beard."

"Seditious talk, Miss Beale. Your social arbiters would be scandalized."

"Perhaps it's time they started thinking instead of passing down judgments" is her retort. "I don't intend to be inflammatory. I'm simply attempting to comprehend motives as aberrant as Adelaide's."

Kelman doesn't reply at once; instead he strokes her hand while studying the river lying below the plateau, a band as shiny as quicksilver. "Motives are myriad, dear one; I don't believe they can be explained without comprehending a person's history. A dog that was beaten as a pup becomes vicious as an adult, because it knows no other behavior; conversely, one that's been cosseted has a sweet nature. What's true of animals is true of men and women as well."

"Then how does someone like Findal Stokes, whose history was brutal, emerge as the opposite? Or Susannah Rause, who had every advantage, emerge as callous and cold-blooded?"

"I don't know. I imagine I never will."

In tacit understanding, they turn away from the shoreline and wend their way back to Beale House. The abnormally bright sky, with its wisps of moonlit clouds, makes the home's Gothic-inspired tracery and turrets seem all the darker in comparison. Gazing up, Martha smiles with bittersweet recognition. The edifice should look foreboding and forbidding; her father, not one for liberality, built it to impress. Instead, the walls and roofline appear to yearn upward: a human construction attempting to re-create glory and wonderment out of hand-cast bricks and hand-hewn stone.

"I wonder," she says at length, "whether Heaven, with God enthroned, and Hell, ruled by a merciless Satan, have different configurations than the simplistic locations we've been taught to envision."

"More subversive notions?"

"No, not subversive. Rather, it's an inquiry...similar, perhaps, to the theories you posit in order to solve what seems inexplicable." She pauses, her footsteps keeping pace with his. "What if Heaven isn't an airy retreat hidden high above us in the clouds, as comforting as that notion seems, and Hell's not a giant cauldron sizzling beneath our feet?" She grows quiet, her eyes focused first on the path before them and then on the dark bulk of Beale House. "Sacrilegious though you may find the concept—"

"I told you I'm not a regular churchgoer."

"Yes, you did, although you have attended services with me."

"And will again, no doubt."

"I trust so."

He doesn't respond at once. When he does, his tone has a lighter air, though Martha's remains as serious as her expression.

"So, Heaven and Hell aren't locales in this theory of yours?"

"No. At least, not as we've been taught. Instead, the place where an act of violence occurs becomes Hell for a period of time. Adelaide's house, for instance. Or any other space in which cruelty is practiced. And wherever good triumphs and love is expressed, then that spot is transformed into Heaven."

"So, thousands of Heavens and thousands of Hells, is that your hypothesis?"

She nods as she looks into his eyes. "Yes. Throughout the earth, and all at once."

"And God and the Devil?"

"Perhaps they walk beside us. Always. Now and all our lives."

"Hardly comforting, Miss Beale."

"No? I find it so."

"With all those devils and fiery pits?"

"But an equal number of Heavens, or maybe more...vastly more...as well as the breath and heart and sustaining love of God. If that doesn't inspire joy, then I don't know what will."

Listening to her, Kelman makes a decision. The awkwardness he experienced before has miraculously disappeared, and he feels both comforted by his resolution and empowered. *Isn't this what I've long desired? Isn't this what Martha wishes, too?*

Almost in the house's shadow now, he drops to his knees. "This may be an odd moment to ask this of you, Martha, but I haven't found a more suitable one; in fact, none better may exist than this space and this singular time."

Pausing only to draw breath, he takes her hands in his. "Will you become my wife? You're already the joy of my every waking moment."

Made in the USA
Monee, IL
30 April 2021